evil spy school

Also by Stuart Gibbs

The FunJungle series

Belly Up

Poached

Big Game

The Spy School series

Spy School

Spy Camp

The Moon Base Alpha series

Space Case

Spaced Out

The Last Musketeer

STUART GIBBS
evil spy school

A spy school NOVEL

Simon & Schuster Books for Young Readers

New York London Toronto Sydney New Delhi

SIMON & SCHUSTER BOOKS FOR YOUNG READERS
An imprint of Simon & Schuster Children's Publishing Division
1230 Avenue of the Americas, New York, New York 10020
This book is a work of fiction. Any references to historical events, real people, or real places are used fictitiously. Other names, characters, places, and events are products of the author's imagination, and any resemblance to actual events or places or persons, living or dead, is entirely coincidental.
Text copyright © 2015 by Stuart Gibbs
SIMON & SCHUSTER BOOKS FOR YOUNG READERS is a trademark of Simon & Schuster, Inc.
For information about special discounts for bulk purchases, please contact Simon & Schuster Special Sales at 1-866-506-1949 or business@simonandschuster.com.
The Simon & Schuster Speakers Bureau can bring authors to your live event. For more information or to book an event, contact the Simon & Schuster Speakers Bureau at 1-866-248-3049 or visit our website at www.simonspeakers.com.
Also available in a Simon & Schuster Books for Young Readers hardcover edition
Book design and illustration by Lucy Ruth Cummins
Map illustration by Ryan Thompson
The text for this book was set in Adobe Garamond Pro.
Manufactured in the United States of America
0317 OFF
First Simon & Schuster Books for Young Readers paperback edition April 2016
10 9 8 7 6 5 4
The Library of Congress has cataloged the hardcover edition as follows:
Gibbs, Stuart, 1969–
Evil spy school / Stuart Gibbs. — First edition.
pages cm
Sequel to: Spy camp.
Summary: After getting expelled from spy school for accidentally shooting a live mortar into the principal's office, thirteen-year-old Ben finds himself recruited by evil crime organization SPYDER.
ISBN 978-1-4424-9489-3 (hardcover) — ISBN 978-1-4424-9490-9 (pbk) — ISBN 978-1-4424-9491-6 (eBook)
[1. Spies—Fiction. 2. Schools—Fiction.]
I. Title.
PZ7.G339236Ev 2015
[Fic]—dc23
2014006329

In memory of Stephen Gibbs, who brought so much joy into so many lives. I miss you, buddy.

acknowledgments

I am greatly indebted to the Filus family—Drew, Andrea, Dashiell, and Sasha—for their exceptional reconnaissance work. And huge thanks to Yusuke Kimura, who taught me the word "swawesome."

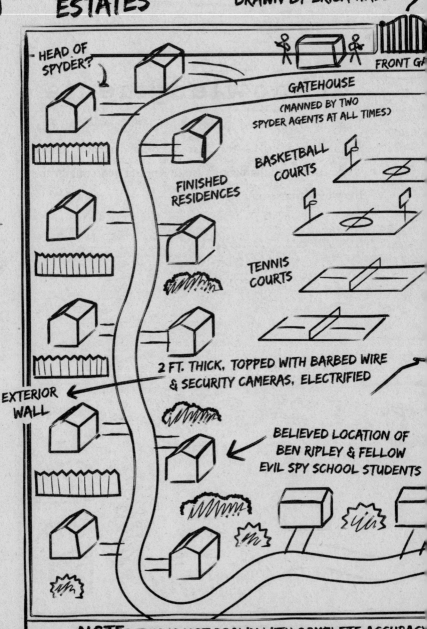

STATE ROAD 11

LOOP ROAD

? BOCCE BALL COURT

CONSTRUCTION ZONE

RECREATION CENTER (LIKELY COVER FOR SOME NEFARIOUS PURPOSES)

SITES OF HOMES STILL UNDER CONSTRUCTION →

→

.28 MILES

THWARTED SPYDER AGENT!

CIA KICKING BUTT!

ALEXANDER DREW THIS, NOT ME. — ERICA

? CROQUET LAWN

UNFINISHED ROAD ↓

THIS IS ONLY BASED UPON EXTERIOR OBSERVATIONS.

contents

August 30

To: ▮▮▮▮▮▮▮▮▮▮▮▮▮▮

Re: ▮▮▮▮▮▮▮▮▮

My covert field research has confirmed the worst. SPYDER definitely has a new diabolical plot under way—and they have started ▮▮▮▮▮▮▮▮ ▮▮▮▮▮▮▮ to staff it. Steps must be taken immediately to determine ▮▮▮▮▮▮▮▮▮▮▮ and ▮▮▮▮▮▮▮▮▮.

Given that the three of us are known to SPYDER and thus unable to infiltrate their organization effectively—and that the CIA has certainly been compromised by enemy agents—we are left with no choice but to activate Benjamin Ripley for Operation Bedbug.

This mission is unsanctioned and unapproved. It is not to be discussed with anyone, anywhere, no matter how much you think you can trust them. This is especially true for ▮▮▮▮▮▮▮▮▮▮. For his own safety, even young Mr. Ripley cannot be informed of what is truly going on until we are sure that ▮▮▮▮▮▮▮▮▮▮▮▮▮▮▮▮▮▮▮▮▮▮.

If anyone has any doubts about Mr. Ripley's ability to serve in this capacity, now is the time to voice them. The consequences of his failure on this mission would be disastrous.

Unless I hear from you, the mission will commence on September 3 at 1100 hours.

God bless America,

▮▮▮▮▮▮▮

HEAVY ARTILLERY

Battle Zone
September 3
1100 hours

I ran as fast as my legs could carry me, seven enemy agents in hot pursuit.

I had spent a great deal of time preparing for this moment. I had practiced self-defense. I had studied how to remain calm under pressure. I had read everything I could find on mortal combat. And so I had hoped that when the time came and I found myself in the thick of battle, I would be able to handle myself with cool, spy-like aplomb.

Instead, I was screaming.

Thankfully, it wasn't a girly shriek. It was more of a

sustained "aaaaaaaaaaaaaaaaaaaaaah!" Which could be roughly translated as: "I'm in serious trouble. Someone please help me."

It's one thing to study action sequences. It's a whole other thing to find yourself in the middle of one.

I dodged through piles of dirt and debris, aware the agents were gaining on me. They were all screaming too, although this was more of a war cry. Translation: "Once we catch you, you're dead meat." I was dressed for combat, clad from head to toe in camouflage gear, but it obviously wasn't working, because the enemy could see me perfectly well. Sniper fire whistled past me. Something screeched through the air high above and exploded in the distance.

Not far ahead, a foxhole came into view. To most people, it would have looked like just a big, grubby hole in the dirt, but to me, it was beautiful.

I shouted into my radio headset, "Erica! I'm coming in hot!"

"Okay," Erica replied calmly. "I'm ready." She didn't sound like she was in the heat of battle at all. Instead, she sounded bizarrely relaxed, as though she were lounging in a hammock at a beach resort.

I leapt into the foxhole. It was four feet deep. Erica Hale sat inside, leaning against the dirt wall, casually leafing through a *Guns & Ammo* magazine despite all the chaos around her. Like me, she was wearing camouflage gear, but somehow she looked stylish in hers. Then again, Erica would have looked stylish in a potato sack. She was the most beautiful girl I'd ever met, as well as the smartest, the most athletic, and the deadliest.

"There's a horde of enemy agents right behind me," I panted. "Heavily armed. They ambushed me as I was nearing the objective. . . ."

"Ben, take it easy." Erica calmly tucked the magazine into her knapsack. "What are you so worked up about?"

"They're going to be here any second!" I exclaimed. "And they're ruthless!"

"They're twelve years old," Erica said flatly.

She had a good point. They *were* only twelve. And the war around us was merely a combat simulation. We were in the midst of our traditional Survival and Combat Skills Assessment exam at the CIA's Academy of Espionage. Our weapons were only paintball guns, and the battlefield was a mock-up on the academy firing range. But it *felt* real enough.

"Some of them are pretty big twelve-year-olds," I said defensively.

Their war cry was growing louder. They were almost upon us.

"How many of them are there?" Erica asked.

"Seven."

In one fluid movement, Erica sprang to her feet and fired her paintball gun over the lip of the foxhole. Five shots, each punctuated by the yelp of someone being hit squarely by a paint-filled projectile.

Erica took cover again, grinning. "Now there's only two," she informed me.

If there was anyone you wanted in your foxhole, it was Erica Hale. Although she was only fifteen, she was easily the most talented spy-in-training at school. She'd practically been preparing for it since birth: Spying was her family business. Most of her ancestors had been spies, going all the way back to Nathan Hale in the Revolutionary War. Her grandfather Cyrus Hale was one of the best there'd ever been, and he'd taught Erica almost everything he knew.

On the other hand, I came from a long line of grocers. I was only thirteen, and until seven months earlier, my entire espionage experience had consisted of watching James Bond movies. Since then, however, I'd twice been involved in thwarting the plots of SPYDER, a secretive subversive organization dedicated to causing chaos and mayhem. Thus, I'd seen far more action than most of my fellow students. But that didn't mean I was comfortable in the heat of battle, be it real or pretend.

Today was a good example. It was our first day back at school for the fall semester, time for the annual Survival and Combat Skills Assessment. When I was inducted, it was the middle of the school year, so my SACSA had been a solo exam. But now the school administration had to assess the entire first-year class—and reassess all the returning students—at the same time. There were six grades (seventh through twelfth) with fifty kids in each. Three hundred people. Thus, the full-scale fake battle. The school had been divided into two teams: red (them) and blue (us). Each was assigned to steal a heavily guarded objective from the other side while protecting their own. It was basically an enormous, potentially painful version of capture the flag. Since it was only a game—and the kids who'd been chasing me were all newbies—I probably should have been as calm as Erica, but I wasn't. I was still on edge, terrified of screwing up in front of the professors, who were watching closely from the sidelines and grading our performance.

"Did you only have five paintballs in your ammo clip?" I asked Erica.

"No," she replied. "I have plenty."

"Then why didn't you take out all seven enemy agents?"

Erica shrugged. "What fun would that be?"

With a primal scream, the two remaining newbies leapt into our foxhole, guns primed, ready to paint us cherry red. One of them was staggeringly large for a boy his age. He was built like a sequoia tree. The other was a surprisingly small girl. She looked like a heavily armed elf.

Thankfully, Erica took the guy. Before he could get a shot off, she'd launched herself into action, sweeping his legs out from under him and wrenching his gun away. Then she dispatched him with a shot to the chest, coating his torso in blue paint.

I attacked the girl. It felt a bit mean to attack an elf, but this one *was* aiming a gun at me. I wasn't as adept as Erica, but my fighting skills had improved at school. Before I'd arrived, I wouldn't have been able to beat a small girl in a fight. Now I could. It wasn't very chivalrous, but my grade was on the line. I shoved the elf's gun aside as she fired. The paintball whizzed past me, leaving a red splotch on the side of the foxhole. Then I barreled into her, knocking her flat as I snapped the gun from her grasp. I swung it around, preparing to blast her.

Only, the elf started crying. "Stop!" she wailed. "I quit!"

"You quit?" I asked, thrown. "Er . . . I don't think you can do that."

"I thought I could hack it here, but I was wrong," the elf sobbed. "It's too hard! I want to go home! I want my mommy!"

I lowered the gun, feeling bad for how hard I'd knocked her down. "Sorry. Spy school's not for everyone. . . ."

"Like you?" The elf's crying suddenly stopped. The whole "I want my mommy" thing had been an act. I tried to shoot her, but she lashed out a leg, catching me behind the knee.

I crashed to the ground, the gun tumbling from my grasp. The elf pounced on it and swung the barrel toward me. . . .

Erica blew her away. She fired six times, coating the elf in blue, then pointed to the sidelines. "Nice try, newbie. But you're out."

The elf now looked like a Smurf. A really angry one. "You got lucky this time," she sneered at me. "Next time, your girlfriend might not be around to save you." Then she stormed off toward the "morgue" on the sidelines, where her fellow paint-splattered corpses watched the battle play out.

"I'm not his girlfriend!" Erica yelled after her.

I staggered back to my feet, brushing myself off. "Man, that girl was devious."

"She was," Erica agreed. "She'll do well here."

I watched the elf trudge past the reviewing stands. Professor Kuklinski, who taught advanced biochemical weaponry, appeared disappointed in her performance, while Professor Greenwald-Smith, who taught counterespionage, seemed to be giving her some words of encouragement. Next to them, Professor Crandall, who taught self-preservation, had dozed off in his chair.

"You know," I said to Erica, "when normal kids go back to school, their first day is all about getting oriented and meeting their teachers. There's no paint guns or fighting or pretending to kill one another."

"Really?" Erica asked. "It must suck to be normal."

I pried a clod of dirt from my ear, then scoped out the battlefield around us. "I'd probably better get back in the game before I get dinged for slacking off."

"Hold on," Erica said. "How'd you end up with all those newbies after you in the first place?"

"Chip and Jawa set up an ambush for me. I thought I had a chance at the objective, but it was a trap."

"You're sure it was their doing?"

"Definitely. I saw them sic the newbies on me." Although they were on the opposing team, Chip Schacter and Jawaharlal O'Shea were two of my closest friends at spy school. Jawa was extremely smart. Chip was extremely sneaky and underhanded. Together, they made a formidable combination.

"They didn't come after you themselves?" Erica asked.

"They probably knew you and I would be working together," I said.

"So let's work together to take them out." Erica started sketching a plan in the dirt with the barrel of her paintball gun.

She'd drawn only two lines when an emergency call came over my headset: "Smokescreen, you out there? We need your help."

It was Zoe Zibbell, another of my close friends, only she was on our team today. Zoe had christened me "Smokescreen" shortly after my recruitment because she had mistakenly believed that my initial incompetence was an act designed to catch my enemies off guard. ("No one could be *that* inept," she'd once explained. "I've seen turtles that could fight better.") Since then, I had gained a considerable amount of skill and savvy, but the nickname had stuck.

I radioed back. "What's the situation?"

"Chameleon doesn't know how to work the mortar," Zoe reported.

"Yes, I do!" shouted Warren Reeves—aka Chameleon— in the background. Warren was gifted at camouflage but mediocre at just about everything else.

The mortar was a new addition to the SACSA exams. The administration at spy school had decided it was time for us to learn how to use heavy artillery.

I chanced a look out of the foxhole toward our mortar base, a makeshift bunker atop a slope at one end of the firing range. From what I knew, the mortar was an actual working cannon; only the ammunition had been altered. Instead of shells, it fired paint bombs big enough to take out a dozen people at once.

There were several red enemy agents between us and the base.

Erica got on the radio with us. "No dice. Smokescreen is assigned to target acquisition, not heavy artillery. You'll have to work this out yourselves."

"No can do, Ice Queen," Zoe replied. "The situation is dire."

"How dire?" I asked.

"Hold on," Zoe said. "You're about to see."

A second later, I heard Warren yell, "Fire in the hole!" followed by a loud explosion. A paint bomb blasted out of the bunker. Only, I could immediately tell something was wrong. Instead of arcing toward the enemy base at the opposite end of the battlefield, the bomb soared almost straight up, then began screaming downward—right toward us.

"Take cover!" Erica yelled.

For once, I was already ahead of her. We threw ourselves into the protected side of the foxhole just as the bomb detonated on the ground above us. A wave of blue paint sailed over our heads and splattered the rest of the hole.

I peered back out of the foxhole. The ground for thirty feet in every direction was a ring of blue. A third-year red team member on her way to the morgue had caught the worst of it. She was now coated with paint.

"That's not cool!" she howled. "I was already dead!"

Several of our own team members had been hit as well. Most had been caught only in the arm or the leg, but that was enough to remove them from the game. They were all shouting things at our mortar base that would have gotten them detention at a normal school.

I got back on the radio. "You guys nearly killed us just now!"

"Sorry," Warren said. "My bad."

Erica took in the carnage and sighed. "All right," she radioed. "I'm bringing Smokescreen in."

"Even though it's not our assignment?" I asked. Erica usually wasn't one to defy orders. Not when her perfect grade point average was on the line.

"It's a calculated risk. If we leave those two cheeseheads in charge of the mortar, we may not have a team much longer. Stay close to me." With that, Erica grabbed her knapsack, sprang out of the foxhole, and raced toward base.

I did exactly as she'd ordered. En route to the base, several opposing team members made the mistake of attacking us. Erica thwarted them so easily, she almost looked bored. I actually caught her yawning while she knocked one enemy agent unconscious.

A few opponents who were older students—and thus familiar with Erica's reputation—didn't even bother to attack. Instead, they simply dropped their weapons and surrendered. This wasn't going to earn them a lot of points on their exam, but it was far less painful than having Erica take them out.

Even though I should have been covering our backs, I couldn't help but watch Erica. In the first place, she could probably cover our backs better than I could, even while being attacked from the front. And second, Erica in action was a thing of beauty. It was like watching a prima ballerina perform *Swan Lake*, only with a lot more screaming. I already had a tremendous crush on Erica, and somehow, watching her wipe out a field full of enemies made her even more alluring.

I was sure Erica knew about my crush. After all, she was our finest spy-in-training; keeping a secret from her was like trying to hide meat from a dog. Erica had never let on the slightest bit, but then, human interaction wasn't her strong suit. She barely deigned to speak to anyone else at school—including our professors—so I knew not to expect too much. Frankly, I was thrilled that she had been willing to team up with me.

Erica calmly took out the last two opponents as we arrived at our mortar base, leaving them whimpering in pain. We clambered over the bunker wall only to have Zoe nearly blast us away.

"It's us, you nitwit!" Erica yelled.

"Sorry!" Zoe apologized, holstering her gun.

It didn't take long to scope out the bunker, as it was only a few feet across. The mortar sat in the center next to a pile of artillery. It was smaller than I'd expected, like a sawed-off cannon. Warren stood beside it, frantically flipping through the instruction manual.

Zoe hugged me with relief. "Thank goodness you're here."

Warren glowered jealously, as he always did whenever Zoe showed me any affection.

"What's the problem?" I asked.

"We're trying to take out the enemy mortar base, but we can't get the targeting right," Zoe reported.

"We'll handle it," Erica said, then pointed to Zoe and ordered, "Stay on guard." Then she pointed to me and ordered, "Work out the trajectory." Then she pointed to Warren and ordered, "Move. You're in my space."

Warren scurried out of Erica's path, meekly holding out the instruction manual. "Do you need this?"

Erica rolled her eyes. "Please. I've known how to operate a mortar since I was in preschool."

With most people, this would have been an exaggeration. With Erica, it probably wasn't. Her father had once showed me a baby picture of her playing with nunchucks. Erica instantly began making adjustments to the cannon.

I turned to Warren and grinned confidently. It was now my time to shine. I might not have been as great a warrior as Erica, but when it came to math, no one else at spy school could hold a candle to me. I had level 16 skills, which meant I could do extremely complex computations in my head and never forgot a phone number. At normal school, this was the kind of thing that not only failed to impress my fellow students but often got me shaken down for my lunch money. At the Academy of Espionage, however, there were sometimes occasions—such as aiming a mortar—where being good at calculus made you kind of cool.

"How far is the enemy base?" I asked.

"One hundred sixty-five meters," Warren replied.

"Charge?"

"Two hundred pounds of thrust."

"Weight of the shell?"

Warren frowned. "Is that important?"

"Only if you actually want to take out the enemy rather than our own team," Erica muttered. Then she told me, "Standard shell weighs sixteen pounds."

"Wind speed?" I asked.

"Fifteen miles an hour," Zoe reported. "Coming directly from the southwest."

I took a second to make my mental calculations, then another second to double-check my work. "We need a launch angle of seventy-three degrees, aiming six degrees right of the target."

"Roger." Erica started orienting the mortar.

"Nice work!" Zoe told me. "Thanks for bailing us out, Smokescreen."

"We don't know if he's right yet," Warren muttered sullenly.

"Of course he is," Zoe shot back. "I'd trust Smokescreen before my own calculator."

I started for the pile of ammunition, but Warren leapt into my path. "I'll handle that!" he snapped. "Firing this is *my* job!"

I stepped back, knowing Warren was desperate to prove his worth. While he grabbed a paint bomb, I jammed in some earplugs and borrowed Zoe's binoculars to scan our surroundings. Below us, the battlefield was laid out in an oddly perfect rectangle. At the edges, the dirt and debris stopped abruptly and the green lawns of campus began. It was like a little slice of Beirut had been dropped in the middle of Washington, DC. Behind me, the Gothic buildings of the academy ringed the north end of the battlefield, dominated by the five-story Nathan Hale Administration Building. For a mile on each side around us was untouched forest, providing plenty of land for our normal war games—as well as a barrier between us and the outside world, which swallowed up the sounds of battle. (The academy's official reason for existence was a highly guarded secret, so the campus had its own secret identity: St. Smithen's Science Academy for Boys and Girls.) The reviewing stands sat on the western side of the field. Beside them, the students who'd been "killed" were gathered, rooting on their respective teams. Since most of the "corpses" were now colored blue or red, they had the look of game pieces gathered along the edge of a Risk board.

There were a lot more blue-spattered corpses than red ones, which meant our team was winning. This was mostly due to Erica, who had more kills than everyone else on our team put together. However, Chip and Jawa were currently leading the remaining reds in an assault on our flag, aided by their own mortar, which their team was doing a decent job of operating. As I watched, a red paint bomb detonated only a few feet from our flag, taking out half of our defenders.

Erica observed this too. "Are you sure you're right, Ben?" she asked. "If we don't take out their mortar with this shot, they'll win with their next blast."

I *was* sure, but I rechecked my math one last time, not wanting to make a fool of myself in front of Erica. "It'll work," I assured her.

"All right." Erica stepped away from the mortar and joined Zoe and me at the edge of the base. Rather than watch Warren set off the mortar, she lifted her paintball gun to her shoulder and began picking off the red team members swarming toward our flag.

"Stand back!" Warren warned us, clutching the remote trigger. "Detonation in five seconds. Four . . ."

Erica suddenly stopped shooting, concerned. She spun back toward the mortar, sniffing the air.

"What's wrong?" I asked.

"That idiot put a live round in there!" Erica cried, springing at Warren.

I leapt into action as well. There was no time to ask Erica *how* she'd determined Warren had screwed up; knowing her, she could smell the difference between a live munition and a fake one. The fact was, I'd calculated the right trajectory, meaning the mortar was about to reduce several of my fellow students to tiny pieces.

Thankfully, before Warren could fire, Erica slammed into him, knocking him flat. Unfortunately, Warren interpreted this attack as some sort of spy school trick.

"Help!" he squawked, struggling for control of the trigger. "She's a double agent for the red team!"

In Warren's defense, this was exactly the sort of ruse the faculty at spy school played all the time. If it had been anyone but Erica, I might have doubted her intentions as well.

I left Erica to handle Warren and turned my attention to the mortar itself. The cannon sat on a rotating platform. I pulled the pin that locked it into place, then threw my shoulder into the barrel. It spun more easily than I'd expected, swiveling quickly away from me . . .

Just as Warren wrenched the trigger away from Erica and depressed it. "Fire!" he screamed triumphantly—and only then bothered to check to see where the cannon was aimed.

The mortar roared. It was so loud that even with my

earplugs in, I felt as though my brains might vibrate out of my head. The shell exploded out of the barrel, arcing into the air away from the battlefield.

And right toward the Nathan Hale Building.

The entire war zone immediately fell silent. Every student and faculty member stopped what they were doing to watch the disaster unfold.

The bomb peaked several hundred feet in the air and then whistled downward, slamming into the Hale Building's roof directly above the principal's office.

Erica had been right. It wasn't a paint bomb. It was a live round.

The explosion blasted a huge chunk out of the building. Brick and tile flew through the air. A gargoyle rocketed across Hammond Quadrangle and embedded in the wall of the armory.

When the smoke cleared, there was a divot thirty feet across right where the principal's office had been.

I cringed and looked to Erica. "What's the chance that the principal was up there?"

"Well, he's *supposed* to be down here in the reviewing stands," Erica said. "But the chances of the principal being in the right place at the right time aren't usually very good."

A howl of rage suddenly echoed from the blast site.

I raised the binoculars and saw the principal stagger

out of the remains of his office bathroom. His clothes were charred black and the toilet seat was around his neck, but he appeared to be all right. Enraged, but all right.

"Who is responsible for this?" he bellowed. "Find them and bring them to me!"

Zoe and Erica looked to me with genuine concern in their eyes. Warren, however, couldn't hide his glee. "Oooh," he taunted. "Ben, you're in trouble!"

And for once, I knew Warren was actually right.

EXPULSION

CIA Academy of Espionage

Nathan Hale Administration Building

September 3

1145 hours

Ten minutes later, I was in the principal's office.
Or at least what was left of it.

It probably wasn't the best idea to be in a fifth-story room that had just suffered severe structural damage, but the principal, who didn't think clearly on normal occasions, was so enraged that he'd apparently ceased thinking at all. I'd seen him angry plenty of times before (not to mention confused, baffled, perplexed, dumbfounded, and completely flummoxed), but those were mere drizzles of irritation compared to the thunderstorm of fury he was experiencing now. He was so determined to unleash his wrath on me that he hadn't even changed out of his scorched clothes. Bits of his tie and sports jacket were still smoldering, leaving tiny contrails of smoke as he paced around the remains of the office. His toupee had been fried black and looked like an overdone steak perched atop his head. But then, the principal's toupee was normally so awful, this was actually an improvement.

"Look at this room!" the principal shrieked. "Look what you did to it! Do you see what you've done to my desk?"

"Er . . . no," I said. "Your desk isn't there anymore." Instead, where the desk had been, there was only blue sky and a massive hole in the floor leading to the dean of Chemical Warfare's office below.

"Exactly!" the principal screamed. "That desk was an extremely important piece of espionage history. It was first used by Sidney Grimble, the founder of this academy, and it has been used by every principal since! It was a priceless artifact—and you blew it to pieces!"

"I'm sorry."

"I should say you're sorry! If it hadn't been for my keen ears and my lightning reflexes, I would have been killed!"

This was a lie. Since I'd seen the principal emerging from his bathroom after the blast, I knew that he'd literally been caught with his pants down. It was only sheer luck that he'd been seated on the toilet, rather than at his desk, when the bomb struck.

It might be surprising that, even though the principal worked in intelligence, he wasn't actually that intelligent himself. Or that, of all people, he'd been the one selected to run a school. But the fact was, no one joined the CIA to become a principal. It was a job no one wanted—and therefore, a dumping ground for agents no one wanted. Most other organizations would have just *fired* an incompetent employee. But the CIA was run by the government, where incompetent people didn't merely avoid being fired; they were often elected to high offices.

"I wasn't *trying* to hit your office," I explained. "I was trying to prevent some students from getting blown up."

The principal paused for a moment, as though weighing whether saving a few students' lives was worth the loss of his desk. "Why were you even firing live ammunition during a fake battle in the first place?"

"*I* wasn't. Another student loaded the cannon."

"It's not very professional to shirk responsibility," the principal scoffed. This, from a man who'd swiped the dessert from his secretary's lunch bag for a year and then tried to pin it on the janitorial staff.

"I'm not shirking anything," I argued. "I'm telling you the truth. Warren Reeves was in charge of the mortar. Erica

Hale and I were helping him. Or trying to. Warren insisted he could load and fire the mortar by himself. But he put a live shell in, rather than a paint bomb. . . ."

"How?"

"I have no idea. You had me brought up here before I had a chance to find out." Less than two minutes after the misfire, two very big men from campus security had arrived at the mortar base and demanded I accompany them to the principal's office. "Erica was the one who realized the ammo was live."

"And yet I notice that *she* didn't blow up my office."

"She was trying to stop the triggerman. While she handled that, I reoriented the mortar from the other students."

"And you aimed it at a building instead? Because the whole point of buildings is that they generally have people inside of them."

"Not today," I protested. "This building was supposed to be empty. The SACSA exams were mandatory for all students and faculty."

"What idiot said that?"

"Uh . . . *you* did."

The principal was already crimson with anger, but now he shifted into a color of red I hadn't known humans could be. A kind of blazing molten-magma red. Before he could explode at me, I reached into my pocket and pulled out the letter that had been sent to my home at the end of the summer. The one stating that attendance at the SACSA exams on the first day of school was mandatory for all students and faculty. It was signed by the principal himself. "You see?" I asked, holding it up.

The principal froze, mouth agape, a half second from reading me the riot act. He was so red already, I couldn't tell if he was embarrassed or angry at me for revealing that he'd messed up. I could almost hear the wheels in his brain turning as he tried to figure out what to do next. Finally, he said, "You're expelled from school."

"What?!" I gasped. "Why?"

"Because you blew up my office!" The principal waved a hand at the space where his wall had been. "You honestly think I'd let you stay here after a screw-up like this?"

"But it wasn't my fault!"

"You just admitted that you aimed that cannon here."

"There were people in danger," I protested. "I had to do *something.*"

"Well, you should have done something else," the principal countered.

"Like what?"

"I don't know. Something that didn't involve nearly killing me while I was on the toilet!" The principal caught his mistake, then desperately tried to backpedal. "I mean, something that *could* have killed me while I was on the toilet, had I been there . . . which I wasn't. I was here, in my office, doing important things, and then cleverly took cover in the bathroom when I heard the incoming mortar round. The point being, your behavior was rash and poorly thought out. . . ."

"There was no time to think!"

"That's never stopped me," the principal snapped. "I rarely take any time to think at all, and yet you don't see me blowing up people's offices."

With most people, I would have chalked a statement like that up to them being too angry to get their thoughts straight, but the principal's thoughts were usually more jumbled than a plate of linguini.

"So," I said, "if I had just stood there and let those other students get killed, then I wouldn't be getting expelled right now?"

The principal mulled that over, then completely dodged the question. "Look, I'm not in favor of killing students. In fact, I'm against it. But we are training people to be spies here, and when you're a spy, there are many instances where life hangs in the balance. The CIA needs people who can handle those situations, people who won't crack under pressure, people who can save lives without nearly killing other people."

"I've done that," I said sullenly. "In fact, I've done it *twice*. I defeated the plans of SPYDER two times. . . ."

"SPYDER?" the principal asked blankly.

"The evil organization that tried to blow up this school a few months ago," I reminded him. "Only I thwarted them, saving dozens of lives—including yours. And then I thwarted them again last summer, saving even more people—including the president of the United States. In fact, I'm the only student at this school who has done anything like that. And you're expelling me? Because I blew up your stupid office?" It probably wasn't the best tone to take with the principal, but I was upset and angry and already expelled, so it wasn't as though I could get into *more* trouble.

"This isn't because you blew up my office!" the principal said defensively. "It's because you nearly killed me! You might have defeated SPYDER, but you are also reckless, dangerous, and insubordinate. There is no place at this school for students like you. Therefore, you are officially dismissed from the Academy of Espionage. Go clean out your dorm room. Security will escort you off campus."

With that, the principal turned his back on me, signaling that our conversation was over. Normally, he would have turned his attention to something on his desk, but now he realized he had no desk—or much of anything else left in his office—so he simply stood there, unsure what else to do, while waiting for me to leave.

I was heading for the door when the principal spoke again. "There's one more thing."

"Yes?"

"We are taking a very big risk by turning you loose into normal society. Even though you are no longer welcome at this academy, it is still imperative that you keep its existence a secret. If you tell anyone of its true nature—or that you were ever training to be a spy at all—there will be consequences."

"Go jump in a lake," I said. It wasn't like he could expel me again.

Then I walked out the door.

Behind me, I could hear the principal screaming something else in rage, but I tuned him out. I walked away, down the long, dark corridor of offices.

This part of the building had withstood the blast quite well. There were a few new cracks in the walls, and most of the portraits of famous spies were now a bit crooked, but other than that, everything looked just the way it always did.

As I passed the last office, Alexander Hale exited it, holding a cardboard box. He froze upon seeing me, looking embarrassed and unsure what to do. Alexander was Erica's father. When I'd first met him, on the day he'd recruited me to spy school, he'd been the most decorated agent of his generation:

suave, dashing, and debonair. However, I had soon learned that Alexander was a fraud. In truth, he was a lousy spy who'd based his entire career on stealing the credit from others—and he'd made several critical mistakes that had severely jeopardized our missions. After Erica and I mentioned these in our debriefings, Alexander's career had taken a nasty hit. He'd been stripped of his medals and commendations and fired from the Agency. I hadn't seen him since. Now it appeared he'd returned to clear out his office. He looked like a mere shell of the man he'd been before. His normally pristine suit was rumpled, his shirt was untucked, and there was a mustard stain on his tie. He had a week's growth of beard on his chin and a great deal of sadness in his eyes.

"Hello, Benjamin," Alexander said meekly. "How's your first day of school so far?"

"Not so good," I told him. "I just got expelled."

Alexander's eyes widened in surprise. "For what?"

"I sort of blew up the principal's office."

"Oh. So that's what that loud boom was."

I nodded. "Yes. He just kicked me out."

The old Alexander Hale might have volunteered to go to bat for me. Or at least pretended that he was going to. Instead, he sighed. "We all fall from grace sooner or later, don't we?"

"I would have preferred later." I noticed what was inside the box Alexander was carrying. Office supplies. And then I realized that the office Alexander had been exiting wasn't his. It belonged to Nathan Kagan, the dean of Survival Skills. "Is all that stuff yours?"

"Er . . . Kind of." It was suddenly evident that Alexander hadn't been embarrassed about running into me; he'd been embarrassed because I'd caught him swiping office supplies. "Kagan filched plenty from me over the years. I can't even count how many bullets I lent him. But was he there when I needed someone to stand up for me? No. He threw me to the wolves. So at the very least, he owes me a stapler." He grinned at me weakly. "I really should go. If anyone asks, you never saw me."

Alexander ducked away before I could say another word, probably intending to use one of the secret exits off the campus to avoid running into anyone else.

I headed down the main staircase to the first floor, where there was a big, open lobby, the grand entrance to the Hale Building.

My friends were gathered there. It was a good-size crowd, with Zoe, Jawa, and Chip at the front. I spotted Warren as well, lurking off to the side.

"I can't believe they're booting you for this," Zoe said, and everyone echoed the thought.

"How'd you even know?" I asked. "The principal just told me. . . ."

"We're studying to be spies," Jawa explained. "It's our job to know things."

I nodded, realizing I should have expected that.

"You want to get even with the principal?" Chip asked. "I'd be happy to handle that for you. Just say the word and his car ends up in the Potomac River."

"Thanks for the offer," I said. "But I'll pass."

"How about his cat, then?" Chip asked. "I could do something bad to his cat."

"Chip!" Zoe gasped.

"I don't mean kill it," Chip told her. "I mean shave it or something. To send a message to the principal that you don't mess with our friends."

In truth, I would have loved for my friends to get even with the principal. After all, the man had just dashed all my hopes and dreams. When I'd first arrived at the academy, I had desperately wanted to become a great spy but had feared I might not be qualified. But now, after several months of school and camp—not to mention two successful confrontations with SPYDER—I really felt I had what it took. And now I was being dumped back into the real world. The principal wasn't tossing me for any real reason; he was just being petty, and I hated him for it. And yet it seemed that having my friends prank him in response was equally petty. Plus, there were cameras everywhere at spy school. If I asked anyone to do anything illegal, it'd be recorded.

"There is *something* I'd like you all to do to the principal," I said.

"Really?" Chip asked, excited. "What?"

"Tell him he's making a mistake."

Chip frowned, deflated. "You mean, like write a petition or something?"

"Yes."

"We could do that!" Zoe proclaimed eagerly. "And we could send it to the top brass at the CIA too! They should know they're losing one of their best spies-to-be for a dumb reason. If anyone should have been booted for this, it's Warren."

Lots of people seconded this.

"Hey!" Warren cried. "This isn't my fault!"

"You loaded the mortar," Zoe said pointedly.

"There were only supposed to be paint bombs in the ammo pile," Warren replied. "I'm not the idiot who put a live shell in there with them."

"But you *are* the idiot who didn't notice the difference," Chip told him.

"They looked exactly the same!" Warren cried.

"They shouldn't have," Jawa chided. "A paint bomb and a shell are nothing alike."

"These were," Warren snapped. "I swear. Any one of you would have made the same mistake!"

"Well, we didn't," Zoe said. "*You* did. And now Smoke-screen's getting sacked because of it."

Warren cringed, looking wounded. Everyone on campus knew that he carried a serious torch for Zoe—except Zoe. I almost felt bad for the kid. Not quite, but almost.

Now that I thought about it, something seemed wrong about the whole mortar incident. I tried to place what it was, but before I could, a hush fell over the room.

Erica had arrived.

I hadn't seen her come in, but that wasn't unusual. Erica had a way of seeming to suddenly materialize. One moment, she wasn't there—and the next, she was.

The crowd parted like the Red Sea, allowing her to pass through it.

Erica didn't look at anyone else as she passed them. She kept her eyes locked on me until we were face-to-face.

I expected that she was there for moral support, like everyone else. She was going to tell me that the administration was doing the wrong thing. She was going to admit that she'd really miss me. Maybe she'd even show a rare spark of emotion and hug me good-bye.

But she didn't. Instead, she said, "You really screwed up."

"Me?" I asked, surprised. "Don't you mean the principal?"

"No." Erica's gaze remained steely and cold. "You cracked under pressure and made a huge mistake. Yes, you saved some people, but in doing so, you nearly killed someone else—and did serious damage to this building. Who knows what might have happened if you'd behaved like this on a *real* mission."

"But you've been with me on a real mission," I protested. "And I didn't screw up then!"

"That's not exactly true," Erica said. "In fact, you made plenty of mistakes."

"Like what?"

"Accidentally alerting potential suspects that you were spying on them, getting captured by the enemy, allowing yourself to be led into an ambush . . ."

"All of those weren't entirely my fault. . . ."

"And refusing to accept responsibility for your failures. Now, I chalked some of that up to you being young and naive, hoping you'd get better. But today's events proved me wrong. I'm sorry, Ben, but it doesn't look like you have what it takes to be a spy."

Erica couldn't have hurt me more if she'd punched me in the face. And to make matters worse, she'd done it in front of my friends. I gaped at her, trying to figure out what to say, but no words would come. I felt completely empty inside.

"Take my advice," Erica said. "The next time someone comes to you with an offer to change your life, accept it—and then try not to mess it up like you did this time."

She spun on her heel and started back through the crowd. Everyone else looked as shocked as I felt.

"All of you know the rules," Erica told them. "After today, in order to protect the secrecy of this institution, none of you can have any more contact with Ben. Anyone who violates that directive will suffer the same fate as he did. As far as this school is concerned, Agent Benjamin Ripley no longer exists."

Then she melted into the crowd and vanished from sight.

CIVILIAN LIFE

Robert E. Lee Junior High
September 4
1200 hours

I didn't think it was possible to feel worse than I did after being expelled from spy school, but I was wrong. Less than twenty-four hours later, I found myself in one of the most horrible places I could have ever imagined.

Middle school.

After packing up my belongings in my dorm room, I had taken a cab to my parents' home in Vienna, Virginia. Spy school had already established a cover story for my return: Due to some unforeseen cutbacks, St. Smithen's Science Academy could no longer afford my scholarship.

My parents were at once upset by this news and thrilled to have me home. Mom had quickly whipped up a celebratory welcome-back dinner while Dad had done his best to assure me that it wouldn't be so bad to return to my old life.

The next morning, they reenrolled me at my old middle school. It wasn't difficult, as the school year had begun only the day before.

I wasn't very happy about this.

Although spy school had been extremely challenging and people had occasionally tried to kill me there, it had still been significantly more enjoyable than middle school. Junior high was mind-numbingly dull, socially distressing, and potentially dangerous as well; it was common to be threatened with physical harm by the roving gangs of bullies there. In addition, the cafeteria food was toxic, the bathrooms were putrid, and many of the teachers were dumber than dirt. (For example: Mr. Godfrey, my American history teacher, who hadn't known when the War of 1812 took place.)

As far as I was concerned, there was only one good thing about middle school: My best friend Mike Brezinski was there too.

Mike and I had met in first grade and been friends ever since, even though we'd grown into very different people. I worked hard and studied hard. Mike didn't. In fact, he tried to get away with doing as little as possible. Things always worked out for him, though. He was popular, happy, and dating Elizabeth Pasternak, the most beautiful girl in school.

"It's good to have you back, buddy," he told me at lunch the first day.

I poked at the grayish slab of meat I'd gotten in the hot lunch line, checking it for insect parts or stray cafeteria-lady hairs. "It's good to be back," I agreed, doing my best to sell the lie.

Mike saw right through this. "I know you're bummed that you can't go to that science school anymore, but trust me, it's way better here."

"I already went to this school," I reminded him. "It sucked."

"More than science school? Please. What'd you do there for fun, dissect worms?"

"Not exactly," I said. If there was anyone I wished I could tell the truth about spy school, it was Mike. Throughout our lives, he'd been the cool kid while I'd been the dork. And now I'd fought bad guys, been in death-defying action sequences, and saved the life of the President of the United States—and Mike *still* thought I was a dork.

"I'll tell you why this is better," Mike said. "We have girls here."

I took a tentative bite of my mystery meat, then spit it right back out again. It tasted as though it had gone bad several months earlier. "There were girls at St. Smithen's."

"I mean *attractive* girls. Not science girls."

"They *were* attractive. You saw Erica."

Mike paused, then nodded agreement. "True. Erica was smoking hot. But you're not seeing her anymore."

I frowned. I'd never really been seeing Erica. Mike had once spotted us together and mistakenly assumed we were dating—and I hadn't exactly tried to convince him that wasn't true. It was the one time in my life he'd actually seemed jealous of me. However, since I was barred from ever seeing Erica again for security reasons, I'd had to claim things were over between us.

"You know how you get over losing a hot girlfriend?" Mike asked. "You get another hot girlfriend."

"Just like that?" I asked, dubious.

"Just like that," Mike said. Like it was easy.

As if on cue, Elizabeth Pasternak arrived at our table with her best friends: Chloe Appel and Kate Grant. Back in sixth grade, I'd had crushes on all three of them. Although they paled next to Erica, I still felt my heart rev up when they sat with us.

All of them seemed slightly annoyed that I was crashing their table.

Elizabeth gave Mike a peck on the cheek. "Hey."

"Hey," Mike said back. "You all remember Ben, right?"

"Kind of," said Elizabeth.

"Maybe," said Chloe.

"No," said Kate.

I'd been in the same grade with all of them since kindergarten.

Mike said, "Ben just transferred back here from private school."

"Really?" Chloe asked, trying to be nice. "What school?"

I started to say, "St. Smithen's Science Academy," but before I could, Mike said, "You wouldn't have heard of it. It's top secret."

The girls all perked up, intrigued.

"Why was it secret?" Chloe asked.

"Because Ben was training to be a spy," Mike told them.

I turned on Mike, worried, wondering if he really knew my secret or was simply trying to make me sound cool and had guessed the truth by accident.

"Liar," said Kate. Then she looked at me. "He's lying, right?"

I couldn't believe I had to lie to the three hottest girls in the school—about *not* having trained to be a spy—but I did it anyhow. "Yes, he's lying."

"I knew it!" Kate exclaimed.

"Oh, come on," Mike said. "You can't expect him to admit the truth, can you?"

The girls all took a moment to think about that.

"I thought you were at some dorky science academy," Elizabeth said.

"It was his cover," Mike told her.

I tried to deny this, but before I could, Chloe asked, "If you were in spy school, what are you doing back here?"

"He's undercover," Mike said.

He was surprisingly convincing. The girls all now looked intrigued. It took everything I had to tell them, "That's not true. I *did* go to a science academy. I was never training to be a spy."

Chloe said, "That's exactly what I'd expect someone who *was* training to be a spy to say."

I started to deny this, but Mike gripped my arm tightly and pulled me aside. "What are you doing?" he whispered.

"What are *you* doing?" I shot back.

"I'm trying to get you a new girlfriend."

"By lying to them?" I asked.

Mike shrugged in a way that could have either meant, "You know I'm not lying" or "So I'm lying; who cares?" Then he told the girls, "Sorry. Ben's upset at me for blowing his cover. Apparently, now that you know the truth about him, we're all in mortal danger. So we have to stop talking about this."

Elizabeth and Chloe nodded in understanding. They didn't look concerned about being in mortal danger. They looked excited.

Kate fixed Mike with a skeptical glance. "You're so full of garbage."

I couldn't believe the irony of my situation. The one person who thought Mike was lying was actually wrong. While the other girls, who'd been theoretically misled, now believed the truth. It was so screwed up, I could barely keep track of right and wrong.

Before I could even begin to sort it out, though, someone grabbed me by the collar from behind, dragging me away from the table and hoisting me to my feet.

It was Dirk Dennett. Otherwise known as Dirk the Jerk. Dirk wasn't the toughest bully we had at our school, but he made up for that by being the meanest. Before I'd gone to spy school, he'd made my life miserable every chance he got, and now that I was back, he seemed eager to make up for lost time. "I heard you got kicked out of your science school," he taunted.

"N-no," I stammered. "I lost my scholarship."

Mike was suddenly on his feet beside me. "Leave him alone, Dirk."

Dirk didn't take his eyes off me. "Why do you insist on hanging out with this loser, Brezinski?"

"'Cause it's better than hanging out with a jerk like you," Mike shot back. "Now let him go."

Elizabeth, Chloe, and Kate all cooed, impressed by Mike's chivalry.

Dirk shifted his attention to Mike, but kept a vise grip on my collar. "You gonna make me?"

Mike wasn't really a fighter; he tended to get by on charm. He sized Dirk up, a bit daunted, but then stood up for me anyhow. "I might."

Dirk shoved me aside and clenched his fists.

"Mike," I said quickly. "You don't have to do this."

"Yes, I do," Mike replied. "I'm not letting this bozo ruin your first day back."

Without warning, Dirk suddenly took a swing at Mike. Only, something caught his fist en route.

To my surprise, it was me.

I'd learned some things over the past few months at spy school. For starters, I wasn't completely helpless when it came to self-preservation. I'd hoped to keep all that a secret, given the official directive I'd received to not reveal anything about my training, but the instant I saw Mike in jeopardy—for trying to help *me*, no less—my instincts had taken over.

Dirk seemed even more surprised that I'd caught his fist than I was. Then he turned on me and attacked.

Right up until that point, I had never considered myself a good fighter. I'd been one of the worst at spy school. But then, I'd been measuring myself against other spies-to-be, many of whom had been studying martial arts since preschool. I'd never fought a normal person before.

In truth, even a bully like Dirk didn't fight that much. He merely threatened smaller kids and hoped they'd fork over their lunch money. Or he sucker-punched them and put them out of commission before they even knew what was happening. The only reason he attacked me then was that, after all my years of letting him bully me, he was sure he'd win.

He was wrong.

Without even thinking about it, my training kicked in. First, I went with the Sneaky Cobra defense. I quickly side-stepped Dirk's punch and wrenched his arm behind him. He buckled at the knees and I slammed his face right into Chloe Appel's hot lunch. His face splatted in her mashed potatoes, flecking gravy onto her blouse.

"Sorry," I said.

"Don't worry about it," Chloe replied, then flashed me a coy smile.

I twisted Dirk's arm a bit more, making him yelp in pain. "Are you going to behave now?"

Dirk whimpered and nodded, which was hard to do with his face in the potatoes.

"All right, then." I released my grip on him.

Dirk immediately went back on his word and attacked again. He came up roaring—which might have been scarier if there hadn't been French-cut green beans jammed up his nose. Then he charged me, swinging his fists wildly. I quickly went with the Angry Monkey counterattack, spinning away, then delivering a quick elbow to the solar plexus. When Dirk doubled over, gasping for air, I gave him a good, quick thwack to the back of the neck, which laid him out for good on the cafeteria floor.

The entire room erupted with cheers.

Every single person—most of whom had been picked on by Dirk at some point—was applauding. Even the lunch ladies. Mike was grinning proudly, like a dad who'd just watched his son hit a home run. And Elizabeth Pasternak's friends seemed much more interested in me than they had before.

"You expect us to believe you learned *that* in science school?" Chloe asked.

"Karate's really just physics," I replied.

"What are you gonna do to the other three guys?" Kate said, excited.

"What other three guys?" I asked.

The girls pointed behind me.

It was only now that I noticed Dirk had brought backup. Three guys, each considerably bigger than I was, were lurching toward me, cracking their knuckles.

"Get him!" Dirk gasped from the floor, where he was still curled in the fetal position. "And make him pay!"

I hadn't studied fighting three opponents at once yet. That was to be covered in Self-Preservation 102, which was a second-year class at spy school. Although I'd still learned one useful thing about this situation in S-P 101: When severely outnumbered by the enemy, running away is always a good call. And so I went with the Frightened Rabbit defense and turned tail.

The three thugs followed, knocking hapless students aside and sending lunch trays flying as they came after me.

"Wait!" Mike yelled to me, but there was no way I could do that.

I barged out of the cafeteria and raced through the halls, which were now empty for lunchtime. I'd been hoping to outrun the bullies, but they were surprisingly fast for guys so big. They kept pace as I zigged and zagged through the halls. Then I rounded a corner, expecting to find an exit ahead of me . . .

And found a wall instead. Either there had been some new construction at school or I hadn't remembered the layout right. Either way, I was at a dead end.

I had no choice but to turn around and brace for the oncoming attack.

Only, it never came.

Around the corner, the sound of the three brutes storming down the hall toward me was interrupted by the sound of them all reacting with surprise, followed by the sounds of them getting thrashed in a fight: the muffled thuds of fists hitting flesh, the metallic clangs of heads caroming off lockers, the wet slaps of bodies landing hard on a linoleum floor.

Then there was silence.

I peered around the corner, wondering who had come to my rescue, expecting Mike—or perhaps Mike and a few other guys—or maybe even Erica, who'd reveal that she'd been keeping an eye on me out of habit.

The three bullies were laid out, unconscious.

And standing in the middle of them, brushing a bit of blood off his sleeve, was Joshua Hallal.

This was a considerable shock to me, as Joshua worked for SPYDER. Plus, the last time I'd seen him, he'd been plummeting to his death.

He looked up and smiled politely, as though there was nothing insanely abnormal about his being there at all. "Hello, Ben," he said. "We need to talk. I have a proposition for you."

RECRUITMENT

Robert E. Lee Junior High
September 4
1245 hours

"I thought you were dead," I said.

"I'm not," Joshua replied. "Surprise." Although he was trying to be civil, there was a bitter edge to his voice, which made sense, given that I was partly responsible for his plunge off a cliff. I had just thwarted SPYDER's plans and Joshua had been trying to escape when he'd fallen to what I'd *thought* was his doom. Although he hadn't died, he hadn't come out of it unscathed, either. In fact, he was extremely scathed. Joshua was only eighteen, and he'd been a student at spy school before defecting to SPYDER. Back then he'd been renowned for his good looks, with piercing green eyes, a mane of dark hair, and flawless skin. Now his once-handsome face was a maze of scars. In addition—or perhaps, subtraction—he was missing an eye (covered by a patch), a hand (replaced by a high-tech hook), and a leg (now a robotic prosthetic). And yet he carried himself with grace and style, sporting designer clothes and a watch that probably cost more than my father's car. He looked like an extremely well-dressed pirate.

"How'd you survive?" I asked.

"I landed in a bog. Or a marsh. Something squishy. It broke my fall enough to spare my life." Joshua spoke with a clipped, somewhat snobbish accent that made him sound like he'd spent a lot of his life at a country club. That, combined with his battered body, made him seem older than he actually was. "SPYDER's agents found me later, and the doctors did the best they could to fix me."

Voices echoed through the school halls. It sounded like a lot of other students were coming our way, probably wanting to see what the bullies had done to me—or vice versa.

I could hear Mike's voice among them, leading the pack. "I think they went this way! Come on!"

"We need to go," Joshua told me. "I can't be seen here."

"I'm not going anywhere with you," I said.

Joshua produced a gun from his pocket. "Does this change your mind?"

"Yes," I admitted. "It sure does."

Joshua motioned me toward a classroom with the gun. "Move."

I did as ordered, and found myself in a chemistry class. Joshua came in behind me, locked the door, and then pointed to the window with his hook. "Open that."

I did this, too. We were only on the first floor, so it was easy to clamber out onto the school lawn.

Through the door behind me, I could hear my fellow students discovering the trio of unconscious bullies in the hall. There were lots of gasps of surprise.

"Holy cow!" Mike whooped. "Ben wiped the floor with them!"

"You weren't kidding!" Chloe gasped. "He *was* a spy!"

"Is he dating anyone?" Kate asked.

Joshua slipped out the window with surprising grace for a man missing half his limbs. A gray sedan idled nearby, a man in sunglasses in the driver's seat. "Get in," Joshua demanded.

There was no one else outside the school, no one I could signal to for help. And while I could outrun bullies, I couldn't outrun a bullet. So I got in the car.

There was a thick glass partition between us and the front seat, like in a taxicab. It was soundproof, so the driver couldn't hear us. The backseat was spacious and comfortable.

There was a small cooler with some drinks on ice for us. It might have all been very pleasant if I wasn't being forced to be there against my will.

Joshua climbed in, keeping the gun trained on me. The car started moving before I even had my seat belt fastened.

"It's good to see you again, Ben," Joshua said. "You look like you've kept yourself in good shape."

"Thanks." Seeing as he had a gun, I tried to be polite. "You look . . . um . . . well, not good exactly, but . . ."

"I think the word you're looking for is 'terrible.'"

I frowned. "Did all that happen in the fall?"

"Most of it. I lost the arm and the leg, but not the eye."

"Oh. How'd you lose that?"

"A bug flew into it."

"Er . . . You don't lose your eye if a bug flies into it."

"You do if it's your first day with the hook."

I winced. I almost apologized, but then it occurred to me that I hadn't directly caused Joshua's misfortune. All I'd done was defeat his evil plans. The damage he'd experienced as a result was all due to his own actions as he tried to escape. "So," I said. "What's this proposition?"

"You're a smart kid. You can't figure it out?"

There was only one reason I could think of that I was still alive. "You want me to come work for SPYDER."

Joshua smiled. "Yes."

"You guys have already made me this offer," I said. "Twice."

"I know. And you've rejected us twice. Not to mention thwarting our plans twice, causing us considerable embarrassment and costing us a great deal of money. But we don't see that as a problem. When the New York Yankees get repeatedly shut out by a great pitcher, they don't hate the pitcher. Instead, they try to recruit him."

"This isn't baseball."

"True."

"So what makes you think I'm going to accept this time?"

"The way spy school treated you, for starters. You're one of the finest students they've produced in years. Not just anyone could have undone our plans. And how do they repay you? With expulsion. I assure you, we would never treat you that way at SPYDER. In fact, we are prepared to treat you far better than the Academy of Espionage has treated you all along."

I didn't want to work for SPYDER. Not in the slightest. And yet Joshua had struck a nerve. Spy school *had* treated me badly. So I couldn't help but ask, "How so?"

"For starters, we'd compensate you very well financially. While your friends from spy school will be struggling to make ends meet on measly government salaries, you'll soon make millions with us—tax free. Enough to be extremely comfortable for the rest of your life. But more important, we'll give you *respect*. The respect you deserve. The respect the CIA should have given you for your amazing work, but didn't."

I glanced out the window. We were passing through the suburbs of Washington, DC. I saw a Starbucks and a McDonald's slide past. It occurred to me that I probably should have been keeping better track of where we were going, but I'd forgotten to. It was hard to focus on my location when Joshua Hallal still had a gun aimed at me.

"Are you going to shoot me if I say no?" I asked.

"Of course not. This was only to make sure you'd get in the car." Joshua slipped the gun back into his pocket. "If you say no, the only punishment we'll give you is returning you to your normal life. You'll be free to go back to middle school and join the chess club and spend your weekends at the arcade like a regular boring teenager."

I was quite sure Joshua was lying. SPYDER didn't seem the type of organization that would simply let bygones be bygones. My mouth was getting dry from fear, so I fished a root beer out of the cooler and cracked it open. "What would I be doing for you?"

Joshua smiled, pleased I'd taken the bait. "Given your age, we wouldn't activate you right away. Even though you've shown some mettle, you still have things to learn. So for the time being, you'll be sent to our training facility."

"Training facility?"

"Yes. Being a bad guy isn't easy, you know. In fact, it's considerably harder than being a good guy. There is a great array of skills and abilities that you'll have to master. Many of them are similar to those which you began studying at the academy: self-preservation, cryptography, facility with weapons. But there's also duplicity, conniving, subterfuge, and killing without making it look like murder, to name just a few things."

"So . . . it's kind of like evil spy school."

Joshua frowned. "I suppose. Although we prefer to call it the Wiseman Preparatory Academy."

"Why?"

"Because 'Evil Spy School' sounds a little suspicious, don't you think?"

I glanced out the window again, just in time to see us go past a Starbucks and a McDonald's. I had no idea if they were the same Starbucks and McDonald's we'd passed before or different ones that merely looked the same.

I took another sip of root beer. "Where is this academy?"

Joshua chuckled. "You don't honestly think I'd tell you *before* you accepted our offer?"

"I was only wondering if it was far. I just got done unpacking. . . ."

"So you'll pack again. This isn't some pedestrian commuter

school. Should you say yes, we will return to your home and inform your parents that Wiseman Prep sees an opportunity where those fools at St. Smithen's no longer do. You now have a brand-new scholarship that will require you to reside at another school, effective immediately."

"Immediately?" I repeated.

"Yes. The sooner you can begin your training with us, the better."

"I understand, but . . . You're asking me to make a really big decision here. Can I at least have a little time to think it over?"

"Of course. You can have three minutes." Joshua plucked a book of crossword puzzles out of the seat back pocket in front of him and turned his attention to it.

I stared out the window again. Another Starbucks slid by, although I was relatively sure this was a different one.

I *really* didn't want to join SPYDER. Even though the Academy of Espionage had treated me badly, it still seemed wrong to go to the dark side: I simply wasn't an evil person. But a few things made me think I shouldn't reject SPYDER's offer.

First, Joshua would kill me if I did. Which was a very powerful incentive to say yes.

Second, as bad as going to evil spy school sounded, it would probably still be better than normal middle school.

Third, Erica's final words kept coming back to me.

The next time someone comes to you with an offer to change your life, accept it—and then try not to mess it up like you did this time.

In retrospect, it had been kind of an odd thing to say. Now it made me wonder. Had Erica suspected this was going to happen all along?

I thought back to the mortar incident that had gotten me in trouble, realizing what had been bothering me about it.

There was a very good chance that Erica had planted the live round.

She'd been carrying a knapsack throughout the SACSA. She could have easily smuggled in a live round designed to look like a paint bomb, then tricked Warren into loading it. It would certainly explain how she'd known the round was live so quickly. And, now that I thought about it, it also explained how Warren had been able to wrest the remote trigger away from Erica. On an average day, Erica could have outfought Warren in her sleep; there was no way he'd have ended up with the trigger unless she wanted him to have it. Everything seemed to indicate that I hadn't randomly fired that bomb at the Nathan Hale Building; I'd been manipulated into doing it.

Could it all have been a setup to make SPYDER think I'd been kicked out of spy school?

Or was I deluding myself, inventing evidence to make myself feel better after getting expelled for real?

If it hadn't been for those last words of Erica's, I would have figured I was deluding myself. But this was certainly an offer to change my life, and she'd given me specific instructions on what to do if such an offer came along.

I still had a thousand questions. Was Erica working with someone else, or had she gone rogue and dragged me in? Did the principal know about this, or was he just a pawn like me? Did Erica know Joshua Hallal was still alive? If I did go to evil spy school, what was my assignment? Was I supposed to only be a mole, or was there something more specific? What was I supposed to be looking for? Was this really an under-cover mission? If so, why hadn't anyone told me about it? And did I actually have what it took to succeed?

"Time's up," Joshua said.

I turned back from the window, where another Star-bucks was passing.

Joshua was looking at me expectantly. The bulge of his gun was barely visible inside his pocket.

I took a deep breath, hoping that I'd interpreted everything correctly and that I wasn't making the worst decision of my life.

"I'm in," I said.

IMMERSION

SPYDER Agent Training Facility
Location Unknown
September 5
1030 hours

I woke in a strange room.

I felt groggy, like I'd been drugged. It took me only a few seconds to figure out why: I *had* been drugged.

A thirteen-year-old kid probably shouldn't have been drugged enough times to recognize the sensation, but that was life when you were a spy-in-training. My head was pounding and my mouth felt like it was stuffed with cotton.

Joshua Hallal had done this to me. Even with my mind cloudy, I had no doubt of that. There wasn't anyone else who could have done it. Immediately after I'd accepted his offer, we'd driven to my house, where he'd presented my parents with an official-looking contract stating that I had been accepted with a full scholarship to another school for gifted children. Joshua had claimed to be my new student adviser, shown them some glossy promotional brochures, and had gone on at length about how Wiseman Preparatory Academy was an even better school than St. Smithen's. He sold it well—although Mom and Dad seemed just as impressed by him as the school. My parents were at once pleased by my prowess and saddened that I'd be leaving again—though they were perhaps a bit more prone to accept the offer as my middle school principal had just informed them that I'd received six weeks of detention for fighting and then skipping school. We had a farewell meal, where Joshua was the perfect guest, charming and graceful and not the slightest bit evil, and then . . .

Well, I wasn't quite sure what had happened after that. The whole point of drugging someone is to leave some blanks in their memory. Joshua must have slipped me something shortly after dinner, probably in the apple pie Mom had made for dessert.

My eyelids were so heavy, it felt like they were made of steel. I fought to keep them open and took in my surroundings.

I was in a bedroom. A nice bedroom, bigger than mine back home—and several times larger than my dorm room at spy school. But then, I'd been in closets bigger than my dorm room at spy school.

The room was bare save for a twin bed, which I was currently lying on, a dresser, a desk, and my suitcases. Apparently, I'd packed my clothes. Or someone had packed them for me. Except for the suitcases, everything in the room seemed to be brand-new, including the room itself. There wasn't a scratch on the walls—which smelled faintly of fresh paint—or a stain on the carpet. The bedsheets were crisp and still had the creases that indicated they'd recently come out of the package.

The walls were bare, too, except for a framed inspirational poster: a photo of a mountain climber standing atop a snowy peak and the mantra OPPORTUNITY IS ALWAYS KNOCKING. MOST PEOPLE JUST DON'T OPEN THE DOOR. There was a closet, a private bathroom, and a large window.

The sun was streaming through the blinds from a high angle, indicating it was well into the morning. I generally had an extremely good sense of time, knowing exactly when it was without needing to check my watch—one of the perks of my innate math skills—but it didn't work so well after I'd been drugged. So I used my watch. It was 10:34 a.m. I'd been out for at least sixteen hours.

I struggled to my feet and started running in place. The best way to fight off a drug haze was to get your blood flowing. The moment my legs began pumping, I felt better.

I jogged over to the window.

Evil spy school didn't look a thing like I'd expected. I'd figured it would appear, at least in some way, like a campus. Perhaps the classic, Gothic style of the Academy of Espionage—or maybe more architecturally modern—but at least something with stately buildings and gymnasiums and grassy expanses where students could hang out and play ultimate Frisbee. But of course, evil spy school wasn't like that at all. SPYDER never did anything that anyone expected.

I was in a brand-new gated suburban community. Or at least, it *looked* like a brand-new gated suburban community. I was on a street lined with homes that were almost identical. There were subtle differences between them, but they were all two stories with tile roofs and wide front porches and manicured lawns. I could tell it was all new because the street was perfectly black, the sidewalks were perfectly white, and the lawns looked like they had been put down that morning. The trees hadn't had any time to grow: They were mere saplings, sprouting every twenty feet along the road.

A few years before, my parents had considered moving to a community like this. We'd visited several. This looked like every single one of them.

My mind was now cleared from my exertion. Or at least, I thought it was. My surroundings were so odd, part of me wondered if I was hallucinating them.

I tested out the bathroom. After all, it had been more than sixteen hours since I'd last urinated.

The toilet worked perfectly. It was also nice and clean and smelled like ammonia. This was a change from spy school, where the dormitory toilets probably hadn't been cleaned since the Clinton administration.

Having a private shower was pretty cool, too. The ones at spy school were all shared, which meant cleaning off was rarely relaxing, because someone was always clamoring for you to vacate the stall. Plus, the hot water tended to run out, usually right at the point when you were completely lathered up.

I turned on my sink to check the water. It was nice and hot.

While I was washing my hands, I noticed I was still in the same clothes I'd worn to school the day before. However, something seemed different. I felt my pockets and realized what was wrong: My phone was gone.

I returned to my room and quickly rooted through my suitcases. The phone wasn't there.

I had no doubt it had been taken from me. Which meant that, for the moment, I had no way to contact anyone on the outside—or determine where on earth I was.

I tried the door to my room, expecting it to be locked.

It wasn't.

The hall outside was equally new-looking, with fresh carpet and paint. One end led to three other doors, all shut, presumably more bedrooms. From the other end, I could hear someone playing a video game.

I went that way.

The hall led to a staircase, which swept down into a large common area: a kind of living room/family room/kitchen. It looked like teenagers had furnished it. There was foosball, air hockey, and a drum set. Instead of a dining room table, there was a Ping-Pong table, its surface covered with half-eaten bags of chips and unwashed cereal bowls. The only piece of actual furniture was a couch, which was oriented directly at the largest television I'd ever seen.

A kid who appeared to be around fifteen years old was slumped on the couch, playing the video game I'd heard. I didn't recognize the game, but it was some sort of air combat simulator and the kid was extremely good at it, racing fighter jets across digital landscapes and carpet bombing the enemy. He was stick thin with a mop of wiry dark hair, wearing unfashionable glasses and a T-shirt smeared with Day-Glo orange Cheetos dust. His face was a minefield of pimples. His eyes flicked in my direction, but he made no attempt to introduce himself. Or smile. Or be friendly in any way whatsoever.

"Hi," I said. "I'm Ben."

The kid didn't respond. He had returned his full attention to the game, where two enemy planes were now attacking him. He dodged them with ease, then launched two missiles into a bridge, which exploded so violently that the entire room was momentarily bathed in red.

I noticed that his lips were moving, but he wasn't talking to me. He was mumbling softly to himself. It was hard to hear over all the virtual explosions, but it appeared to be a run-on commentary on what he was doing: "Adjustaltitude-employboostersfindtargetsreadymunitions."

I tried to engage him again. "I just got here. I'm not sure when, exactly, because I was drugged. It's nice to meet you."

This was a lie. It wasn't really nice to meet the kid at all. It was sort of like meeting a brick.

"Evadeflak," the kid mumbled. "Lockontargetsbombs-away."

On the TV, two more missiles detonated, reducing another bridge to dust.

"Do you have a name?" I asked.

"Nefarious," the kid said, so quietly I didn't think I'd heard it right.

"Nefarious?" I repeated.

"That's his name," said someone behind me.

I spun around to find a girl there. She looked to be my

age and she was exceptionally perky, with a big smile and wide, bright eyes. She was short, but very physically fit. I could tell this right away, because she was wearing a sparkly pink leotard. She also had glitter in her hair.

"His name's Nefarious?" I asked.

"Right. It's not his nickname or anything. It's his real name. Nefarious Jones. And I'm Ashley Sparks. Nice to meet you." The girl held out a hand. She had rainbows painted on her fingernails.

We shook hands. Ashley's hand seemed to be only about half the size of mine, but her grip was startlingly strong.

"I'm Ben," I said. "Ben Ripley."

"No need to introduce yourself. You're pretty famous around here, given how much trouble you've caused SPY-DER over the last year."

"Oh." I lowered my eyes, embarrassed. "Sorry about that."

Ashley waved this off. "Hey, they weren't *my* missions. Anyhow, it's swawesome to have you on our side now."

"Swawesome?" I asked.

"Yeah. Sweet plus awesome. 'Swawesome.' Are you hungry? I'll bet you're hungry."

I realized this was true. My stomach was grumbling.

Ashley waved to the kitchen. "Help yourself to anything you want."

"Not the Cheetos," Nefarious said quickly.

"Except the Cheetos," Ashley corrected. "Nefarious is a big old scrooge with his snacks, even though he doesn't even pay for them. SPYDER covers the bills—and they have a staff that does all the shopping for us, so if there's anything you want and we don't have it, just fill out a requisition form and they'll get it."

I opened the kitchen cabinets. One was fully stocked with sugared cereal, instant pudding, and a staggering amount of Cheetos. The other was filled with large canisters of powder. I took one out and examined the label. The ingredient list was filled with words I had never seen before, even though I was relatively sure they were English. Ergocalciferol. Phytonadione. Pyrophosphate.

"What is this stuff?" I asked.

"Power Powder!" Ashley exclaimed. "One scoop provides me with all the probiotics, antioxidants, and digestive enzymes I need each day—though I like to throw in a little chia seed to boost my omega-3s. I use it to make energy shakes. Want one? They're telicious."

I took a moment to figure that one out. "Tasty plus delicious?"

"Exactly! And they give you a ton of energy! They're all I eat, every day."

"Really?" I asked. "You don't eat food?"

Ashley shook her head. "Oh no. These are better than food."

I was pretty sure that, as far as meals were concerned, there wasn't anything better than food, but I kept this to myself. I didn't want to offend Ashley right after meeting her. "Sounds great, but I'm kind of in the mood for cereal right now. I always want carbs after I've been sedated." I grabbed a box of Lucky Charms, which was the only cereal I could find that didn't have chocolate flavoring in it. "Is there any fruit?"

"Uh . . . no," Ashley admitted. "And I think we're out of milk, too."

I opened the fridge and confirmed she was right. There was, however, an entire convenience store's worth of soda.

"Milk wouldn't have done you any good anyhow," Ashley said. "I just realized all the bowls are dirty. The maids don't come until noon."

"Maids?" I asked.

"Yeah. To clean up after us. You didn't have maids in spy school?"

"Er . . . no."

"Ooh. That stinks. Guess you're even happier that you're not at that lousy place anymore."

"I sure am," I lied.

Nefarious was acting as though we weren't even there, his full attention riveted on his video game. He was strafing an enemy base, mumbling to himself the whole time. "Avoid-enemyfirestaycalmdepresstriggers." More explosions rocked the room.

"So," Ashley said. "Have you had a chance to poke around yet, or would you like the tour?"

"A tour would be great." Seeing as there were no bowls or spoons, I dug a handful of Lucky Charms out of the box. "This is as far as I've gotten. I only regained consciousness a few minutes ago."

"Cool!" Ashley led me across the room. "Obviously, this is the living area. Our bedrooms are all upstairs. . . ."

"There were four rooms up there," I said. "Does someone else live here?"

Ashley hesitated the tiniest fraction before answering. "Nope. That one's empty. It's only the three of us here for now."

"Where do all the other students live?"

Ashley looked at me curiously. "There are no other students."

"You mean . . . we're the entire school?"

"Joshua didn't tell you?" Ashley laughed. "I guess he thought you knew or something. Yeah, it's only us here. This is a much more elite organization than the CIA. That place will let practically anyone in. No offense."

"None taken."

"But SPYDER's different. They're not recruiting future

desk jockeys here. Our projects are complex and devious, requiring exceptionally intelligent employees with highly specialized skill sets. It's harder to get into SPYDER than it is to become an astronaut. You can't just be the cream of the crop. You have to be the cream of the cream of the cream. So you should be darn proud of yourself for making the cut. Plus, SPYDER doesn't want to be some giant, bureaucratic organization anyhow. They want to stay lean and mean and under the radar. There's not many people in it, period."

"How many?"

Ashley shrugged. "No idea. That's confidential. But most of the people you see working around here: security guards, maids, groundskeepers, and such . . . They're not official SPYDER employees. In fact, they don't even know SPYDER exists. They're just subcontractors who think they've been hired by a legitimate homeowner's association. Okay, here's the gym." She led me into a surprisingly large room. There were treadmills, stationary bikes, and a weight bench—although most of the space was given to gymnastic equipment: uneven bars, a balance beam, a pommel horse, a trampoline, and a lot of tumbling mats.

Suddenly, the leotard made sense. "You're a gymnast?" I asked.

"I *was*." For the first time, the smile faded from Ashley's face. Her eyes narrowed.

"Did something happen?" I asked.

"Something *didn't*," Ashley said. "I tried out for the U.S. Olympic team—and didn't make it. I came in sixth. You've never heard of me?"

"No," I admitted.

"Exactly. No one ever hears about the *sixth* best gymnast in the United States. They only hear about the five best. The ones who get to go on and represent the country. Do you have any idea what it's like to spend your whole life working toward a goal, ten hours a day, seven days a week, giving up any semblance of a normal life, putting everything you have into it . . . and then not getting it?"

"Sort of. I just got booted from the CIA."

"Well, imagine you'd been training for that since you were four. It totally blinks."

"Blows plus stinks?"

"Yes. And it blinks big-time. I came in sixth by one hundredth of a point. One judge thought I didn't stick the landing on the dismount from my balance beam routine, even though I did. I totally stuck it. But that's gymnastics for you. One lousy hundredth of a point makes all the difference between living your dreams—and having them dashed to pieces. Sure, they say you can come back and try out again in another four years, but you know they're only snowing you. By then you'll be four years older and there'll be a whole new crop of younger gymnasts who can't wait to crush your dreams again. I didn't want to spend another four years setting up for another heartbreak. But I didn't know what else to do either."

"So you turned to crime?" I asked.

"Sure did!" The anger seemed to evaporate from Ashley, and she was suddenly chipper as a chipmunk again. "I took all that rage and hatred and bad energy and refocused it into this. Joshua came to recruit me right after the trials. Apparently, it's a pretty common route from Olympic sports to crime. I hear one of the higher-ups at SPYDER is a decathlete who barely missed the cut a few decades ago." Ashley led me back into the main room and shut the gym door.

Nefarious had paused his air raid mission to get another bag of Cheetos. Now that he was standing, I could see he was far less physically impressive than Ashley. His legs were as skinny as chopsticks. He looked like a strong breeze could knock him over.

"Ashley just told me her story," I said. "What's yours? Why are you studying to be a criminal?"

Nefarious didn't make eye contact. He stared at the floor instead. For a moment, I thought he was going to return to his game and start mumbling again, but instead he said, "My parents named me Nefarious. What else was I supposed to do?"

"That's it?" I asked.

Nefarious shrugged, then headed for the couch again. As he did, though, he shot a sidelong glance at me, allowing me to catch the look in his eye. He seemed livid. Maybe it was the thought of his parents, or the idea of his own ridiculous name—or maybe he was angry at me for bringing it all up. But whatever the reason, it was extremely unsettling.

"Let's go see the rec center!" Ashley suggested.

"There's a rec center?" I asked, surprised.

"Oh yeah! It's swawesome! Want to come, Nefarious?"

Nefarious made a noncommittal noise. It sounded like "Mneh." Then he plopped back in front of the TV and resumed his game.

"Okay. See you later, then." Ashley found a pair of sweatpants in a wad by the front door and yanked them on before leading me outside. "You're gonna love the Rec," she said as we crossed the lawn. "It's so much fun. There's a spa and bowling alleys and a rock-climbing wall and a pool with two water slides."

"Wow." My excitement was genuine. "Our pool at spy school didn't have water slides."

"Really? What did it have?"

"Bacterial contamination. They had to shut it down last spring. A couple kids who'd gone swimming ended up covered with hives. They looked like raspberries in Speedos."

Ashley giggled, which was kind of weird. I hadn't

expected someone training to be a criminal mastermind to giggle. "Guess you're happy you transferred here, huh?" she asked.

"I sure am." This time, I didn't have to try quite as hard to lie.

Now that we were outside our house, I saw that it looked pretty much like all the others. The homes across the street had yards that backed up against the wall surrounding the property. Meanwhile, the houses on our side backed up to a large common space. We took a landscaped path that ran past our neighbors to get to it.

"How long have you been here?" I asked.

"A little over a year," Ashley replied. "And Nefarious came a few months before me."

"And it's been only the two of you training for that whole time?"

"Yeah. So it's pretty exciting to have someone new here. Someone fun." Ashley grinned widely and batted her eyes.

She was cute, which made me uneasy. "How do you know I'm fun?"

"Anyone's fun compared to Nefarious. I mean, he's nice enough, but frankly, the guy has the personality of an eggplant."

We emerged into the common area. It looked like the best public park I could have ever imagined. In addition to several wide lawns, there were brand-new tennis courts, bas-ketball courts, batting cages, and a soccer field.

"Does Nefarious do anything besides play video games?" I asked.

"Not much. He's pretty introverted. You got more words out of him just now than I have in the last month."

"You're joking, right?"

Ashley shook her head. "He's an odd duck. Something seriously messed him up. I'm betting it was his parents."

"Could be. What kind of people name their kid Nefar-ious?"

"Exactly. Although, believe it or not, Nefarious actually got off easy. According to his file, his folks named his little sister Placenta."

"Ooh. That's rough." Given how Ashley had just gone on about how rigorous SPYDER's selection process was, it sur-prised me that they'd chosen someone as socially awkward as Nefarious. But then it occurred to me that his awkwardness might actually be tied to his selection. After all, there was a flip side to the argument that SPYDER recruited only the elite: Most teenagers weren't inherently evil. Sure, there were plenty of bullies, nimrods, pinheads, and other assorted jerks out there, but still, it'd probably be rather hard to find kids willing to commit large-scale assassination, chaos, and may-hem, no matter how much you were offering. That'd leave a pretty small pool of potential recruits—meaning SPYDER might have to settle for a kid like Nefarious, someone so socially maladapted that maybe he couldn't quite tell what was evil and what wasn't.

We passed between an archery range and a croquet lawn. On both, the grass was so perfectly maintained that it looked like green carpet.

"Do you actually ever go to classes here?" I asked.

"Oh, sure," Ashley replied. "But they don't start until noon. The mornings are for training on our own schedules."

"Nefarious didn't look like he was training at all."

Ashley paused a moment before answering. "Nefarious has a very distinct skill set. He does what he needs to do."

"And how does doing gymnastics count as training for you?"

Ashley grinned in response. "Boy, you're just full of questions, aren't you?"

"I'm new here," I explained. "No one's told me anything. Is there an introductory pamphlet or something I'm supposed to get?"

"No. SPYDER doesn't print anything if they don't have to. That stuff can fall into the wrong hands."

We arrived at the rec center. It was a large building with huge glass windows through which I could see the rock-climbing wall, which had a three-story spire, and the indoor pool, which had several hot tubs. The Rec sat at the top of a small hill, so I could see the whole gated community from there.

According to the big sign at the entrance, the whole place was officially called Hidden Forest Estates. It wasn't very large. There was only one street, a loop on which all of the houses were built. The rec center was in the very middle of it all. I counted twenty-four homes—although the community wasn't finished yet. Halfway around, the asphalt road became dirt. A few houses were under construction, though many of the lots were still empty. The bang of hammers echoed from the building sites while bulldozers rumbled around them.

The wall was finished, though. It swept around the entire community, topped by barbed wire and security cameras, except for two imposing gates and a guardhouse at the front. Although the security was there to protect SPYDER, it didn't look any different from what I'd seen at plenty of other gated communities.

"Are those houses all for our teachers?" I asked.

"Some of them," Ashley replied. "Though our teachers aren't *just* teachers, like at your old school. They all have real jobs for SPYDER, doing all sorts of important stuff for our projects, but they take a little time every week to teach us about their areas of expertise."

"So . . . there's more to this place than just the school?"

"Oh boy, yes. A lot more. This is SPYDER's world head-quarters."

I looked around the property again, stunned by SPY-DER's brilliance. Unlike James Bond villains, they hadn't built a giant secret lair on some remote island. Instead, the organization was hiding in plain sight. They'd built a gated community that looked like every other gated community in the country. There was nothing about it that seemed remotely unusual, or that would grab the attention of the USA's spy satellites—although I suspected that, as with everything in the spy game, there was a lot more going on at Hidden For-est beneath the surface.

I asked, "Does everyone who works for SPYDER live here?"

Ashley giggled again. "Of course not, sillypants. SPY-DER has operatives all over the world. But this is command central, the heart of the organization. All the important stuff happens right here."

I looked at the land beyond the security wall. There was a farm on one side of the community, a bucolic place that looked straight out of a picture book, with a red barn and green fields. On the other side, there was only forest. Lots of deciduous trees, which meant we were probably somewhere in the eastern United States.

"Any idea where we are, exactly?" I asked.

"I'm not authorized to divulge that information to you at this time. Sorry."

I nodded, having expected this. "I'm guessing that I can't just walk out the front gate, either."

"Now, why would you want to do that?" Ashley waved a hand toward all the great things around the rec center. "We've got everything you could possibly want right here."

I glanced back at the security wall again. There *was* something unusual about it, something that made it different from the walls at other gated communities, although I hadn't noticed it until now. The barbed wire at the top angled over both sides of the wall, meaning it wasn't there just to keep people out. It was also there to keep people *in*.

I was trapped at evil spy school.

EDUCATION

SPYDER Agent Training Facility

September 5

1200 hours

My evil training began at noon.

The first class was advanced weaponry. This took place on the indoor shooting range, which was in the rec center, tucked between the squash courts and the sauna. Our instructor was Mr. Seabrook, who reminded me a great deal of my advanced weaponry instructor back at regular spy school; both men were tough, tightly wound, and constantly annoyed with how bad I was at advanced weaponry. Or even basic weaponry, for that matter. (While I was skilled at figuring out how to aim a weapon, firing one was a whole different ball game.)

"Ripley!" Mr. Seabrook yelled after watching me empty an entire clip of ammunition at a target silhouette and only graze its elbow. "My grandmother can shoot that gun better than you can—and she's dead! How on earth did you ever manage to defeat our organization twice with skills like those?"

"I've always been more of a problem solver than a shooter," I explained.

"Well, you'd better start practicing," Mr. Seabrook grumped. "Right now, there's no way in heck I'd trust you with a gun. In fact, with those hands, I'm surprised you can even use a fork."

I did much better in my other subjects. Over the next few days, I was quickly immersed into the routine of evil spy school. Although we had our mornings free, instruction and training started immediately at noon and went straight until dinnertime. Even on weekends. Classes occurred in a variety of ways. For some, an instructor came to our house. For others, we went to the instructor's house. And for yet others, we telecommuted, connecting with someone via the giant TV in our living room. (For most of these, our instructors' identities were kept secret and we saw them only as silhouettes.) Plus, we spent a great deal of time doing physical training, either in our home gym or at the rec center.

For the most part, our instructors didn't appear to be

blatantly evil. Instead, they were disturbingly normal. In fact, they were considerably more normal than my teachers at spy school had been. Mrs. Henderson, who covered mathematics, science, and bomb construction, was a doting, motherly woman who often cooked dinner for us as well, while Mr. Garabindian, our coach (who insisted we just call him "Mr. G") was supportive, cheerful, and friendly, even when showing us how to kill someone with his bare hands. The only instructors who were even a bit nasty were Mr. Seabrook and Joshua Hallal, who oversaw many of our lessons and still seemed bitter with me for making him lose a few parts of his body.

My classes, like my teachers, were bizarrely normal as well. There was surprisingly little that was evil about them. Many of the self-defense, explosives, and weaponry courses were eerily similar to those at spy school, while other subjects were tweaked only slightly. For example, while spy school taught counterespionage (activities designed to thwart spying by an enemy), evil spy school taught *counter* counterespionage (figuring out the methods the good guys were using to thwart you spying on them and then thwarting those so you could get back to spying on them in the first place).

Some classes weren't much different from those I would have had in regular middle school. For example, advanced mathematics was just advanced mathematics—although Mrs. Henderson did try to spice up the word problems with the occasional evil scenario. ("If Ernst Blofeld has a thirty-ton surface-to-surface missile and he wants to destroy a government installation thirty-five miles to the north with a twenty-mile-per-hour wind coming from the east, how many pounds of thrust will he need to launch the missile and demolish his target?") The only class that seemed remotely illicit was Lying Low 101, which taught us how to set up fake personas, forge government identification, and establish bank accounts in countries with loose financial regulations—and that wasn't really evil so much as moderately sneaky.

It was all kind of disappointing. I hadn't expected evil spy school to be crawling with jackbooted minions and run by a maniacal genius fiendishly plotting to overthrow the world—but I'd figured it would be at least a little less ordinary. I began to wonder if SPYDER was cooking up any sort of evil plot at all. Had they merely recruited me in the hopes that I'd be of some future service? And if they hadn't, what was the point of Erica—and whoever she was in cahoots with—railroading me into going undercover right then?

Which led to another, even more unnerving question: What if Erica hadn't been behind my ouster at all? What if I'd blown up the principal's office on my own, truly been expelled from spy school, and misinterpreted Erica's final words to me? If that was true, then I had enrolled in evil spy school by accident. Not only would this have been a terrible mistake on my part, but there was probably no way to undo it. I couldn't just go to Joshua Hallal and say, "Here's a funny story: I only agreed to come to this school because I thought the CIA wanted me to be an undercover agent here and find out what your evil plans were. But it turns out, they didn't. So, do you think I could just drop out and go back to normal life? I promise I won't tell the CIA anything about your secret hideout."

It would never work. If I wasn't really an undercover agent, there were only two ways to leave evil spy school: as a graduate or as a corpse.

This put me in the strange position of actually hoping SPYDER was plotting something. If the organization was truly hatching an evil scheme, then there was a reason for me to be undercover, which meant Erica might have really sent me there. Unfortunately, during my first few days, I hadn't seen any evidence that SPYDER was plotting anything at all.

But maybe that was evidence in itself. Even though they'd recruited me to their school, SPYDER was taking great pains to keep secrets from me. True, SPYDER was an extremely secretive organization to begin with—and true, they might not fully trust me, seeing as I had been recruited from their rival school—but I got the distinct sense that they were hiding something.

For example, no one would even tell me where Hidden

Forest was located—and I wasn't allowed the chance to find out, either. My phone hadn't been returned to me, and I was barred from using anything that would allow me access to a global positioning system. I was given a computer, but it was only for writing papers. I wasn't even allowed to go online. If the compound had Wi-Fi, no one had given me the access code for it.

"This is ridiculous," I groused at dinner on my third night. "Without the Internet, I can't even do any research for school. There must be a wireless connection *somewhere* around here, right?"

"Maybe," Ashley said, dumping Power Powder and almond milk into the blender. "But if there is, I can guarantee you, we're not allowed to use it."

"Why not? Doesn't SPYDER trust us?"

"It's nothing personal. It's for our protection. They can't just let us all surf the web. Because any line out is also a line in. The government could use it to access our computers."

"That's not true," I argued.

"It is! That's how SPYDER accesses the government's computers."

This bit of news was disturbing to me, but not exactly a surprise. SPYDER was a subversive and technologically advanced organization. Frankly, it would have been more startling to hear that they *hadn't* accessed the government's computers.

I pulled the pizza I was making out of the oven. It was the frozen, store-bought kind, although SPYDER's purchasing department had at least sprung for an expensive brand. I would have preferred delivery pizza, but of course, no outside companies were allowed past the front gates for security reasons. "There's no way they can give us any kind of secure access?" I asked. "Even for a few minutes a day? I'm not gonna watch YouTube or anything. I just want to send my folks an e-mail. Let them know I'm okay."

"Oh, you've been doing that plenty," Ashley said.

I looked up from slicing my pizza. "What are you talking about?"

"SPYDER handles all communication with your parents for you!" Ashley fired up the blender.

I had to shout to be heard over the appliance. "How?"

"They send a communications representative to a remote secure site to handle all personal correspondence!" Ashley shouted back. "You're not the only one here with family, you know!"

"And it doesn't bother you that they do this?"

"Are you kidding? I love that I don't have to deal with my parents!" Ashley flipped the blender off and returned to her normal voice. "It's one of the best perks at this school."

"I'd be happy if I never had to talk to my folks again," Nefarious said from the couch.

I'd forgotten he was there even though his standard air-strike video game was on the TV. This was because, with Nefarious around, a video game was *always* on the TV. After a while, it became background noise. I'd already begun tuning it out, the way that people who lived near airports tuned out the jet planes roaring overhead. Nefarious was such a fixture on the couch, I tended to not notice him—or to at least think he was in his own world and not paying any attention to Ashley and me. As it was, he hadn't even taken a break from his gaming for dinner. He had a bag of Cheetos in his lap and a can of Pepsi wedged between his knees.

Nefarious didn't even seem to be aware he had spoken. The words appeared to have slipped out of his subconscious. He was now entirely focused on the game, doing his standard mumbling commentary. "Adjustflapsincomingmissile-evasiveaction."

"What do they say in these e-mails?" I asked.

"Oh, the standard stuff, I guess." Ashley poured her shake into a glass. "School's great. You're making friends. Learning a lot. Blah, blah, blah. If anything serious happens, like your grandma dies, they'll let you know. Want some shake?" Ashley held the glass out to me.

I cringed reflexively. The shake didn't merely look disgusting—a thick brown slurry—it also smelled bad enough to kill a canary. "Er . . . No thanks."

"You sure?" Ashley pressed. "I made plenty. And it's super healthy for you."

"Maybe," I said. "But it looks like stuff that ought to be coming *out* of you, rather than going in."

Ashley stuck out her tongue in disgust. "Laugh now, but I'm gonna live to be one hundred and fifty, drinking this stuff. The way you two eat, you'll be lucky to make it past your thirties."

If SPYDER finds out I'm a double agent, I won't make it past thirteen, I thought. Then I said, "What about our friends? Does SPYDER handle all communication with them, too?"

Ashley hesitated a moment too long before answering. "Sure."

"Do they really?" I asked, as pointedly as I could.

Ashley looked to Nefarious, who remained fixated on his game. Then she looked back to me and cracked. "They do, but . . . It's pretty hard to have friends on the outside when you work for SPYDER. Too many secrets to keep and all. So after a while, SPYDER kind of weeds them all out of your life."

"We have to give up all our friends?" I gasped.

"You gave up most of them when you ditched spy school, didn't you?"

"I was thinking more about the friends I had from outside spy school," I said, which was only half-true.

"Yeah, you kind of have to drop them." Ashley seemed sad for a brief moment, then perked up again. "But on the other hand, we're gonna get really rich at SPYDER. And *we* can be friends, right?"

"Right," I agreed, though it took everything I had to paste a smile on my face. Down inside, I was overcome with anguish. If I really had mistakenly enrolled at SPYDER, there were a lot of bad things that would result, but losing my friends would be the worst. Having to cut ties with Zoe, Jawa, Chip, and Erica—who I still considered a friend even if she might not have thought of me that way—had been bad enough. The idea of losing Mike as well was soul-crushing. For all its faults, spy school had allowed me to have friends on the outside, provided that I followed strict secrecy protocols with them. Even though evil spy school had plenty of perks—free food and private bathrooms and water slides and the promise of riches ahead—there was no way those could ever compensate me for a life without friends.

Now I found myself desperately hoping I hadn't made a mistake—and that I was on an actual undercover mission. I was determined to find out what SPYDER was up to, thwart them, and be reinstated in regular spy school, where I could resume my old life, surrounded by my old friends, as quickly as possible.

The first step was to find a way out of Hidden Forest.

If I was really undercover, I needed to be able to get in touch with the CIA. If I wasn't really undercover, then I needed a way to escape. I had to get close to the perimeter wall and see if there was any way to breach it. And while I was at it, I had to examine the rest of the grounds more closely as well.

Unfortunately, doing this was more difficult than I'd expected. I didn't want to attract attention by nosing around too much—and I couldn't find a chance to sneak away. I was never alone at evil spy school. There was always someone keeping an eye on me.

SPYDER's watchfulness was subtle but effective. During class times, I was always with my instructors. And during free time, Ashley was always nearby. I wasn't sure if she was staying close because SPYDER had asked her to watch over me or if Ashley was just really clingy, but the result was the same. Most of the time this didn't bother me, because Ashley was surprisingly nice for someone studying to be evil, and quite fun to hang out with—as opposed to Nefarious, who remained as cold and distant as Antarctica. In fact, I suspected that Ashley's constantly wanting to hang out was a direct result of having only Nefarious for company for the past year: Living with someone so remote was practically the same as being assigned to solitary confinement. Even though Ashley had said she was fine with cutting off ties to her outside friends, she seemed to be dying for company.

However, it would have been nice to have some time alone now and then. Ashley tagged along whenever I went to the Rec. She was with me at every meal, offering to whip up another vile protein shake. And at night, after our homework was done, she hounded me to play cards or watch movies.

Virtually the only time I wasn't with Ashley was at bedtime, but I could never slip out then because my window was bolted shut and Nefarious was inevitably parked on the couch in the living room, blocking the route to the doors. Although he was always riveted to the TV screen and mumbling to himself, I wondered if he secretly was keeping an eye on me as well. It didn't matter what time of night it was, he'd be there, preventing me from sneaking out. As far as I could tell, the kid never slept. Or at least, he needed far less sleep than I did.

So I was forced to wait for the right opportunity. In the meantime, I tried to be the best student possible, hoping to allay any suspicions SPYDER might have that I was a mole. I studied hard. I trained hard. I did well in all my classes—except advanced weaponry. But I at least tried my best in that class and earned a glimmer of respect from Mr. Seabrook.

And then, on my seventh night at evil spy school, I finally got my chance.

EXTRACTION

Even though I'd never found a chance to explore Hidden Forest on my own, I stayed up late every night, hoping for one anyhow. I'd sit in my room, studying or reading, waiting in vain for Nefarious to vacate the living room and go to bed, until I passed out from exhaustion. Ashley was the opposite. Since she used a tremendous amount of energy every day, she tended to crash early. She was usually out cold by nine p.m.

On my seventh night at spy school, that didn't happen. Ashley *acted* like she was turning in early, wishing us a good night right after dinner and disappearing into her room. She stayed so silent afterward, I'd assumed she was asleep. But then, at 12:45 in the morning, I heard her creeping about quietly in her room—the same way a teenager did when they were trying to slip out of the house without waking their parents. I pressed my ear against the wall we shared. It sounded like she was getting dressed. Then I heard her door creak open softly, followed by the sound of her feet padding slowly toward my room.

I leapt back in bed and pretended to be asleep.

My door opened. I felt Ashley's eyes on me. Then the door closed again and her footsteps receded down the hall, toward the stairs. Thirty seconds later, the front door opened and closed. Outside, a car pulled up in front of the house. Its doors opened and banged shut and then it motored on.

I pretended to be asleep for another fifteen minutes just to play it safe.

Then I got out of bed and dressed in the darkest clothes I had: jeans and a black T-shirt. I slipped out of my room. Nefarious's door was closed and locked, but then, I'd never seen him actually enter his room. I checked downstairs. Nefarious wasn't on the couch. He'd been such a fixture there that this was quite startling to me, sort of like going to the National Mall and discovering that the Washington Monument had disappeared.

I slipped out the door.

Outside, Hidden Forest was eerily dark. The lights were out in all the other homes, and while there were streetlamps, SPYDER had either installed them just for show or had forgotten to turn them on. We were far enough into the countryside that there wasn't much light pollution. The sky was shrouded in black clouds.

I stuck to the shadows anyhow. Even though I was finally out of the house, I still wasn't in the clear. SPYDER doubtlessly had surveillance cameras everywhere, and there were people patrolling the compound as well. I spotted two of them wandering about in the distance. I was too far away to tell if they were the normal security guards who mistakenly believed they were working for an average, everyday gated community or actual SPYDER agents, but it didn't really matter. Whoever they were, I needed to avoid them.

Fortunately, I was quite good at this. At spy school, I had aced my exams in Avoiding Observation 101 and been highly commended on my skulking about. Now I stole through the compound with stealth and speed.

The backyards of the homes across the street ran right up to the security wall, so there was no way I could get close to it without venturing onto someone else's property. I didn't want to wake anyone in the houses or trip any alarms, so I headed for the far side of the community instead, where the homes were still under construction and the wall was more accessible.

The construction site was even spookier in the dark. The frames of the unfinished homes loomed like skeletons of enormous beasts and the construction vehicles looked like killer robots. The ground was an obstacle course of hazards: plumbing trenches, two-by-fours with nails spiking out of them pointy-end up, minefields of abandoned building supplies and broken glass. I almost toppled right into a giant hole for a septic tank. Even though it was ten feet wide, it was invisible in the darkness. No one had bothered to put up any sort of protective barrier, so I didn't see the thing until I was right on the lip, pinwheeling my arms wildly to keep from tumbling in. The septic tank was already installed in the pit, but it was still a four-foot drop onto a hard cement surface, the kind of thing that could easily twist an ankle or snap a bone. It was only after I'd regained my balance that I noticed the CAUTION: OPEN PIT sign lying on the ground nearby.

I encountered more septic pits as I continued on, but now that I knew they were there, I was able to avoid them more easily.

To my dismay, the security wall around the community was impossible to breach. It looked normal enough—like any other wall around a gated community—but it might as well have been around a maximum-security prison. It stood twelve feet tall and the surface was perfectly smooth and unscalable. The barbed wire at the top canted back three feet on my side. Once I finally got close to it, I noticed there was yet another type of wire strung among the barbed kind. This was smooth and thin, and it connected to small transformers at regular intervals. I could hear the occasional faint pop coming from them.

The top of the wall was electrified.

The construction crews had apparently been ordered not to leave any ladders around—or, for that matter, any large lengths of wood I could have built a ladder out of—but the electric wire would prevent me from climbing the wall anyhow. If anything I was holding so much as touched the wires, I'd get myself flambéed.

I spent the next two hours cautiously prowling along the wall, scoping it out for weak spots. I couldn't find a single one. Every now and then, one of the guards would wander down the road and I'd have to lurk in the shadows for a few minutes until they were gone.

The front gates were even more imposing than the wall. There were dozens of cameras focused on them and two guards stationed in a small booth, even in the middle of the night. This was the only spot in the entire community where there was any light at all. In fact, it was lit as brightly as a baseball stadium, with klieg lights all around, making it impossible to get anywhere close to the guard booth without them seeing me coming. And I knew they wouldn't let me just saunter out the gates. Not at three in the morning. Instead, they'd report me and any goodwill I'd earned with SPYDER over the past week would be blown.

It was time to get back to my room. I'd probably been out too long as it was.

I decided to steer well clear of the gates, carefully looping back through the construction area and then cutting through the park in the middle of the community. I had just passed the rec center when I heard someone coming.

I dropped to the ground, following the First Law of Camouflage: Quite often, the best place to hide is right in plain sight. On a pitch-black night, all I had to do to stay unseen was flatten myself on the lawn next to the tennis courts.

A minute later, Joshua Hallal came along. Although he was too far away for me to make out his face, I could tell it was him; he moved with a slight limp due to his fake leg—and even in the faint light, his metal hook gleamed. He strolled along casually, not looking the slightest bit furtive, even though it was now three thirty a.m.

Joshua was only fifteen feet away from me when a cricket chirped right by my foot. Joshua froze and looked my way suspiciously. His one good eye shone in the night. I held as still as possible, knowing that a mere twitch of my leg or a rustle of the grass would give me away for good.

Joshua stayed still for an unnervingly long time, until the cricket chirped again.

"Freaking cricket," Joshua muttered, and finally continued on. He headed to the rec center, typed the entry code on the security keypad at the door, and went inside. He didn't bother turning on the lights, so it was difficult to make him out—he was one shadow against another—but I could do it. He headed right for the three-story rock-climbing spire and twisted one of the handholds.

A secret door hidden in the spire slid open.

Joshua stepped inside and flipped on the lights. In the otherwise dark night, the sudden brightness was almost blinding. Joshua became a silhouette, which immediately began lowering into the floor. It took me a few seconds longer than it should have to realize that he was descending a spiral staircase concealed inside the spire. He was only halfway gone before the door slid shut, plunging the world back into darkness again.

I stayed flat on the lawn, wondering what to do next. Following Joshua through the secret door seemed dangerous and reckless—but it was also what Erica would have done. Going home and waiting for another day—when Joshua wasn't in the secret room—was certainly more prudent, but when would I get the chance to investigate again? The secret door was right out in the open, which would make it difficult to access during the day, especially when Ashley was always hovering nearby. And for all I knew, it might be weeks before Nefarious abandoned the couch again, allowing me to leave the house at night. Plus, Joshua was up to something *now*. Why else would he be creeping about in the middle of the night?

The point of my mission was to find out what SPYDER was planning. If I wanted to ever get out of evil spy school, I had to act.

I sidled over to the rec center, entered the code, and slipped inside. It took me a few minutes to find the right handhold on the climbing wall. I fumbled with dozens, trying to twist them one way or the other, but they were all bolted on firmly. Finally, I felt one give slightly. I jiggled it, felt something catch, and then rotated it clockwise.

The secret door opened with a hiss, revealing the spiral staircase. I tentatively stepped onto it and the door slid shut behind me.

The staircase wound down two stories, leading to a surprisingly well-decorated underground hallway. At spy school, the subterranean tunnels were drab and dingy, but this one looked straight out of a five-star hotel. The walls were wood-paneled, the floors were carpeted, and every few feet, there was a vase with fresh flowers. If you were going to spend a great deal of time underground, this seemed like the way to do it.

I crept down the hall. Through the door on the right was a conference room, currently empty, with an imposing oval table and eight ergonomic chairs. Oil paintings adorned the walls. It looked like the sort of room you could imagine diabolical villains discussing world domination in.

On the left side of the hall, there was a small kitchen. In it were a refrigerator, a sink, a microwave—and a frozen yogurt machine with a toppings bar. Apparently, the folks at SPYDER really liked fro-yo sundaes: There were dozens of toppings, ranging from crumbled toffee to rainbow sprinkles. The kitchen was empty, although there were a few fresh drips of strawberry yogurt on the floor, indicating someone had used the machine recently.

There was one last room at the end of the hall. I cautiously peered into it.

It was a command center.

It looked a bit like the living room back at the house I shared with Ashley and Nefarious, only significantly larger and with much nicer furniture. A fancy leather couch sat before an array of four high-definition TV screens. Soft jazz played from a surround sound system.

Joshua Hallal sat on the couch, typing on a laptop computer, a frozen yogurt sundae on the coffee table in front of him. The laptop appeared to be connected to all four TV screens at once. A great deal of information was scrolling across two of them, thousands of lines of letters and numbers. The third screen was full of words, but I couldn't read them, because they were in Russian. The fourth screen showed a satellite map of a country road. Two blips were moving along it, one blue, one red.

Joshua wasn't a very fast typist on account of the fact that he had only one hand. Plus, he kept stopping to eat his yogurt. And he spent a lot of time watching the screen with the satellite map.

I tried to focus on the other screens, hoping to catch a glimpse of something that made sense. However, on the first two, the information was scrolling too quickly to comprehend, even for me—and I was better at memorizing strings of numbers than most people.

So I focused on the screen with the Russian words. Back during the Cold War, Russian probably would have been the first language I'd have learned at spy school. These days, it wasn't something you studied until later years. I'd been told to focus on Chinese and Arabic instead. Unfortunately, Russian wasn't like French or Spanish, which were somewhat related to English and could be partially worked out, even if you couldn't speak them. The Russian words—and even some of the letters—were completely unfamiliar. It might as well have been Egyptian hieroglyphics.

However, there were some numbers as well. Numbers were the same, no matter what language you spoke.

And Joshua was entering even more numbers. As I watched, he slowly typed them with his good hand, pausing now and then to check them against a piece of paper in his lap. I memorized them, although sadly, I could find no pattern in them.

243.657

94.1

40.7057

73.9964

A message in Russian suddenly flashed on the screen. There were two buttons to click on. I couldn't read the word on either one, but it looked like the standard computer choice between "save" and "cancel."

Joshua clicked "save."

Three seconds later, that screen and the two with the lines of code on them went blank.

Joshua had turned them off. For a moment, I was terrified that he'd spotted me, but it turned out, he was fixated on the map screen again. On it, the red dot raced past the blue one. Ahead of them, the road suddenly disappeared from view, indicating a tunnel.

Joshua quickly downloaded something to an external

drive, ejected it from his computer, and hurried to where a safe was built into the wall, the door wide open. Joshua slid the drive inside, shut the safe, and locked it.

The safe had an electronic combination lock with fifteen digits.

Joshua returned to the couch and polished off the last of his sundae.

On the map screen, the blue dot entered the tunnel far ahead of the red one and vanished from sight.

The soft jazz suddenly cut out and was replaced by the sound of a phone ringing. The words "Incoming Call" flashed over the screen with the map.

Joshua clicked a button on his laptop, answering the phone over the surround sound system. "I see you're in position," he said.

"T-minus sixty seconds." I recognized the voice. Ashley.

"Going live." Joshua typed a command.

Views from four video cameras suddenly appeared on the TV screens, showing the inside of the tunnel from different angles. I figured SPYDER had installed the cameras well ahead of time in preparation for this event. They had extremely good picture and sound quality.

Joshua said, "Your practical exam in extraction is about to begin. If you do not succeed in this task, you will flunk the course."

"We're not going to flunk," Ashley said confidently. "Relax. This is gonna be incrazing."

"Incrazing?" Joshua repeated.

"Incredible plus amazing. Sit back and enjoy the show."

A sedan skidded to a stop inside the tunnel, angled across the center line. It looked like the type of car my parents would have bought if they'd had a little more money. Sensible, with a bit of luxury.

Nefarious was driving. Ashley got out of the passenger side. Both were dressed casually in T-shirts and jeans, like typical high school students—except for the fact that they had fake blood all over their faces. They looked like they'd just been in a terrible accident.

Nefarious floored the gas and leapt from the car. It sped away, then plowed into the tunnel wall hard enough to crumple the front end. The windshield shattered and the airbags deployed. Nefarious then ran back to the car and climbed into the driver's seat, wedging himself behind the airbag. He slumped over and closed his eyes, pretending to be unconscious.

An armored car now entered the tunnel: the vehicle that had been represented by the red dot on the map. The doors were marked with the seal of the U.S. Department of Justice.

Ashley staggered toward it, waving her arms wildly, acting like a desperate car wreck survivor. "Help!" she cried. "Help us!"

The armored car slammed on the brakes. The driver and the federal agent from the passenger seat leapt out. Although both had weapons in their holsters, neither one removed them. They both looked concerned, rather than on guard, which made sense. After all, Ashley didn't look remotely like an enemy agent. She looked like a terrified teenage girl who'd just been in a car wreck.

She sounded like one, too. She was so convincing, I almost bought her act myself. "Please!" she screamed. "My brother's hurt! He needs help!"

The armored car's driver grabbed a medical kit and raced toward Nefarious. Meanwhile, the other agent tried to calm Ashley. "I need you to relax," he told her. "You might be hurt, too."

"I'm not!" Ashley said, faking hysteria. "I'm not hurt at all!"

"You could be," the agent warned. "Try to calm down."

The driver reached Nefarious, who remained slumped in the driver's seat. Concerned, the driver set the medical kit down and leaned in to take his pulse.

Nefarious suddenly lashed out, spraying him in the face with a small vial of aerosol. The driver gasped in shock, then collapsed to the ground.

The agent with Ashley turned toward the driver, startled. "Jim?" he asked. "What's . . . ?"

Before he could even finish the thought, Ashley gassed him the same way. He reached for his gun, but the spray acted too fast and he went down on the road, too.

"I told you I wasn't hurt," Ashley said, dropping the scared-little-girl act. Then she raced toward the armored car.

Two more agents burst out of the rear doors. These guys knew what had just happened to their partners and were ready for trouble.

But Ashley got the jump on them. Literally. She attacked with a martial arts style I had never seen before. It was part karate, part Olympic gymnastics: a mix of handsprings, flips, chops, and kicks. Even though she was only half the size of the agents, she quickly overwhelmed them. Within seconds, both were out cold on the ground.

Nefarious came running, only to find that Ashley had handled everything fine without him. Rather than congratulate her, he awkwardly looked at the ground and said, "Mneh."

"I'd like to see any of those little twits who made Team USA do *that*," Ashley muttered, then checked her watch. "Twenty seconds to rendezvous. Let's get the package."

Nefarious nodded, then climbed into the back of the armored car. Ashley followed him.

Twenty seconds after Ashley had spoken, a minivan squealed to a stop beside the armored car. I couldn't see the driver, but I had no doubt it was another SPYDER operative, driving the most innocuous vehicle possible. Hiding in plain sight.

Ashley and Nefarious emerged from the back of the armored car. The "package" wasn't a thing. It was a person: a federal prisoner, wrists and ankles cuffed together.

The passenger door of the minivan slid open for them and they bundled the prisoner inside. As they did, one of the cameras caught his face, revealing the identity of the fourteen-year-old boy they'd gone through so much trouble to rescue.

It was my nemesis. Murray Hill.

REUNION

SPYDER Agent Training Facility

Student Housing

September 12

0830 hours

Murray made his dramatic entrance back into my life during breakfast.

I was having cereal. Ashley was drinking a shake. Nefarious was cramming Pop-Tarts into his mouth while he played video games. We were all trying to act normal, like we hadn't been doing things in secret the night before. Ashley and Nefarious were pretending like they hadn't subdued four federal agents and sprung Murray Hill, while I was pretending like I had no idea that they had subdued four federal agents and sprung Murray Hill.

I was the one who had caught Murray in the first place. In fact, I'd caught him *twice*. The first time was right after I had figured out he was SPYDER's mole at spy school—although he hadn't gone to jail then. SPYDER had intercepted him on the way, freeing him to participate in their next plot. I'd thwarted that one too, capturing Murray again (with a little help), and this time, the CIA had made absolutely sure he ended up in prison. But now, after only three months, he was out once more.

After watching Murray's rescue, I had hustled back home and climbed into bed, though I'd been too amped to sleep and was still awake when I heard Ashley and Nefarious return at five a.m. I faked being out cold when Ashley peeked into my room to check on me, and didn't really doze off until almost six, but to allay any suspicion that I'd been up all night, I'd pried myself out of bed at eight and headed down to breakfast.

Ashley and Nefarious had done the same thing. Despite the events of the previous night, neither looked tired at all. In fact, Ashley was humming with more excitement than usual. She couldn't sit still or keep the self-satisfied smile off her face.

"Why are you in such a good mood?" I asked.

"I rocked an exam yesterday." Ashley took a big gulp of probiotic sludge.

"What exam?" I demanded. "How are you taking exams that I'm not taking?"

"Surprise!" Murray yelled from the top of the stairs, then slid down the banister. He tried to hop off suavely at the bottom, but he wasn't nearly as coordinated as Ashley. Instead, he tripped over his own feet, clocked his head on the foosball table, and collapsed on the floor.

As nemeses went, Murray wasn't particularly imposing. His hair flopped over his eyes, he had the posture of a question mark, and he believed physical exertion was something that should be avoided at all costs. In addition, he'd never come across as particularly devious or malevolent. Instead, he behaved more like a criminal fanboy, raving about the brilliance of SPYDER's plots—or giving me respect when I figured them out. Murray had cleaned himself up since his rescue, but he still looked disheveled, wearing a stained T-shirt, torn jeans, and mismatched socks. Now he hopped back to his feet with a flourish, acting like he'd meant to crash into the foosball table all along. "How's it going, Ben?"

I did my best to look stunned. I stared at him in fake astonishment and did some Oscar-quality stammering. "What . . . ? How did . . . ? I thought you were in prison."

"I *was*—until last night. The Feds were transferring me to a new maximum-security penitentiary, but your pals here sprang me en route."

I spun toward Ashley and Nefarious, letting my jaw hang open in shock. Nefarious didn't look up from his game. Ashley shrugged and blushed.

I stared at her accusingly. "You sprang Murray? And you didn't tell me?"

"I asked her not to," Murray explained. "It wasn't any sort of top-secret, hush-hush, for-your-eyes-only kind of a thing. I just wanted to surprise you. You should have seen your face! I totally got you!"

"You sure did," I admitted, then dug back into my cereal.

Now it was Murray's turn to look surprised, only his was genuine. "That's it? That's the welcome I get? How about, 'Hi, Murray. Long time no see. Sorry I sent you to prison. Twice.'"

"I'm not sorry about that," I said. "In fact, I'm kind of upset you're out." I'd given a lot of thought to what my reaction to seeing Murray again should be. It was one of the many things that had kept me awake the night before. Acting was a big part of being undercover. The wrong emotion might make everyone suspicious. I'd rejected excitement, anger, sadness, guilt, and joy, finally opting for mild annoyance.

It worked. Murray sat across from me, looking hurt. "I thought we were friends."

"You only pretended to be my friend while working for SPYDER."

"It wasn't all pretend. I really did like you."

"You locked me in a room with a ticking bomb!"

"That wasn't personal. You were a good spy; I was a bad spy. That's how the business works. But we're both working for the bad guys now! We're on the same team! We should be friends. You're friends with Ashley, right?"

"Yes," I said. "But Ashley never tried to kill me."

"And yet she works for the organization that ordered *me* to kill you," Murray countered. "In fact, *you're* working for the organization that ordered me to kill you. So, if you're going to be angry at anyone, it should be yourself."

I hated to admit it, but there was a bizarre logic to Murray's argument. "It's not that simple."

Murray started to reply, but Ashley cut him off. "Give Ben a break. You know what they taught us in Psychology of Evil. Transitioning to being a bad guy is morally complex. It's hard enough to do without the person you sent to prison surprising you at breakfast all of a sudden. I told you that wasn't a good idea."

"Only like a thousand times." Murray rolled his eyes. "So you know, Ben, I don't bear any grudge against you. Although I am a bit ticked at Erica Hale for giving me this." He pointed to his right front tooth. It was made of gold, to replace the real one. "There was no point in her knocking it out. She did that just to be mean."

"Well." I sighed. "You'd tried to kill her, too."

"And seeing as she's on the other team, I'd do it again if I had to. But as far as you and I are concerned, everything's copacetic. No ill will on my part at all. Do you guys have any bacon?"

"Sure!" Ashley nodded. "We've got tons. Help yourself."

"Thanks!" Murray hurried to the fridge. "They didn't have any real bacon in prison. Only that weird veggie bacon junk."

"Why?" Ashley asked. "For health reasons?"

"No. Cost cutting." Murray dug through the deli drawer. "They don't give a hoot about your health in prison. They've got guys serving life sentences in there. The longer they live, the more it costs. Frankly, it'd make financial sense to give them *more* bacon. They'd die much sooner, which would be a substantial cost savings, but they'd be happier. It's a win-win for everyone." He gave a cry of joy and pulled out a fresh packet of bacon. "Ooh! Thick cut! Excellent!"

"Why'd SPYDER spring you?" I asked.

Murray flashed a smug grin. "'Cause I'm a nice guy."

I shook my head. "Springing someone's a big risk, right?" I turned to Ashley. "I'll bet whatever you did last night, it wasn't easy."

"It wasn't," Ashley said proudly. "If it wasn't for my swawesome fighting skills, Nefarious and I could've ended up in jail ourselves."

"SPYDER never takes risks it doesn't have to," I told Murray. "They wouldn't have gone through all the trouble to get you out unless they had to."

Murray laughed, then shook a finger at me. "You always were a smart one. Man, I'm glad you're working for us now. You're right. I wasn't sprung just for my sparkling personality." He set a pan on the stove and turned the flame on under it. "There were two other reasons."

"What?" I asked.

"Aw, come on, brainiac. I'm sure you can guess at least one of them." Murray dumped the entire package of bacon into the pan at once.

"Hey!" Nefarious snapped. "Don't eat all of it! Some of that's mine!"

Everyone turned to him, startled he'd spoken.

"Cut him some slack," Ashley said. "He's been in jail."

"Darn straight." Murray opened the cabinets and poked through our food. "While you guys have been living it up here in the burbs, I've been suffering for our cause. The least you could do is let me have a nice breakfast. Ooh! Doughnuts!" He pounced on a pack of powdered ones he'd discovered in the cupboard.

Nefarious turned back to his game, muttering under his breath. "Fine. Eatallthebacon. Butyou'dbetterkeepyourhandsoffmyCheetos."

The interruption had given me time to think about the answer to my own question. I told Murray, "SPYDER was worried the CIA would get you to talk."

"Ding, ding, ding! Give the kid a prize!" Murray grinned, his lips now ringed with powdered sugar. "I didn't talk, of course. But your pals were gonna keep trying to crack me. It's not easy doing the old clam routine. Sooner or later, everyone blabs. It might take a couple years, but they do it. And as you're certainly aware, SPYDER has plenty of secrets."

"What's the second reason?" I asked.

"The government has plenty of secrets itself." Murray shuffled the bacon around in the pan with a wooden spoon. "And sometimes, the only way to get those secrets is from the inside."

I stiffened in surprise. "Are you saying SPYDER *wanted* you to get captured?"

Murray laughed. "You mean, like the thing that happens in practically every spy movie, where they catch the bad guy halfway through, and they're all proud of themselves, but then it turns out that getting caught was part of the bad guy's plan all along? That he wanted to be in jail because then he could attack the system from the inside?"

"Yes."

"No, that's just something they do in the movies." Murray had the heat on too high and was now enveloped in a cloud of bacon smoke. "And if you ask me, it's a pretty lousy plan. Jail stinks. The food's bad, the accommodations are cramped, and the service is deplorable. Any evil scheme that involves sending you there needs to go back to the drawing board. Our last plan was much better: We blow up Camp David, we get paid a lot of money, and everyone's happy. Only, you screwed it all up. Believe me, I did not want to end up in the can. But since I *did* end up there, thanks to you, SPYDER figured I might as well nose around and see what I could turn up."

"What were you supposed to find out?" I asked.

"How much the CIA knows about our current plans."

"And what do they know?"

"Nothing." Murray flashed another powdered-sugar grin. "Zilch. Nada. Zippo. They don't have the slightest idea what we're up to."

"That's it?" I asked. "That's all you learned?"

"What else did I need?" Murray asked.

Ashley polished off her shake with a loud slurp. "Well, I can see you guys have a lot of catching up to do. So I'm gonna go work out." She plunked her dirty glass in the sink and headed for the gym.

"Thanks for springing me last night," Murray told her.

Ashley waved this off. "I'm sure you would have done the same for me."

"Probably not," Murray said. "Rescues are dangerous."

Ashley laughed, thinking this was a joke, although I was quite sure it wasn't. She disappeared into the gym, and a few seconds later, her workout music began to filter through the door, a mix of upbeat dance tunes.

"She's amazing," Murray said. "Maybe not quite as gonzo as your girlfriend Erica . . ."

"Erica isn't my girlfriend," I corrected.

". . . but she's still pretty darn awesome. And, unlike Erica, she's actually nice."

"Erica can be nice when she wants."

"How often is that? Once a decade? I went to school with her for two years and she never so much as smiled at me. Not once. And she knocked out my tooth!"

"You were the bad guy! She was taking you into custody!"

"It was malicious. Ashley's not malicious at all. She's sweet. That girl wouldn't hurt a fly—unless she had orders to hurt it. Have you ever seen her in action?"

"No," I lied.

"It's unbelievable. SPYDER developed this whole gymnastics/kung fu kind of thing for her. It's why she was recruited, but she's turned out even better than we'd hoped. She's like Bruce Lee in spandex." Murray used a pair of tongs to fork the entire load of bacon onto a plate. He tested a piece and groaned in ecstasy. "Oh, man, have I missed this! I have no idea what vegetarians are thinking, saying no to bacon. Want some?"

"Sure," I said.

Murray grabbed the plate of bacon, the box of doughnuts, and a can of Dr Pepper, carried it all over to the Ping-Pong table, then waved to it graciously. "Help yourself."

I plucked a piece of bacon off the stack. Now that I had Murray alone—Nefarious was riveted to his video game—it seemed like the perfect time to question him about SPYDER's current plans. But I realized I had to proceed with caution. If I was too nosy, he'd get suspicious. Then again, he might also get suspicious if I wasn't nosy enough. After all, the only person who wouldn't ask *any* questions would be an undercover agent trying to act like they weren't interested. Luckily, it wasn't terribly hard to get Murray to talk. He loved to hear the sound of his own voice. If I led him to the subject, he might simply tell me everything I needed to know.

"So, you're now living in the fourth bedroom here?" I asked.

"That's right. We're housemates!"

"And you're going back to school with us?"

Murray frowned. "No. Although, SPYDER might ask me to sit in on your courses, just to brush up on a few subjects. My skills have gotten a bit rusty, seeing as I've been in jail and all, but I'm not a student like you guys."

"It *sounds* like you're gonna be a student like us," I said, knowing that the best way to get under Murray's skin was to wound his pride.

It worked like a charm. "I'm not," he snapped. "I'm well beyond being a student. I've been sent on a mission for SPYDER! Twice!"

"I've defeated your missions," I pointed out. "Twice. And I'm still a student."

"That's different. You were working for the good guys. Now you need to unlearn everything the CIA taught you and relearn everything SPYDER's way. And Ashley and Nefarious haven't been activated at all, save for last night. Meanwhile, I've been out in the field for SPYDER. I've been a mole. I've planted bombs. I've arranged for the smuggling and delivery of stolen missiles. I've even been shot at, for Pete's sake!"

"I know," I said. "I was the one who shot at you."

"I've done my time as a student here." Murray made a sandwich, cramming half a package of bacon between two doughnuts, and took a huge bite. "Last spring, when the CIA *thought* I was at that juvenile correction facility, I was actually here, prepping for my mission. But now I've been baptized by fire. Gunfire. I'm part of the brain trust here now."

"Then why are you living with us students instead of getting a house to yourself?"

"Because my house isn't built yet," Murray said peevishly. "But it's under construction. I'll have one soon enough, just like Joshua and all the other big shots."

I didn't quite believe what Murray was telling me—though it wasn't because Murray was inherently untrustworthy. There was an edge to his voice, like I'd struck a nerve. Murray *was* being sent back to school, and he had a big chip on his shoulder about it. This time, he wasn't lying because he was under orders to do so. He was lying so I'd think he was cool.

So I called him on it. "That's not true. Those houses are for other people."

"They're not! I've got mine picked out already. It's gonna be ready any day now—and it'll be even better than Joshua's. It has a Jacuzzi tub in the master bathroom. Joshua doesn't have a Jacuzzi tub. If he wants bubbles in his bath, he'll have to eat a whole bunch of beans first."

"I'll bet you don't even know what SPYDER's plotting this time."

"Of course I do!"

"Then what is it?"

Murray started to say something but caught himself. Then he broke into a knowing smile and pointed at me.

"You sly devil. You're playing me. You almost got me to spill my guts. But it's not gonna happen. For the time being, only those of us in the brain trust are allowed to know the future plans. You *students* will have to wait."

This time, I couldn't quite get a reading on Murray. He might have really known what SPYDER was up to and been following orders to keep it secret. Or he might have merely been pretending to do this so that I'd believe he had more access than me. I decided to take one more shot at cracking him. "I wasn't trying to get you to spill your guts. I just didn't think you were being honest with me."

Murray held his hands up in surrender. "I know I haven't always been straight with you in the past. But things are different now."

I shook my head. "No, they're not. You're lying to me right now. Just like all the higher-ups at SPYDER have lied to me."

Now Murray looked offended. "Oh, and the CIA was always completely honest. Like when they brought you in as bait to catch a mole without even telling you they were doing it. You could have been killed!"

"By you!" I pointed out. "You were the mole!"

"Water under the bridge," Murray said dismissively. "Point is, SPYDER is a million times better than the CIA. "Look around you! Look what we give you: free housing, a rec center, all the bacon you can eat. Total and complete awesomeness. Meanwhile, what does the CIA give you? Criticism, angst, and ulcers. And then they kick you to the curb."

There were only two strips of bacon left. I grabbed one before Murray wolfed the rest down. "I'm not saying that SPYDER isn't better than the CIA. It is. I should have listened to you and switched sides months ago. . . ."

"Darn straight," Murray said proudly.

"However," I continued, "SPYDER still hasn't been completely honest with me."

Murray paused in the midst of taking the last piece of bacon. "What are you talking about?"

I had to fight the urge to smile. I might have failed to get SPYDER's plans out of him, but I still had him hooked. "Don't get me wrong. I don't want to sound ungrateful, but . . . Well, sometimes I still get the feeling that SPYDER doesn't completely trust me. Maybe it's because I just defected from spy school and they think I'm some sort of double agent. . . ."

Murray shook his head wildly. "No. SPYDER would never have recruited you if they thought for a moment that you'd do that. To be honest, they'd written you off after you thwarted us the second time. You were too much of a Goody Two-shoes to flip. But then those idiots at spy school ousted you and the top brass here reconsidered. Nothing makes for a better bad guy than wanting revenge on the agency that dumped him."

"Then why doesn't SPYDER let me have a cell phone?" I asked. "Or an Internet connection?"

"That's nothing personal. That stuff's just too easy for the CIA to crack. E-mailing, texting, cell phone messages, Internet searches . . . It's all traceable. We didn't go through all the trouble to build this secret community to have someone accidentally blab its location to the CIA on Twitter."

"And yet someone's using the net. You guys are communicating with my parents for me."

"Yes, but from an extremely secure location, far away from here. Which reminds me, I have some messages for you." Murray fished some crumpled pieces of paper out of his pocket and tried to decipher his own handwriting on them. "Your parents are very proud of you but miss you very much. Your aunt Sadie had her archaeopteryx removed. . . ."

"You mean her appendix?" I asked.

Murray squinted at his notes. "Oh yeah. Her appendix. That makes a lot more sense. And Mike B-something says he can't believe you're going to another lame private school and that some girl named Kate is still asking about you."

Once again, I had to wonder how much Murray actually knew. SPYDER wasn't connecting to the Internet through a distant secure location; Joshua had been online the night before in the secret underground lair. Either Murray wasn't aware of this or he was trying to keep me in the dark, but I couldn't tell which.

My inability to get him to cough up any solid information was frustrating, but there was one last thing I could try to get him to do: spring me from Hidden Forest for a while. Once I was outside the compound, there was a chance I could figure out how to contact Erica—or at least figure out where Hidden Forest was in the first place.

"Okay," I said. "I guess there really isn't an Internet connection here. But SPYDER definitely doesn't trust me."

"Sure they do." Murray popped the last of his bacon and doughnut sandwich into his mouth.

"Then how do you explain the fact that SPYDER won't even let us leave the property?"

"We can leave."

"*I* can't," I shot back. "This place is like a prison. A really nice prison . . . but still, a prison."

"How many prisons do you know of that have their own rec center?"

"How many communities do you know of that won't let you leave whenever you want?"

Murray started to argue, but before he could, Nefarious said, "Ben has a point."

We turned to him, surprised as usual that he'd actually spoken, wondering how much of our conversation he'd listened to.

He had turned away from his game, although he wasn't really looking at us. He was looking down at the floor, avoiding eye contact. "We *can* leave, but we need permission," he mumbled. "And we haven't had permission in a long time. It'd be nice to get out of here."

"See?" I told Murray. "Even the guy who never gets off the couch is feeling trapped."

"What are you talking about?" Murray asked Nefarious. "You got out of here just last night to rescue me!"

"Mneh," Nefarious said.

Murray turned to me, unsure what to make of this.

"I think he means it'd be nice to leave the compound for something fun," I translated. "Not just for a mission."

Nefarious nodded agreement.

"Fun?" Murray asked. "Have you guys seen that rec center? That place is the capital of fun city! Anything you could possibly want to do, you can do there."

"You're making excuses," I told him. "I thought you said you had some clout at SPYDER, but it sounds like you're trapped here just like the rest of us."

Murray looked as though I'd insulted his honor. "I *do* have clout. If you want to get out of here, I'm your man. Where do you want to go, the beach?"

Before I could respond, Nefarious said, "Okay."

"Great!" Murray agreed. "The beach it is! I'll make it

happen." He shoved back from the table and hopped to his feet.

I didn't want to go to the beach. I'd been hoping for something more urban. A restaurant or a mall. A place where I could clandestinely slip a message to a policeman. A place with Internet access. A place I wouldn't have to wear a bathing suit. "Hold on . . . ," I began.

"No can do." Murray was already heading for the door. "I'm already late for some meetings today. Postincarceration briefings, reorientation, and all that jazz. Ben, it's good to see you again. Glad to have you aboard. Oh, and thanks for the bacon."

He grinned, flashing his gold tooth, and then slipped out the door.

TARGET PRACTICE

SPYDER Agent Training Facility
Recreation Center Firing Range
September 15
1400 hours

"Our business is not an easy one," Joshua Hallal said. "We must always work in the shadows. Our successes must always remain secret. And, of course, there is always the issue of law enforcement."

He looked right at me as he said this. Not so much accusing me of still working for law enforcement (I hoped) as much as indicating that I used to work for the other side.

It was early afternoon, right after lunch, and Joshua was lecturing us. We were on the firing range at the rec center. It had started as a normal class, with Mr. Seabrook teaching us the basics of weaponry (or at least in my case, *trying* to teach us the basics of weaponry), but Joshua had shown up suddenly and taken over. Mr. Seabrook obviously wasn't happy about this, but he relented and now sat in the corner behind us, grumbling to himself.

Ashley, Nefarious, and I all stood at attention while Murray slumped beside us. It had been three days since he'd arrived at evil spy school, and despite his claims that he wasn't a student like the rest of us, he'd been at every one of our classes. He'd claimed he was just auditing them—or brushing up on some information he'd forgotten while imprisoned—but it definitely appeared that he was under orders to be there and he made no secret of being annoyed about it. At the moment, he was making a show of being bored for Joshua, stifling yawns and checking his watch repeatedly, but Joshua barely glanced at him.

Instead, Joshua kept his gaze riveted on me. Or, at least, it seemed like it was riveted on me. It was kind of hard to tell because he had only one eye. "There is no other business in the world that must contend with what we do," he continued. "No other business that has so many people actively trying to stop it from making a profit. No other business that has multiple government agencies, at both the local and federal level, working against it."

"Well," I said. "That's because our business is illegal."

Joshua stared at me for a long moment, then nodded. "A valid point. And yet the fact remains that, no matter what we do, one branch of law enforcement or another is always determined to muck it up. Unfortunately, they sometimes succeed. But then, we often succeed as well. In fact, we have succeeded far more than law enforcement knows. And that is the way it will always be. They try to thwart our plans. We try to stay one step ahead of them. Or more, if possible. Quite often, this results in direct conflict. So the question I have for you today is: In the event that you do encounter a law enforcement agent, what should you do?"

Ashley's hand shot up in the air. "Ooh!" she cried. "I know! Pick me!"

Joshua pointed to her with his hook. "Yes, Miss Sparks?"

"Capture them!"

"I'm afraid that's incorrect," Joshua said.

Ashley sagged, disappointed.

I raised my own hand. Ashley raised hers again at the same time, having thought of another answer, but Joshua made a point of calling on me. "Yes, Mr. Ripley?"

"Kill them," I said. Merely pronouncing the words made me feel sick to my stomach, but I hid this behind as stony a face as I could muster.

Joshua gave me an amused smile, like I was a dog who'd just mastered a trick. "That's exactly right."

I did my best to look pleased with the praise.

Since Murray had arrived at evil spy school, life had gone on exactly as before. Classes had continued. Ashley worked out. Nefarious played video games.

The only thing that had really changed, it seemed, was me.

I was growing more worried by the day. SPYDER was definitely up to something. The underground lair and Murray's rescue indicated that. But no one seemed willing to let me in on the secret. I still hadn't learned a thing about SPYDER's plans—and yet, even if I did find out what they were plotting, I had no idea what to do about it. Because I still hadn't heard one word from Erica. Or anyone else at the CIA.

"Capturing enemy agents might *seem* like a good idea," Joshua explained. "After all, you can always use them as hostages. Or as bargaining chips: 'Give us safe passage out of the country and we won't hurt your friends.' But the fact is, capturing them is never worth the headache. You have to imprison them somewhere, and prisons are expensive. You have to feed them, and that's a big hassle. And worst of all, enemy agents have an annoying habit of escaping. It's much less trouble to just kill them. And to kill them as quickly as possible."

"Kill them quickly?" Murray asked, without bothering to raise his hand. "Really? Isn't it more fun to draw their death out a little? To make them suffer?"

Joshua sighed. "No. We're not James Bond villains here, kids. The more you draw out your enemy's deaths, the more chance they have to escape. So no lowering them into pools full of crocodiles or trying to slice them in half with lasers or anything like that. Just shoot them and be done with it."

Ashley nodded appreciatively, like she was cataloging this information in a mental file. Nefarious simply stared at the floor. Murray slumped against the wall, looking ashamed that Joshua had dismissed his ideas so quickly.

The silence from the CIA was really starting to eat at me. I'd been assuming all along that they knew where I was, even if *I* didn't know. I'd figured they were out there behind the walls of Hidden Forest somewhere, watching me. But now I wondered if something had gone wrong. What if they'd sent me into the lion's den but lost me en route? Or worse, what if they hadn't really sent me at all? In either case, I was on my own, surrounded by the enemy.

Joshua stared us all down with his one good eye. "If you found yourself facing an enemy agent, could you kill them?"

"You know I could," Murray groused. "You've seen me in action."

"Mneh," said Nefarious.

Joshua shifted his attention to Ashley, who grew uneasy. "Do we absolutely have to *kill* them?" she asked. "Can't we just knock them unconscious? Because I'm good at that."

"Yes, you are," Joshua agreed. "You were quite adept on your mission the other night. However, there is a big difference between facing a lowly delivery boy for the prison system and an enemy agent who has uncovered information that could compromise our plans. There are cases when one must take drastic measures. Can you do that?"

Ashley's features suddenly hardened. Any trace of doubt disappeared. I guessed she was channeling her huge reservoir of anger about the Olympics. "Yes," she said. "I can."

Joshua turned to me. "And you?"

"Sure," I said confidently. "I can do that."

"Really?" he asked. "Because you didn't kill *me* when you had the chance."

"Ah," I said. My fake confidence faded a little. "Well, you know, the CIA has this whole policy about *not* killing people. They're more of a capturing organization. Although, in my defense, I *did* arrange for you to fall off of a very high cliff. You were really very lucky to have survived that."

"Still, you didn't come down and make *sure* I was dead," Joshua pointed out. "That was sloppy."

I fidgeted uneasily. "Um . . . are you saying that you'd be more convinced if I had actually killed you?"

"Yes."

"But then you'd be dead."

"But I'm not." Joshua's gaze, which was already cold,

now grew significantly colder. "That was a big mistake on your part. A rather fortunate mistake where I'm concerned, but a mistake nonetheless. And I need to know that, the next time you find yourself in a similar position, you won't be as careless. Because next time, there's a very good chance that your enemy is going to be someone you know. One of your friends from spy school, perhaps."

I nodded understanding. Of course, I'd known all along that something like what Joshua was suggesting could happen—but I was really hoping it wouldn't. I had never liked the whole idea of shooting anyone to begin with, which was something my weaponry instructors back at spy school had always found frustrating. In my confrontations with the enemy so far, I'd always found ways to subdue them without personally inflicting any harm. But now I was in much deeper than before. And I didn't have anyone else— like Erica—to protect me.

I tried to mimic Ashley's stony glare. "You can count on me."

Joshua held my gaze for a long moment before nodding. "I hope, for your sake, that you're all being honest with me. Because when the moment of truth comes, any hesitation on your part means *you're* the one who ends up dead. I can assure all of you that if I were to find myself in a situation where I was face-to-face with someone who I knew was working for the enemy"—here, he stared directly at me, as if issuing a challenge—"I would not hesitate to take them out."

"Good to know," I said, trying to sound nice and casual, like the entire exchange hadn't been absolutely terrifying. Did Joshua still have suspicions about me? I wondered. Or was I just being paranoid? "I can assure you, I'm being honest. Those people from spy school . . . they're not my friends anymore. If I have to take care of them, I can handle it."

"Let's put that to the test, shall we?" Joshua flicked the lights on, illuminating the entire firing range. Hanging at the far end, instead of the standard silhouette of a human body, was a full-size photograph of Erica Hale. Joshua then plucked the gun from his holster and placed it in my hand. "Show me what you'd do to her."

I suddenly felt sick to my stomach. I had never liked guns much—and I liked the idea of aiming them at people even less. (Although this was infinitely preferable to having people aim guns at *me*.) So the idea of aiming at someone I cared about—even if it was only a photograph of them—was nauseating.

But I knew I couldn't reveal this. I ignored my queasiness, spun toward the target, and pulled the trigger repeatedly, emptying the clip.

I missed with every shot. The closest I got was a bullet hole six inches from Erica's knee—and that shot had actually ricocheted off the floor.

Mr. Seabrook rolled his eyes in exasperation.

"Your marksmanship could use some work," Joshua observed dryly. "However, the intent was still impressive." A tiny smile flickered across his face, as though he was actually pleased with me.

A tinny beeping suddenly echoed in the firing range.

Mr. Seabrook snapped to his feet, eyes wild with fear. "Is that a bomb?"

"Don't have a heart attack," Murray chided. "It's just my watch alarm. Class time's over." He turned to Joshua. "Are we done here? Because we've got a beach to go to."

"Really?" Ashley asked, surprised. "We're going today?"

"Right now." Murray grinned. "Unless you'd all rather continue this lecture."

"No way!" Ashley exclaimed, then seemed to think better of it and turned to Joshua. "No offense."

"It's okay. I understand," Joshua said, though he looked quite annoyed. Whether he was annoyed at Ashley or Murray was hard to guess.

"Go pack your bathing suits," Murray ordered us. "I've already got everything else in the car. Towels, snacks, sunblock, you name it."

"All right!" Ashley bolted out of the firing range, so excited that she executed two handspring flips en route.

Nefarious shuffled out after her. It seemed he might have

been excited too. He looked the same as he always did, but he seemed to be shuffling faster than usual.

I followed them, although by the time I was out the door, both had already disappeared down the hall.

So I paused there, out of sight of Murray and Joshua, and listened, wondering what I might hear.

Back inside the firing range, Joshua said, "Your orders were to do a surveillance run, not lead a field trip."

"I *am* doing the surveillance run," Murray shot back. "But I made a judgment call. I'll blend in better with everyone else than I will alone."

"You didn't make this call. You allowed Ben to manipulate you into it."

"No. I had to go to the beach anyhow, and I let him *think* it was his idea."

"I don't like it."

"Well, your boss approved it, so it doesn't matter if you like it or not."

There was an uncomfortable pause. Then Joshua said, "Murray, I know you like to pretend that you're at the same level I am, but you're not. I'm a full-fledged member of SPYDER, while you still have a great deal to learn. Humility, for one thing. In addition to your surveillance, you'd better keep a very close eye on Ben Ripley."

Murray sighed. "I know you've got issues with Ben

because he turned you into half the man you used to be, but I know him. And I promise you, we can trust him. He's on our side now."

"You can't trust anybody."

"Whatever the case, he doesn't know what we're planning and he doesn't know what today's really about. He and Ashley and the Video Freak were all just champing at the bit to get out of here for a little while. They've been working hard, seven days a week. If you don't give them a little time off, they'll go psycho."

"That's a bad thing?" Joshua asked. "We could use a few more psychos at this place."

"They deserve some fun. It's good for morale to let them have it. And besides, I have to check out fifty-six anyhow. So why not kill two birds with one stone? I know how much you like killing things."

I didn't get to hear Joshua's reply. Instead, I heard footsteps coming my way. Given the heavy, plodding nature of them, it sounded like Mr. Seabrook was on his way out of the firing range.

I slipped away before he could catch me eavesdropping and raced home to get dressed for the beach. I had no idea what "fifty-six" was, but I was determined to find out.

I finally had my first lead.

RECREATION

Sandy Hook National Seashore
September 15
1600 hours

It turned out that SPYDER's gated community—
the headquarters for the most malicious, dangerous, subversive enemy organization in the world—was in New Jersey.

There was no way Murray could keep me in the dark about this once we'd driven out the gates. There were too many signs: signs for highways, signs for turnpikes, signs indicating how far it was to New York City and Philadelphia. Even a master of obfuscation like Murray couldn't keep me from noticing at least a few of them.

However, he did try very hard to keep me from figuring

out exactly *where* in New Jersey Hidden Forest was. Murray had procured a sedan from the SPYDER motor pool for us and was driving himself even though he was only fourteen. (Given that Murray had once been part of a plot to assassinate multiple world leaders, driving without a proper license probably didn't seem like much of a crime to him.) In order to keep an eye on me, he'd assigned me the shotgun seat—over the protests of Ashley, who claimed she had seniority—and he spent the entire drive trying to distract me from paying attention to my surroundings. He insisted I work the radio, asked me to dig through his beach bag in search of his sunglasses (which turned out to have been in his pocket all along), and repeatedly dropped his gun between the seats, which I then had to recover before it discharged and wounded someone. By the time we hit the New Jersey Turnpike, I'd deduced that we were somewhere around Plainfield, but I had no idea how to get back to Hidden Forest from there. Adding to my confusion was the fact that SPYDER had been brilliant in choosing to disguise their compound as a gated community. There were gated communities *everywhere* in suburban New Jersey—and most of them looked exactly like Hidden Forest.

Murray probably could have dispensed with all the tricks; his horrible driving was more than enough to distract me. He was constantly getting distracted himself, veering out of his lane, blowing through stop signs, and nearly plowing into other cars, until Ashley, Nefarious, or I—and often all three—screamed at him to watch what he was doing before he killed us. By the time we reached the beach, I'd clenched the armrest in fear so many times that I'd dug furrows into it with my fingernails. Ashley was so thrilled that we'd survived the trip, she kissed the ground when she got out of the car.

Murray had brought us to a national seashore called Sandy Hook, which was the northernmost beach on the Jersey Shore, a thin peninsula that jabbed northward into Lower New York Bay. I'd never even heard of Sandy Hook before. It was beautifully pristine, especially compared to the other Jersey beaches we'd passed, where homes were crowded up right onto the sand. New York City was surprisingly close across the bay. Coney Island in Brooklyn was only six miles across the water, and to the west of it, I could see the towers and bridges of Manhattan peeking up from behind Staten Island.

As it was mid-September, summer was still lingering, providing perfect beach weather. It was also a Tuesday, so the beach wasn't horribly crowded, although there were still a good number of adults who had slipped away from work for the afternoon and students who had come down after school. Murray had apparently selected our parking place, in part, due to the large concentration of teenage girls in bikinis in the area. He seemed particularly taken with a group of blondes who were tanning close by and chatting about shoes in classic Jersey accents.

Ashley quickly snapped off her T-shirt and shorts, revealing she was in a bikini herself. Nefarious opted for significantly more sun protection, pulling on a long-sleeved rash guard. It was probably a good idea, as his flesh was pale and white as the belly of a flounder.

The Jersey girls noticed him and snickered cruelly.

Nefarious stared at the sand, trying to hide his wounded expression. I still saw it, though, and got the sense this was an all-too-familiar experience for Nefarious.

I wondered if this had played into his decision to join SPYDER. A kid who'd spent his life being teased and tormented might have a pretty big grudge against the world.

Ashley didn't notice. In fact, she teased Nefarious as well. "See that big bright thing up there?" she asked, pointing at the sky. "It's called the sun. Apparently, you've never been out in it before."

"You're hilarious," Nefarious muttered.

I peeled off my shirt, pried off my sneakers, and dropped everything in the sand.

Ashley bolted for the water. "Last one in is a federal agent!"

Nefarious and I took off after her, but with her muscular

legs, Ashley beat us soundly. She plunged directly into the surf, then came up whooping with delight.

I came in second with Nefarious far behind. He entered the water tentatively, as though afraid it might be poisonous. It was perfect, though, just the right temperature, refreshingly cool without being cold. I caught up to Ashley where it was knee deep.

"Losers!" Ashley taunted. "You guys are slame! Slow plus lame!"

"You gave yourself a head start," I pointed out. "That's cheating."

"Last time I checked, we were training to be bad guys, not Girl Scouts," Ashley replied. "And I wasn't even running my fastest. Maybe you guys should spend a little less time doing math problems or gaming and a little more time at the gym."

Nefarious finally caught up to us. He looked extremely uncomfortable in the water. I guessed that, if the Jersey girls hadn't been there to laugh at him, he probably would have stayed back on the sand. "You know there's a reason for all my gaming," he mumbled.

I started to ask what this was, but before I could, Ashley asked, "Want to play Sneak Attack?"

"Sure," I said gamely. "How do you . . . ?"

Ashley suddenly lashed a foot out and knocked my legs out from under me. "Sneak attack!"

I toppled into the ocean, but rather than give Ashley the pleasure of seeing me come up sputtering, I stayed below the surface. I fumbled around in the silty water until I found Ashley's ankle, grabbed on tight, and yanked her off her feet. Then I surfaced, crowing triumphantly. "Sneak attack back at you!"

"Not quite," Ashley said behind me.

I spun around, startled. I had barely a moment to register that I'd actually dunked Nefarious, rather than Ashley, before she took me down again.

This time, I *did* come up sputtering. Nefarious did the same thing right beside me. He glared in my direction.

"She did it," I said, pointing at Ashley.

Nefarious bought it. "Not cool," he said, then lunged at her.

While they chased each other around in the surf, I looked back to the beach to see what Murray was up to. Instead of coming into the water with us, he'd parked himself in a beach chair beneath an umbrella, a cooler full of sodas by his side. There was a book in his lap, but with his sunglasses on, there was no way to tell if he was actually reading it—or merely using it as a prop while he spied on something else nearby.

I looked up and down the beach, wondering what the "fifty-six" was that Murray had orders to survey. Beyond the road we'd come in on, a scrub-covered hill rose from the sand.

There were a few low buildings behind it. I couldn't tell what they were, but they didn't appear to be residential.

I returned my attention to Murray. He was looking around now, not even pretending to read his book. He polished off a soda and tossed the can aside, then got to his feet and picked up a camera.

It was a big camera with a long lens. The kind serious photographers used. Not the kind you brought to the beach to snap a few pictures with your friends.

My feet were suddenly yanked out from under me. It happened from behind this time, so I face-planted directly into the ocean, catching a noseful of salt water.

I came up, gagging, to find Ashley grinning impishly. "Sneak attack!" she cried.

Nefarious staggered up behind her, looking like he'd been dunked several times himself. "I hate this stupid game," he muttered.

I tried to snort the salt water back out of my sinuses. "Any idea what Murray's taking pictures of?"

The others glanced toward the beach quickly, as though afraid this was a ruse I was using to distract them from a sneak attack. When they realized Murray was really taking pictures, they dropped their guard and watched him a bit longer.

"Looks like he's photographing those girls," Nefarious mumbled.

Indeed, the bikini-clad blondes were now up and about, slathering on more tanning lotion.

Ashley made a face. "Ick. That's pretty greevy. Gross plus skeevy."

"You think that's why he suggested coming here?" I asked. "To scope out girls?"

Ashley looked to me, slightly suspicious. "What are you getting at?"

"Nothing," I said innocently. "I'm only asking. I mean, if he just wanted to see girls, there are probably girls at the mall. And it would've been a lot closer."

"These girls are wearing bikinis," Nefarious pointed out. Despite the fact that they'd laughed at him, he seemed pretty interested in them himself.

I looked back to the beach. Murray wasn't aiming his camera at the girls anymore. He was aiming the opposite way, toward the scrubby hills. "What's he shooting now?" I asked.

"He's probably only *pretending* like he's not taking pictures of the girls anymore," Ashley said. "So they don't realize that he *is* taking pictures of them and think he's a pervert."

"Maybe he's not taking pictures of girls at all," I said. "Maybe he's taking pictures of those buildings over there."

"What buildings?" Ashley asked.

"The ones behind that little hill," I said.

Ashley and Nefarious looked that way, seeming to notice the low-slung buildings for the first time.

"Why would Murray want to take pictures of buildings?" Ashley asked.

I shrugged. "Beats me. It just looks like he's doing it is all."

"Why are you so interested in what Murray's doing?" Ashley demanded.

"Shouldn't we *all* be?" I shot back. "You guys went through a lot of trouble to spring him. And the first thing he does is bring us all to the beach?"

"That's not the first thing he did," Nefarious grumbled. "The first thing he did was eat all our bacon."

"Oh, for Pete's sake, will you forget about the bacon?" Ashley asked.

"Okay, so not the *first* thing," I corrected. "But you know what I mean. He's a wanted man. And you're the ones who freed him. You all ought to be lying low. And then he brings us to the beach?"

"Maybe he's hiding in plain sight," Ashley said. "The beach is probably the last place the Feds would ever expect an escaped criminal to go."

"It's still not as safe as just staying at Hidden Forest," I pointed out.

"I thought the beach was *your* idea," Ashley replied.

"Weren't you the one who pressed Murray to get us out of the compound?"

"Yeah," I admitted, "but I didn't say I wanted to come *here*. This was Murray's suggestion. I didn't even know what country we were in until an hour ago."

"He's taking pictures of the girls again," Nefarious reported.

I returned my attention to the beach. Murray's camera was pointed back toward the blondes, who were now playing Frisbee. Or, at least, they were trying to play Frisbee. They weren't very good at it. As we watched, one accidentally pegged another in the face with the Frisbee from five feet away. Murray kept the camera aimed at them the whole time.

"Yeah. Girls," Ashley said. "That's definitely why he picked this beach."

I frowned. Either my fellow students didn't know Murray's real intentions for bringing us to Sandy Hook—or they were doing a fantastic job of keeping me in the dark.

Whatever the case, I was quite sure Murray hadn't chosen that beach randomly. While he certainly liked girls, if he'd merely wanted to take photos of them in bikinis, we had passed other beaches on the way there.

One of the blondes now misfired a Frisbee terribly, nearly nailing Murray in the head. He didn't even seem to notice it as it flew past.

"See that?" I asked. "If he was really watching the girls, how come he didn't see the Frisbee coming at him?"

"Because he's watching the *girls*, not their Frisbee," Ashley replied.

A blonde in sunglasses ran over to our section of beach to grab the Frisbee. *Now* Murray noticed her. He lowered the camera, flashed a grin, and said something I was too far away to hear, but it was probably supposed to sound suave. The blonde wasn't impressed. She ran right back to her friends without so much as a glance at him.

"Why do we even care what Murray's doing?" Ashley asked. "We're at the beach. Let's have some fun!"

"I'm not playing Sneak Attack anymore," I told her.

"All right," Ashley said. "Let's play Deception instead."

"How do we play that?" I asked.

"It's simple. All you do is . . ." Ashley suddenly turned back toward the beach. "Whoa. What's Murray doing now?"

I turned back that way. The moment I took my eyes off Ashley, she swept my legs out from under me again, plunging me back into the water. "Deception!" she crowed.

I counterattacked. I'd asked too many questions about Murray as it was. Any more and I'd raise the suspicions of my fellow students. Instead, it seemed I should focus on being part of the team and enjoy my precious time at the beach. Or, at least, I should act like I was doing that. So I did my best to dunk Ashley back into the ocean—and when she proved too adept at getting away from me, I teamed up with her and we dunked Nefarious instead. Then Nefarious decided he'd had enough and fled for dry land. Ashley and I bodysurfed for a while, and eventually we returned to the beach and played smashball. Every once in a while, I'd steal a glance back at Murray to see what he was up to, but after a few minutes of snapping photos, he had put the camera away and returned to his beach chair. He stayed planted there with his book for the rest of the time, not doing anything remotely suspicious. He even dozed off for a while.

At six o'clock, he whistled for our attention. "Sorry, guys. But we've got to pack it in."

"Already?" Ashley pleaded. "Can't we have another half hour?"

"We've stayed late enough as it is. I had to twist a lot of arms to get us this free time. If you ever want to do something like this again, we can't push it."

Ashley sighed heavily but gave in. "All right."

We slogged back to where we'd left our things in the sand and grabbed our towels. The sand around Murray was littered with crumpled soda cans.

"You leave anything for us?" I asked.

Murray tipped the lid of the cooler back and peered inside. "Uh . . . no. Unless you like melted ice."

"Are you kidding?" Ashley gasped. "There were two six-packs in there at least. You drank twelve cans of soda all by yourself?"

Murray gave a loud, carbonated belch. "They didn't let us have soda in prison. Only milk, water, and herbal tea. It was horrible."

I grabbed my shirt and sneakers off the sand.

From my right shoe came the sound of something small inside it sliding down into the toe.

It was barely audible. Although the others might not have heard it anyhow. Ashley had coiled her beach towel into a whip and snapped it at Murray, cracking him in the knee. "That's for not sharing," she said.

Murray yelped. Ashley prepared for another assault, but he raised his hands in surrender. "Sorry! How about if we grab some ice cream on the way back?"

Ashley and Nefarious exchanged a look, then nodded agreement.

"Sure," I agreed, then upended my shoe into my hand to find out what was inside.

I was expecting a pebble. Or perhaps a soda can pull tab that Murray had chucked into my sneaker.

Instead, it was a radio receiver.

It was very small, designed to be inserted deep inside your ear. It actually looked a bit like a pebble. I only recognized it because I'd used one in school before. It was an expensive, top-of-the-line model that the CIA favored.

I palmed it quickly, before anyone else could see, and tried to hide the fact that I was completely astonished by its presence.

I didn't quite manage it.

"What's wrong?" Murray asked.

"I got sand in my shoe," I lied, then made a show of shaking it out.

Murray turned back to the others to discuss where to get ice cream. He seemed to have bought my ruse. Of course, there was little reason for him to suspect that I had a high-end radio earpiece in my shoe, rather than sand. After all, there was plenty of sand around. And even *I* was having trouble believing the high-end radio earpiece was there. I couldn't imagine how it had ended up in my shoe. Except for Murray, no one had been anywhere near our things for the last few hours. . . .

No, I realized. That wasn't quite true.

Understanding suddenly descended on me. The truth was so startling, I had to turn away from the others and pretend to be toweling my hair dry so they wouldn't see the shock of revelation on my face.

One of the blond bikini girls had been near our things. The one who had chased the Frisbee over. Only, now that I thought about it, I realized she hadn't been some random teenager.

It had been someone I'd known. Someone I was desperate to see, in fact. But I hadn't even recognized her, because she was a master of hiding in plain sight.

Erica Hale.

COMMUNICATION

SPYDER Agent Training Facility

Student Housing

September 15

2100 hours

I wasn't one hundred percent positive it had been
Erica on the beach. Because if it had, she'd done a staggeringly good job of blending in.

As I'd learned in Avoiding Observation class, there was
more than one way to camouflage yourself. You could make
yourself blend into the surroundings, the way Warren Reeves
specialized in, painting your face and covering yourself with
leaves or bark so you looked more like a bush than a human.
However, this method had its limitations. It was very difficult

to drop a radio receiver into a shoe on the beach when you were dressed like a bush. People tended to notice bushes wandering around. So you could try option two: hiding in plain sight. This involved making yourself so obvious that even a suspicious bad guy like Murray Hill would never think for a moment that you could possibly be an enemy agent. Which was exactly what Erica had done.

At first thought, it seemed outlandishly risky. After all, Murray knew Erica well. But Erica had used that to her advantage. She hadn't merely dyed her hair blond. She'd changed her wardrobe, her voice—and her entire personality. I knew Erica well too—in fact, I probably knew her as well as anyone at spy school—and yet it was almost impossible to imagine her wearing a bikini or talking animatedly about shoes or, for that matter, being friendly at all. In essence, Erica had turned herself into the anti-Erica. And she'd done it so well that, if I hadn't found the radio, it would never have occurred to me that one of the vapid, blond Barbie dolls next to me on the beach was the very person I'd been desperately hoping to have contact from.

The possibility that she'd done it was so amazing, I spent much of the ride home trying to get my mind around it. Plus, I couldn't wait to use the earpiece and check in. These thoughts kept me so distracted, I wasn't nearly as terrified by Murray's driving as I should have been. I barely even noticed when we clipped three cars just getting out of the parking lot at Sandy Hook, or when we drifted across the median of Route 18 and nearly got pancaked by a semi. I did my best to make conversation during our stop for ice cream and to play I Spy on the drive home, but my mind was somewhere else the entire time.

Murray was also up to his usual tricks, trying to divert me from paying attention to the route back. However, this time I wasn't trying nearly so hard to figure out where Hidden Forest was located. If Erica had found me on the beach, she probably knew exactly where Hidden Forest was.

It was after dark by the time we got home. I was worried that everyone would be hungry and that I'd have to sit through dinner with them all, but the moment we climbed out of the car, Ashley announced she was going to take a shower to get all the sand off her.

"Me too," Murray said. "Feels like I've got half of Sandy Hook in my bathing suit."

"Mneh," Nefarious said, which seemed to mean, "I'll shower too."

We all headed upstairs. I listened to the water come on in everyone else's bathrooms, indicating they were too busy to eavesdrop on me, then stuck the radio into my ear and turned on my shower as well. It was possible that SPYDER had my room bugged, so the more noise, the better.

"Anyone there?" I asked.

"Guess you found my present," Erica replied. Her voice was distant and all-business, but it still sounded wonderful to me. It was thrilling to make contact after so much time on my own. "Turn on your shower. Make some noise."

"Already done."

"Okay. Now get in. Don't worry. The equipment is waterproof."

I didn't argue. I was feeling awfully briny anyhow. "So that *was* you on the beach today?"

"Didn't even notice me, did you?"

"No," I admitted. I felt embarrassed, though I wasn't sure if this was because Erica had fooled me, or because I was hearing her voice in my ear while I was naked. Probably a little of both. "How'd you even know we were going to be there?"

"I didn't. We followed you there."

"We?"

"Yes. Me and Granddad."

That would have been Cyrus Hale, Erica's extremely impressive grandfather. "I thought he was retired."

"Well, he unretired himself after SPYDER targeted him last year. He knows they're up to something, and he's determined to bring them down. We tailed you guys from their compound, then passed you on the road into Sandy Hook.

It's a peninsula, so once Murray turned onto it, we knew that was the only place you could be going. Then I got out and tried to blend in."

"You mean, you didn't know those girls?"

"Did those girls look like people I'd *want* to know? I'd just met them."

"Wow. You seemed like you were all best friends."

"It wasn't hard to work my way in. I just walked up, asked if I could borrow some tanning lotion, and then complimented them on their hair. I had no idea Murray was going to set up right next to us, but I figured it was a decent shot. We were the only girls in bikinis on the beach, and he's been in prison for a few months. Don't forget to shampoo your hair."

As usual, Erica's abrupt shifts in conversation caught me off guard. "Why?"

"Because it'll look suspicious if you get out of the shower and don't smell clean."

"Oh. Right." Up until that point, I'd just been standing in the water, focusing on the conversation. Now I grabbed the shampoo and lathered up. Under my hair, my scalp was gritty with sand. "Where are you right now?"

"About a mile away from you."

"And, uh . . . where am *I*, exactly?"

"You don't know?"

"SPYDER's worked very hard to keep me in the dark. No Internet. No phones. I know I'm in New Jersey, though."

"Short Hills, to be exact. Or at least, on the outskirts of it. It's gated community heaven out here. SPYDER couldn't have picked a better spot to build this place."

I rinsed my hair, then lathered again, trying to get all the sand out. "And how'd you know the compound was here?"

"We tailed you and Joshua the day he picked you up. We were watching you the whole time after you left the academy, figuring he might show. Or someone from SPYDER, at least."

"So . . . I was right to accept Joshua's offer, then? This was the CIA's plan all along? Pretend like I'd been booted out of spy school, then have SPYDER come and recruit me?"

"Yes, it was planned. But not by the CIA. They don't have any idea we're doing this."

I gasped in surprise, catching a mouthful of water, which I then sputtered out. "They don't know I'm here? This wasn't their idea?"

"Of course not. The CIA would never have approved sending a second-year student undercover."

"Then whose plan is it?"

"Granddad's."

I had to lean against the tiled wall to steady myself. "Are you telling me that this mission is unauthorized?"

"Well, we couldn't have done an *authorized* mission,"

Erica said dismissively. "SPYDER has moles everywhere in the CIA."

"So, as far as the Agency knows, I really have joined SPY-DER?"

"Keep your voice down. The Agency doesn't know you're with SPYDER at all. They think you're still back at your old middle school. They're completely in the dark here."

"And they really think that I blew up the principal's office by accident? I got expelled for real?"

"Yes. We had to make it look official to SPYDER. And the principal would never have been able to fake it. As you know, the man's an idiot."

"So you *did* set me up. You replaced the fake bomb with a live one?"

"Yes. I wasn't expecting you to nearly blow up the principal, of course. The moron wasn't even supposed to be in his office. But that actually worked out better than expected. Normally, it would take a few days to expel a student. There's usually a lot of paperwork involved. But the principal was so angry, he did it on the spot."

I picked up the soap. "Why didn't you tell me you were going to do any of this?"

"We had to make your part look real, too."

"You mean, you didn't trust me any more than the principal."

Erica paused a moment before answering. "To be honest, we weren't sure how well you'd perform if you knew. I thought you'd be fine, but Granddad doesn't really know you, and my father backed him."

I squeezed the soap so hard, it fired out of my hands, caroming off the wall. "Alexander's in on this?"

"We needed a third person. Granddad and I can't do surveillance twenty-four hours a day by ourselves. Besides, I had to go back to your middle school and mop up the mess you left back there. Your cover story was blown."

I groaned. "That wasn't my fault. First Mike was goofing around—and then Joshua showed up and things got out of hand."

"I'm well aware of what transpired."

"So how'd you fix it?"

"I had to run a disinformation campaign. I showed up at the school, pretended to be your ex-girlfriend looking to make up, and I spread the word that you were the physics king of St. Smithen's, not some undercover junior agent. It took a while to convince some of those airhead girls, but lucky for you, I can be very persuasive."

"Er . . . You knew that I'd told Mike you were my girlfriend?"

"Only for the last six months. I'm a spy, Ben. It's my job to know things."

I quickly changed the subject. "I thought you felt Alexander was a terrible spy."

"He's gotten better lately. He's really trying to prove himself to Granddad. Although we still won't let him have a gun unless it's an emergency."

"I can't believe you had more faith in your father than you did in me."

"If I didn't have faith in you, do you think you'd even be doing this?"

I considered that while picking up the soap again. "I guess not."

"Exactly. Speaking of which, I need your intel. If you stay in that shower too long, they're gonna get suspicious."

I knew Erica was right, but I wasn't ready to move on quite yet. "How long are you expecting me to stay here?"

"As long as it takes you to figure out what SPYDER's plotting."

"What if that takes a year? I'll be stuck here that whole time!"

"You're not the only one making sacrifices here. I'm AWOL from school. And while you've got a bed, a rec center, and fresh groceries every day, I'm crammed in a surveillance vehicle with my father and grandfather, living on fast food and sleeping on the passenger seat."

"At least it was your decision to do this," I said bitterly.

"Listen," Erica told me, "we knew SPYDER was plotting something big, we knew something had to be done about it, and we couldn't trust the CIA to handle it without tipping off the enemy. Like it or not, you're the best option we had. Now, if you succeed, Granddad will be able to go to the Agency, tell them what we've done, get both of us reinstated at the academy, and probably even swing us some distinguished service medals to boot. You'll make a bigger impression on the top brass at Central Intelligence with this one mission than most students will make in six whole years of spy school. So drop the sad sack act and let me know what you've learned."

I sighed. "All right. I guess you've realized that SPYDER controls this whole community."

"Yes. We've scoped it out thoroughly."

"Did you know Joshua Hallal was still alive?"

"Not until he showed up at your middle school. He doesn't look so good."

I was surprised by Erica's lack of emotion here—even though Erica had raised lack of emotion to an art form. I was relatively sure that, back before Joshua Hallal had left spy school, Erica had had a crush on him, if not even stronger feelings. And yet her reaction had betrayed none of this. I might as well have told her that I'd seen a squirrel, as opposed to a crush-turned-enemy risen from the dead.

I decided not to dwell on it. There was too much else to

discuss and my skin was starting to pucker. "Are you aware SPYDER has a whole underground complex here?"

Erica didn't answer right away, which was as close as she ever came to admitting I knew something that she didn't. "Where?"

"Under the rec center. There's a secret entrance in the rock wall."

"What do they have down there?"

"There's a conference room and a kitchenette with a sundae bar. . . ."

"Really?"

"Yeah. With toppings and everything. And then there's some sort of control center. Joshua ran Murray's extraction from there the other night, but I'm sure it must be for more than that. I saw him programming something in Russian."

"What was it?"

"I don't know. I can't read Russian."

"Since when?"

"Since always."

"That's inconvenient," Erica said in a tone that left no doubt in my mind that she could speak Russian—and had probably been doing it since she was three. "Did you see anything you *could* read?"

"A couple numbers, although I don't know what they could mean."

"What were the numbers?" Erica didn't even ask if I remembered them. She knew I had.

I repeated them from memory. She wrote them down, then asked, "What did he do then?"

"He downloaded everything to a flash drive and stuck it in a safe."

"What kind of lock did the safe have?"

"A fifteen-digit electric combination lock."

"Did you see him enter the combination?"

"No. His body was blocking my line of sight."

"Do you have any idea what SPYDER's plans are?"

"Er . . . no."

"None whatsoever?" I could actually hear Erica frowning.

"Everyone's being very secretive around me," I explained. "I did hear one thing, though. Joshua wanted Murray to check out something they called 'fifty-six' today."

"And what is that?"

"Um . . . I was hoping *you* would know."

Erica sighed. "I'll run it past Granddad. He's pretty sharp when it comes to this stuff."

"Whatever it is, I think it's down at Sandy Hook. Murray was taking pictures like crazy down there."

"No kidding. He snapped a couple hundred of my bottom, the scumbag."

"I think maybe he was only pretending to look like a

scumbag to take pictures of what was really important."

"We both know Murray. When it comes to being a scumbag, he's the real deal."

"Still," I said. "There were some **buildings** behind a hill near the beach, but I never got a chance to see what they were. Murray took some pictures of them, too."

"He did," Erica admitted. "I saw that. We'll look into it. Now, even though you don't know what the plot is, do you know who's in on it?"

"Joshua and Murray are, but I doubt they're really in charge. . . ."

"No. The real puppet masters are keeping to the shadows. How about your fellow students?"

"I don't think either of them knows what the plan is."

"Either?" Erica sounded surprised, which was a rare occasion. "You mean there's only two?"

"Yes. They were both at the beach with us today."

"That's the entire school?"

"You didn't know? I thought you were keeping a close eye on us."

"We're doing our best. It's not easy with only the three of us. And a wall surrounding the whole community. We figured we'd missed a few students."

"Well, you didn't."

"Who was the pasty one in the body stocking?"

"Nefarious Jones."

"Cute code name."

"No, that's real."

"You're kidding."

"No. He says it's why he turned to crime. Though I think there might be other reasons. I'm guessing he got picked on a lot back home before he came to SPYDER."

"Makes sense. Social pariahs are good targets for an organization like SPYDER. Kids who grow up thinking the whole world is their enemy and wanting revenge. What's his specialty?"

"I don't know," I admitted. "He spends most of his time playing video games. Although he indicated today that there might be a reason for it all."

"I suppose there could be. And the other student? The munchkin who kept dunking you? That was Ashley Sparks, the gymnast, right?"

"You recognized her?"

"Are you asking if I'm a fan of competitive gymnastics? No. But Granddad took some photos and we ran an Internet search. Let me guess: She got disgruntled after not making the cut for the Olympics and turned to crime."

"Yes. Kind of crazy, huh?"

"Frankly, I'm surprised it doesn't happen more. Having high expectations placed on you at a young age can create a lot of emotional strain." There was something in Erica's voice that made me think this statement was based on experience rather than guesswork. "Let me guess. They've got her doing martial arts."

"Exactly. SPYDER's developed this gymnastics-based kung fu kind of thing for her. I saw her use it when she and Nefarious sprang Murray. It's really amazing."

"Amazing?" Erica repeated. "Do you have a crush on this girl?"

"Of course not!"

"Sounds like you do. And, frankly, it kind of looked like it today, the way you two were frolicking in the surf together. . . ."

"I thought I was supposed to be getting close to the enemy."

"You're supposed to be finding out what they're up to, not falling in love with them."

"I'm not in love!" I snapped, a little too quickly.

"Well, keep it that way. Just remember, Ashley Sparks might seem nice and friendly, but she willingly chose to go work for SPYDER. Under that cute, sparkly exterior, she's evil."

"At least she didn't get me expelled from school and force me to go undercover for the enemy without even caring to ask if I wanted to."

My own words surprised me. It wasn't until I said them that I realized how angry I was at Erica. She had made decisions that put me in danger before, but that had generally been to protect me from even greater danger. This time, she'd gone much further, manipulating me—and my future—for her own agenda. Or her grandfather's agenda, at least. And she didn't even seem to care.

Erica let the words hang there for a while, then decided to pretend as though they'd never been said. "We should wrap this up. You've been in the shower too long as it is."

I looked at my hands. My fingertips were so pruned, they looked like tiny versions of the Himalayas. "Are you going to stay in contact with me, or am I going to be left on my own again?"

"I'll be in contact, but we have to be careful. Can you check in at oh-two-hundred hours tomorrow night?"

"I think so."

"Good. In the meantime, I'll see what I can do about getting you a break-and-enter kit."

"Why?"

"Because I need you to break into the underground lair and enter it. And then find out what's in that safe."

I gulped. "That's going to be dangerous."

"Well, you need to do it—unless you'd prefer that Operation Bedbug run for another few months."

"I'd prefer that Operation Bedbug had never run at all," I said, then thought to ask, "Why's it called Operation Bedbug?"

"Think about it."

I did, then understood. "Because I'm undercover."

"Bingo," Erica said. "Talk to you tomorrow."

And then she was gone.

I turned off the shower, toweled myself dry, and took the radio out of my ear. Then I cased the bathroom for a good place to hide it, spotting the bar of soap on the shower floor. It had been sitting in the water so long, it had turned mushy. I gouged out a divot in the bottom with my thumb, dropped the radio inside, then took the soap I'd removed and spackled the hole back up. After a minute rolling it around in my hands, the soap looked good as new. No one would ever guess the radio was hidden inside.

Pleased with my own cleverness, I slipped into my SPYDER bathrobe, entered my room . . .

And found Ashley sitting on my bed.

"Who were you just talking to?" she demanded.

Suddenly, I didn't feel quite so clever anymore.

OBFUSCATION

SPYDER Agent Training Facility

Student Housing

September 15

2145 hours

"Who was I talking to?" I repeated, doing my best to appear sarcastic rather than terrified. "I was in the shower. How could I have been talking to anyone?"

"You tell me." Ashley narrowed her eyes suspiciously. She was surprisingly intimidating, even though she was dressed in a pink nightgown with unicorns on it. "Because it sure sounded like you were talking to someone."

I pretended to have a sudden flash of understanding. "Oh! I know what you heard! I *was* talking, but only to myself. Sometimes, I practice math when I'm in the shower. Multiplication tables. Long division. That sort of thing."

Ashley's hard stare softened. "You practice that stuff? Your file said you were naturally gifted at it."

"I'm naturally gifted *because* I practice. A lot." This was a massive lie. I'd never had to practice math in my life.

Ashley bought it. Her cheeks flushed as pink as her nightgown. "Oh. Sorry for being so distrustful. It's just that I can hear your shower going from my room, and you were in there forever. . . ."

"I had sand everywhere," I explained. "Thanks to you. Every time you sneak attacked me, I got a pound of it up my ears."

"Oh." Ashley turned even pinker. "I wasn't really trying to spy on you. Your shower was running so long, I thought maybe something was wrong, like you'd passed out in there, so I came in here and then I heard you talking and . . ." She trailed off, then frowned. "This place gets to you sometimes. Joshua always says we're not supposed to trust anybody."

"Even our fellow students?"

"Well, you're new. And you *did* work for the enemy. . . ."

"And look how they treated me. They kicked me out." It wasn't hard to fake the bitterness in my voice. "After all I did for them. At least this school gives us some respect."

"When they're not keeping us prisoner here." The moment

the words were out of her mouth, Ashley seemed to regret them. "Not that I don't like it here," she said quickly. "I do."

"So do I," I said.

Ashley glanced toward the door furtively, then lowered her voice. "It's just that it's not quite what I expected. When I heard SPYDER had a secret headquarters, I kind of figured it'd be on some remote tropical island somewhere. Not New Jersey."

"Yeah. I was pretty surprised by that too," I said. "I was really hoping for the tropics myself. But at least they take good care of us here. My room at spy school wasn't nearly as nice as my room is here. And the food was terrible. And our rec center wasn't anywhere as amazing as this one."

Ashley nodded agreement. Her suspicions appeared to be gone. "You're right. They gave me that whole gymnastics setup. For free. When I was training for the Olympics, my parents had to pay for all my equipment themselves—and when I got sixth place, the U.S. Olympic team didn't give me so much as a certificate." Ashley's gaze hardened again. She unwittingly clenched my bedsheets in her fists, knuckles turning white with anger. "Even though I was robbed. That judge was blind. I stuck that landing!"

"I'm sure you did," I said.

Ashley snapped back to reality and looked embarrassed again. "Oh boy," she said. "I went crycho there for a moment, didn't I?"

"Crazy plus psycho?"

"Yes."

"Maybe a little," I teased.

"Well, that's the last time. I promise." Ashley took a deep breath and then smiled. "Who needs some stupid gold medal, right? SPYDER's gonna make us all so stinking rich, we'll be able to buy our own tropical islands."

I sat on the bed next to Ashley, intrigued. "Who told you that? Joshua?"

"Yeah. When he recruited me. He didn't promise to make you rich?"

"He only said I'd make a lot more than I would in the CIA. I didn't think to ask how much. I was really more interested in revenge."

Ashley laughed. "You're gonna make more than the CIA would pay you, all right. Joshua told me that SPYDER's newest scheme is going to make *billions*."

This struck me as important. As far as I knew, SPYDER was an evil organization that caused chaos and mayhem for a price—and while that price was often very good, it was only in the millions, if that. Not billions. Who had billions to spend on causing chaos?

"Do you have any idea what this new scheme is?" I asked, as innocently as I could manage.

Ashley shook her head. "No. Nefarious said it might

have something to do with mineral rights in Indonesia, but I have no idea where he even got that from."

"Think they're going to tell us soon?"

"Oh sure. They have to. We're going to do whatever it is in the next few days."

I almost tumbled off the bed in surprise. "The next few days?!"

Ashley signaled me to keep my voice down. "Yes."

"When? This weekend? Next week?"

"I don't know. Why are you so freaked out?"

"Because this thing is happening a lot sooner than I thought it was!" I snapped to my feet and started pacing. "I thought it was going to be months away. Years, maybe."

"Why?"

"Because I just started here. I thought we'd need a long time to train to do whatever it is that they need us to do."

"Well, we don't. Or, at least, *you* don't, you lucky duck. Nefarious and I have been here more than a year, working our bottoms off. You get to come in at the tail end, study for only a few weeks, and then hit the jackpot like the rest of us. You should be thrilled, not worried."

I stopped pacing, trying to pull myself together. "You're right. That *is* pretty cool. But I still don't have any idea what SPYDER even expects me to do in this scheme."

"I'll bet it has something to do with that big old

computer brain of yours." Ashley grinned. "Maybe I ought to start doing math problems in the shower. I'll need a mind like yours to count all my money."

I turned back to her. "So, once we've done this . . . What happens then? Do we stay here?"

"I doubt it. What's the point of going to school when you're crazy rich?"

"Where do we go, then?"

"Anywhere we want. I was thinking of Disney World. My family could never afford to go after shelling out for all my training. And now I'll be able to get the biggest suite they have!"

"You don't think we'll have to go into hiding?"

"Nope. Not if we do this right. Know what Joshua always says the perfect crime is?"

"One you get really rich from?"

"No. One that nobody knows you've committed. If no one knows we've pulled this crime off, then no one will be looking for us. We'll be able to keep up our lives just like usual—only, we'll have a ton more money."

"So . . . That'll be it for evil spy school? We'll never see each other again?"

"Not necessarily. You could come to Disney World with me." Ashley blushed suddenly upon saying this, then turned away. "Not like a boyfriend/girlfriend thing. I just had fun with you today . . . and Disney's probably not that great alone. Seeing as we've cut ties with all our old friends, I figured, as long as we're lying low, we might as well do it together, right?"

"Nefarious too?"

Ashley made a face. "King of the Misfits? Nefarious isn't exactly Mr. Fun. He'd spend all day playing video games if he didn't have to eat or poop. Thank goodness you showed up. Nefarious would never have thought to talk Murray into springing us for a day."

"I thought Nefarious said there was a reason for all his gaming."

"Yeah. He's addicted to it."

I studied Ashley for a moment. Despite what Erica had said, she didn't seem to be the slightest bit evil. Bitter, yes. But not evil. If anything, she seemed to be a pawn in Joshua's plans, just like me.

"So we'd just hop on a plane and go down there?"

"Yeah! For a couple weeks! We could stay at the nicest resort, take all the VIP tours, maybe go on one of those cruises they have."

"Sure," I said. "I'd be happy to go with you."

Ashley gave a whoop and leapt off the bed. "Swawesome! We're gonna have so much fun!" She threw her arms around me and gave me a surprisingly strong hug.

Her hair was still wet from the shower and smelled like strawberry shampoo. For a few moments, I found myself thinking that it wouldn't be so bad to score a billion dollars and then go hide out at Disney World with her.

Then I winced, realizing Erica had been right.

I *did* have a crush on an enemy agent.

AQUATICS

SPYDER Agent Training Facility
Recreation Center
September 16
1000 hours

The next day, right after I woke up, I went looking for Murray.

It was well past breakfast time. I'd had trouble getting to sleep after my conversations with Erica and Ashley the night before. Too many thoughts had been rattling around in my brain. What was SPYDER's plan? When were my fellow students and I going to be told about it? Or were we not going to be told at all? What role was I going to play in it? Could I do what Erica and her family expected of me?

What was "fifty-six" and why was it so important?

When I came downstairs, Nefarious was in his usual spot on the couch, but both Ashley and Murray were gone. "Have you seen Murray this morning?" I asked.

Nefarious pointed toward the recreation center and said, "Mneh."

I grabbed a handful of Lucky Charms and set off. Although the Rec was quite large, it didn't take me long to find Murray. He was doing the only thing there that required no physical activity at all: soaking in the hot tub in the pool room. If that wasn't lazy enough, he also had a sandwich, two corn dogs, a Coke, and a bag of Nefarious's Cheetos within arm's reach.

Ashley was in the pool room too, though she was actually exerting herself, doing flips off the high dive. "Hey, sleepyhead!" she yelled as I arrived. "Check this out!" Then she launched herself into a triple somersault with a pike. If I had tried something like that, I probably would have belly flopped hard enough to snap my neck, but she sliced through the water's surface with barely even a splash.

Murray applauded, then waved me over. The hot tub jets were on full force, churning the water so much he had to raise his voice to be heard over them. "Plenty of room in here. Want to join me?"

I shook my head. "No, thanks. I didn't bring my bathing suit."

"Neither did I."

I glanced warily into the hot tub. I couldn't see Murray's private parts through all the bubbles, but knowing he was naked in there made me even less inclined to join him. "Is whatever SPYDER's plotting happening soon?"

Murray shot me a sideways glance. "Who told you that?"

"I figured it out on my own."

"It was Princess Glitterpants, wasn't it?" Murray looked across the room, to where Ashley was climbing out of the pool.

"No."

"Yeah, it was. She likes you, you know."

I felt my ears turning red from embarrassment. "She does not."

"If there's one thing I know, it's women," Murray proclaimed. "I was watching you two at the beach yesterday. Trust me, she's into you."

I watched Ashley scale the high-dive ladder, feeling uneasy. She had been the other reason I couldn't sleep the night before. After she'd left, my whole room had smelled like her strawberry shampoo, reminding me of her.

The crazy thing was, I felt guilty for having a crush on her.

It wasn't because she was evil. It was because I felt like I was being unfaithful to Erica. Even though Erica and I weren't in a relationship at all. We were only friends. Or, at least, I'd *thought* we were friends—up until Erica had sent me on Operation Bedbug and put my life at risk without even giving me so much as a warning.

"Watch this!" Ashley called to us, then did a double backflip and zipped into the water with barely a ripple.

"You like her too, don't you?" Murray asked.

"No," I said, way too quickly.

Murray laughed. "Hey, it's cool if you do. There's no rule at SPYDER that says you can't date your fellow agents. And, frankly, she'd be far better girlfriend material than the Ice Queen you've been carrying a torch for all this time."

I didn't want to admit it, but this had already occurred to me. In fact, I'd thought about it quite a lot while tossing and turning in bed the night before. Around two in the morning, I'd begun to wonder if I was growing interested in Ashley *because* I was upset at Erica. True, Ashley was a SPYDER agent, but she had never betrayed me. Plus, she was always warm and friendly, while Erica was cool and distant and often seemed as if she found the entire concept of friendship baffling. Which made Ashley kind of the anti-Erica—although both of them could have mopped the floor with me in a fight.

"You changed the subject," I told Murray, changing the subject myself. "I want to know what SPYDER's plotting."

"Why?"

"Don't you think that if SPYDER wants me to be part

of an operation, it'd make sense for me to know what that operation is?"

"Not necessarily." Murray took a bite of his sandwich. It was ostensibly bacon, lettuce, and tomato, but it was really more like bacon, lettuce, bacon, tomato, and more bacon. Murray had been consuming an absolutely astonishing amount of bacon since getting out of prison, as well as astonishing amounts of soda, ice cream, candy, cake, and sausage, too. Even though he'd been at Hidden Forest for only a few days, he seemed to have gained several pounds in that time.

Across the room, Ashley hopped out of the pool and headed for the water slide.

"Why would SPYDER want to keep its agents in the dark?" I asked.

Murray said, "When the Allies were about to invade France on D-day in World War Two, do you think the generals told everyone what the plan was? No. Because they knew that if they did, someone might blab it. Not on purpose, mind you. But it happens. People talk. One guy shoots his mouth off, and the next thing you know, the Allies show up on Normandy Beach to find the entire Nazi army waiting to massacre them."

Murray's comparing SPYDER to the Allied Forces made me feel uneasy. After all, if SPYDER was anyone in a World War II scenario, it was the Nazis. "I get the need for secrecy, but at some point before D-day, the Allies told the soldiers what the plan was. They didn't just drop them off on the beach and say, 'Surprise! You're invading France today!'"

"And you *will* find out. When the time is right." Murray took another bite of his sandwich. The single slice of tomato he'd put on it slipped out and plopped into the hot tub, where it quickly disappeared beneath the bubbles. Murray didn't seem to care.

Ashley launched herself onto the water slide and whooped with joy all the way down.

"When's the time going to be right?" I asked.

"Soon."

"How soon?"

"I don't know. It's not my call."

Ashley barreled into the pool with a huge splash, then came up laughing. "That was swawesome!" she yelled. "Ben, don't just sit there watching me! Get your suit and come on in!"

"Maybe in a bit," I called back.

"Notice how she didn't invite *me* to join her?" Murray pointed out. "Only you."

"Because she knows you're too lazy to actually climb the ladder to the slide."

"Because she likes you. You think Erica would ever invite you to go down a water slide with her? Or go down a water slide at all? Or do anything fun, ever?"

"Am I the only one who doesn't know the plan?" I asked.

"You keep changing the subject away from Ashley."

"And you keep changing it *to* her. It sure *seems* like I'm the only one who doesn't know SPYDER's plan."

"That's not true." Murray bit off a huge hunk of corn dog. "Almost no one knows the plan. Not everyone here has the same access as I do. Your future girlfriend over there doesn't. Nefarious doesn't. Even some of your instructors don't. And as for those guys . . ." Murray pointed out the large windows toward the construction zone, which was crawling with workmen. "They're completely clueless about what's really going on here."

"That's another thing," I said. "If secrecy is so darn important to SPYDER that they can't even tell their own agents what they're planning, why would they allow all these other people into their compound? Seems like a lot of loose ends."

"SPYDER doesn't leave loose ends." Murray crammed a handful of Cheetos into his mouth. Several fell into the water, creating a Day-Glo orange slick on the surface around Murray's chest. "Every guard, maid, landscaper, and pool boy here has never heard a single mention of SPYDER. They were all hired by a shell company designed to look like it works for the Hidden Forest Homeowner's Association."

"And the construction crews?"

"Employees of Lew Brothers Construction, which is not—as they believe—run by Rocky and Roman Lew, but is in fact secretly owned and operated by SPYDER. Not one of those hammer jockeys has any idea they've worked on anything other than your standard everyday gated community. Anything we needed built specially was taken care of by an outside contractor, who—again—had no idea they were working for us."

I assumed the secret lair hidden three stories beneath us fell into this category. Whoever had built it wouldn't have necessarily known it was going to be used for evil. There wasn't anything particularly insidious about a few underground rooms and a sundae bar. SPYDER had probably lied and told the builders that it was some sort of high-tech security center. I couldn't ask about any of this, though, since I wasn't supposed to know that the secret lair existed.

Instead, I asked, "So what happens to Hidden Forest after we pull off our scheme?"

"What do you mean?" Murray replied.

"Well, the word is that SPYDER's going to make a lot of money this time around. So much that no one here would ever have to work again . . ."

"Did Ashley tell you that, too?"

I reflexively glanced across the room, where Ashley was rocketing down the water slide again. "No, I figured it out myself. As you might recall, I was training to be a spy until recently."

Murray nodded. "Yes, you were. And so you're wondering, why go through all the trouble to build this place if we're not going to need it anymore?"

"Exactly."

"Because Hidden Forest isn't merely a top-secret base. It's also a lucrative real estate investment."

"You mean, you're going to sell these homes?"

"For a ton of money!" Murray grinned. His teeth were full of bacon bits. "You've got to hand it to the big boys at SPYDER. They're brilliant. They needed a headquarters, but they didn't want to do the whole standard spy-movie bad-guy thing and build an outpost on some remote island somewhere. After all, construction on remote islands is *really* expensive. You've got shipping, travel, labor issues, construction delays. The whole thing's a giant headache. I know of at least one secret evil organization that blew so much on their island headquarters that they went bankrupt. And even if you don't go bust, you're gonna be stuck with the place. Giant complexes on remote islands are notoriously difficult to sell. But Hidden Forest is multipurpose. We can plot and train for an evil scheme here, then turn it around and sell all the homes for quadruple the construction costs. We've already got Manhattan big shots lining up to buy them."

I had to admit the whole thing was pretty clever. "Okay. So SPYDER has a plan for Hidden Forest. Do they have one for us?"

Murray washed down the last of his sandwich with a swig of soda. "How so?"

Ashley climbed out of the pool nearby, then scampered over to the Jacuzzi and plunged inside before I could inform her that Murray didn't have any clothes on. "Aaaah." She sighed. "This is swawesome. Why aren't you in here, Ben?"

"Yeah, Ben," Murray echoed. "Why aren't you in here?"

"If we're going to suddenly be very rich in the next few days," I pressed on, "isn't that going to be suspicious? Does SPYDER have some sort of official story for us?"

Ashley turned to Murray. "Hey, that's a good point. Do they?"

"Of course," Murray told us. "Given that we're kids, it makes the most sense to say that we inherited the money."

"From who?" Ashley asked.

"Our very eccentric, incredibly wealthy long-lost great-uncles," Murray replied.

"And what happens," I said, "when someone decides to check into the story and finds out that I don't have a very eccentric, incredibly wealthy long-lost great-uncle?"

"Leave that to SPYDER." Murray upended the Cheetos

bag and dumped the remnants into his mouth. Half ended up in the hot tub. "We have people working to create our long-lost uncles as we speak. It's really not that hard to fabricate a fictional human being, especially one who's dead. You only need some counterfeit documentation and a corpse to pass off as the body."

"A corpse?" Ashley repeated, flicking a rogue Cheeto away from her. "Where do they get the corpse?"

"I don't know." Murray sighed, sounding exasperated. "That's someone else's job. It can't be that hard, though. Thousands of people die every day. Cemeteries are chock-full of them. That's a lot of corpses to choose from. You don't have to worry about any of this stuff. In fact, the less you know, the better. All you need to do is keep your trap shut as much as possible. If anyone says, 'How'd you get so rich?' you say, 'My long-lost uncle left me the money.' And if they ask more, just shrug and say, 'I didn't really know him at all.' End of story."

"How about our parents?" I asked. "That story won't fly with them. They know we don't have any eccentric, long-lost rich uncles."

"Not necessarily," Murray countered. "I mean, that's the whole point of being 'long-lost,' isn't it? Lots of families have secrets. Why should ours be any different? And once Mom and Dad learn that dotty old Uncle Whoever-He-Was left you a pile of dough, they'll probably be *thrilled*, rather than suspicious."

"No kidding," Ashley agreed, then muttered, "It'll almost make up for me not making the Olympic team."

I had to give the issue some thought. "I guess my folks won't question it."

"Of course they won't!" Murray exclaimed. "Not unless you give them reason to. After all, which story sounds more plausible: that you suddenly got a bunch of money from a long-lost uncle no one knew you had, or you suddenly got a bunch of money by helping a top-secret evil organization pull off the crime of the century?"

"Good point," I admitted. "But don't we have to worry about the CIA, too?"

Murray laughed. "They're not going to thwart us this time. You were their ace, and they cut you loose, the idiots."

"They still know me," I pointed out. "If a huge crime gets pulled off and I'm suddenly stinking rich, someone might start to ask questions. Like Erica."

Murray stopped laughing. This apparently hadn't ever occurred to him.

"You won't have to worry about the CIA coming after you," said a voice behind me.

All of us spun around to find Joshua Hallal standing there. We hadn't heard him come in over the roar of the hot tub jets. He was finely dressed, as usual, in slacks, a button-down shirt, and a crisply knotted tie, which made him look extremely out of place in the pool room.

"Why not?" I asked.

Joshua gave me a hard stare with his single eye. "What is the single best way to ensure that you get away with a crime?"

"Don't leave any evidence behind?" Ashley suggested.

Joshua gave a disappointed sigh. "Don't leave evidence behind? That's child's play. Does this look like evil preschool to you?"

"No, sir." Ashley cringed and shook her head, embarrassed.

I suddenly understood what Joshua was getting at. "You make sure all the evidence incriminates someone else."

The slightest hint of a smile creased Joshua's scarred face. "Exactly. We here at SPYDER have taken meticulous steps to ensure that, when the dust clears, others will take the fall for this crime. The CIA will round them up to great fanfare, the case will be closed, and we will be free to go on with our lives. Our patsies will all claim they had nothing to do with the crime, of course—but then, all criminals make such claims, don't they?"

I asked, "So we're going to get rich while innocent people go to jail in our place?"

"Well," Joshua said, "as you've pointed out before, we *are* evil. And besides, these fall guys won't be *completely* innocent. The evidence against them wouldn't be believable if they were. They are all miscreants: terrorists, mafiosi, and other assorted scum and villainy. The world will be much better off with them in jail. As will we."

I forced a big smile onto my face, hoping it looked authentic. "That's brilliant."

"Yes," Joshua agreed. "It is. There will be no need for us to go into hiding or assume false identities. And even if your old friend Erica *does* have suspicions, no one at the CIA will want to hear them. After all, they'll think they've already caught the perpetrators. The last thing they'll want is for the public to find out they've been duped."

"That doesn't mean Erica will back off," I pointed out.

"Perhaps not," Joshua admitted. "But if she—or anyone else—turns out to be a problem, we'll just take care of them." He said this calmly, without a hint of menace, the same way he might have said that we'd send them a nice note asking them to back off. But the intent of his words was unmistakable. Anyone who caused SPYDER trouble would die.

It was getting harder and harder for me to fake pleasure at all this, but I did my best. "Now I'm *really* glad I switched sides."

"So are we," Murray said, then turned to Joshua. "Is there something else you wanted to tell us? I'm betting you didn't schlep all the way out here just to discuss logistics."

"You're correct," Joshua told him. "I've come to inform you that all systems are go for tomorrow. Phase one of our plan will initiate at eight p.m."

Ashley broke into a huge smile. "That soon? Swawesome! What are we doing?"

"For now," Joshua replied, "you will continue your training as if it were any other day. Your assignments will be given to you tomorrow shortly before initiation."

Ashley sprang out of the hot tub, so excited she was quivering. She didn't even notice Murray's escaped slice of tomato was clinging to her shoulder. "This is so exciting! I can't believe the big day is finally almost here!" She gave me a big, wet hug that soaked through my T-shirt. "How about you, Ben? Aren't you thrillighted?"

"Thrilled plus delighted?" I asked. "You bet."

"I told you guys we wouldn't have to wait much longer." Murray pried himself out of the water and grabbed a towel. He'd been soaking for so long, he was as red as a boiled lobster.

Ashley's enthusiasm dampened when she realized Murray had been naked the whole time they'd been in the hot tub together, but only for a few moments. Then she returned to being exceptionally excited once again. "Can I go tell Nefarious?"

"Certainly," Joshua replied.

Ashley cheered and raced out of the pool room, doing two cartwheels and a handspring en route.

I struggled to fake excitement as well. I pasted on the happiest face I could muster, although inside, my stomach was churning with anxiety. If I was going to stop SPYDER's evil plans, I couldn't wait until right before zero hour to find out what they were. I was running out of time.

Which meant I was going to have to take some risks.

Which meant life was about to get a lot more dangerous.

RETRIEVAL

I set my watch alarm for two a.m. Even though I was nervous and angst-ridden, I was quite sure I wouldn't be able to stay up until then for the second night in a row. For starters, I was exhausted after not sleeping much the previous night. And then there was what was known in spy school as Soforenko's Theory of Inconvenient Narcolepsy: Even if you're an insomniac, if there's something incredibly important that you absolutely need to be awake for in the middle of the night, you'll always fall asleep right before it happens.

I was right to take the precaution. I passed out right

after dinner, while I was doing my math homework. One moment, I was in the middle of one of Mrs. Henderson's word problems, trying to determine the minimum amount of explosive needed to take down a suspension bridge, and the next thing I knew, it was the middle of the night and I was facedown at my desk.

Fearing my room was bugged, I had used the silent alarm mode, so I was awakened by my watch vibrating against my wrist rather than any noise at all.

I'd been dreaming about being chased by bad guys. For most kids my age, this probably would have been a metaphor for some fear or another. For me, it wasn't. There was an extremely good chance that very soon, I was going to be chased by bad guys.

It was a relief to be awake. I quickly snapped into action, heading to the bathroom, digging the radio out of the soap, and jamming it in my ear. Instead of speaking, I coughed. Again, because the room was probably bugged.

"I'm here," Erica said in response. "Good call with the coughing. We can't risk you speaking at all, so let's keep that up. One cough for yes, silence for no. Ready to go?"

I coughed.

"Good. You're two minutes late, by the way."

I wasn't. But there was no way to argue that via coughing. So I had to just suck up the criticism.

"Move outside the house," Erica told me. "Chirp like a cricket when you're out."

I pulled on my darkest clothes and sneakers, then peered under my door. The hallway was dark. I swung the door open quickly—doors tend to creak more when you try to do it slowly—and edged into the hall.

The door to Ashley's room was closed. Murray's too. I could hear him snoring like a chain saw on the other side. Nefarious's door hung open, however. I glanced toward the stairs. A constantly shifting blue glow came from downstairs. The television was on.

I slunk down the stairs carefully, fearing Nefarious would be wide-awake on the couch, blocking my escape. Sure enough, he was there—but to my great relief, he was asleep. He was still sitting upright, but his head was lolled back, a strand of drool oozing from the corner of his mouth. The TV screen had gone into sleep mode, which meant he'd been out for at least ten minutes.

I slipped out the front door.

The night was alive with the chirping of crickets. Which was probably why Erica had asked me to imitate one. One cricket chirp among thousands wouldn't stand out, while a cough would.

It occurred to me only then that I had no idea how to chirp like a cricket. It had never come up before. Mooing like a cow, I could handle. Or bleating like a sheep. After all, like most people, I'd been doing barnyard animal noises since I was barely able to talk. But crickets? Not so much. I gave it my best shot.

"You call that a cricket?" Erica sighed. "That sounded more like a sick chickadee."

Again, there was no way to argue the point.

"Can you get to the northeast corner of the compound?" Erica asked.

I oriented myself with the stars. After my adventures fighting SPYDER the previous summer, I had resumed normal spy camp education, and Woodchuck Wallace had given an excellent seminar on nighttime navigation. Northeast was on the opposite side of the community from where I was, over where the construction was taking place. I cased the street. No one else seemed to be awake.

I tried the cricket again.

"That's a little better," Erica told me. "At least you're in the insect spectrum now. How long do you think it will take? One chirp for each five minutes."

It wasn't far across the compound, but I didn't want to rush myself, either. While I couldn't see any guards at the moment, I knew they were out there somewhere, on patrol. I chirped three times.

"Okay. Talk to you then."

I went the roundabout way, sticking to the shadows as much as possible. It was a relief when I got out of the area where the houses were finished—where any insomniac SPYDER agent might be looking out the window or returning home from a late-night session in the underground lair— and made it to the area that was under construction. There, I was able to move about more quickly, dodging among the bulldozers and skirting the septic tank pits.

Even so, I remained constantly on alert, aware that someone else was probably lurking in those shadows. And I didn't say a word to Erica, even though I desperately wanted to.

I knew I had to tell her that SPYDER's plans were launching the next evening, but I also knew that any word I said placed me in jeopardy. If a bad guy heard me scuffling across the dirt, they wouldn't necessarily know it was a human doing that. It could have been a squirrel or a rat. But if I spoke, that was a different story. Squirrels and rats didn't speak much. The enemy would know a human was out there in the darkness—and more important, they'd know I was in contact with someone else. So I kept the information to myself for the time being, not wanting to tank the operation until I had what I needed.

I reached the northeast corner of the compound in fourteen minutes. This area was the most barren in Hidden Forest: no frames of future homes, only a few cement foundations for homes-to-be with the occasional pit for a septic tank. There was little I could do to blend in save for keeping low to the ground.

I made another cricket chirp.

"You're in position?" Erica asked.

Chirp.

"All right. I have a package I'm sending over. It's a little bigger than a softball. Ready?"

I focused on the top of the wall at the corner of the compound and chirped again. My cricket imitation was getting much better with all the practice.

"Good. Then stay ready. I'm waiting for the right opportunity."

Thirty seconds ticked by. Sixty. Ninety.

At ninety-four seconds, a truck rumbled down the road outside Hidden Forest. In the quiet country night, the sound carried far. It was enough to cover the noise Erica was about to make.

"Incoming," she told me.

A black ball, barely visible against the night sky, sailed over the wall. It just cleared the barbed wire, then hit the ground a few feet away from me and rolled. I went after it, but before I could grab it, it tumbled over the lip of a septic pit and dropped inside.

"Got it?" Erica asked.

There was no way to say "give me a minute" in cricket. So I didn't say anything. Instead, I sidled to the edge of the pit and peered inside. It was about a four-foot drop down to the cement lid of the septic tank.

"Is there a problem?" Erica asked.

I remained silent again, meaning "no." Then I slid over the edge as quietly as possible until my toes touched the cement. It was even darker down in the hole than it was on ground level. The black ball had completely melted away. I had to fumble blindly in the shadows for a few seconds until I found it, nestled between the wall of dirt and a large metal hinge in the septic lid.

I chirped.

"Got it?" Erica asked.

Chirp.

Erica sighed with relief. "You had me worried there. Get that package back to your room ASAP. Your instructions are inside. Contact me tomorrow night at this time for further orders. . . ."

She was signing off. I didn't have any more time to play it safe.

"Erica . . . ," I whispered.

"Shhhh!" she hissed.

"SPYDER's plans launch tonight at eight p.m."

Erica was silent for a moment. Then she said, "Nuts."

A flashlight beam suddenly sliced through the darkness above me.

I froze, terrified. In my hurry to tell Erica about SPYDER, I hadn't checked to see if anyone was around.

The beam crossed over my head once, then went back the other way. Then another one joined it. If I hadn't been in the septic pit, they would have lit me up like a theater marquis.

"What's wrong?" one of the flashlight people asked. A male voice, a good distance away from me. It was deep and ominous. I didn't recognize it.

"I thought I heard something." This voice, I recognized. Joshua Hallal.

"I hear them," Erica whispered in my ear. "Just stay still. Don't move a muscle or make a sound."

I'd already figured that out myself.

"What was it?" the voice I didn't recognize asked.

"I don't know," Joshua replied.

The sound of footsteps crunching across the dirt came my way. The flashlight beams shimmied above my head.

If the SPYDER agents got to the edge of the pit—or even close to it—I was a sitting duck. But if I tried to run, they'd see me too. Which basically limited my options to one thing: praying for a miracle.

The footsteps were frighteningly close now. The beams were getting brighter as the SPYDER agents approached.

A loud feline yowl suddenly pierced the air. There was a soft thump on the ground nearby, followed by the sound of something dashing across the dirt.

The flashlights swung away from me, toward the sound.

"It's just a stupid cat," Joshua muttered. "Sorry."

"There's nothing wrong with being cautious," the mystery man said.

The footsteps started again, but now they were heading away from me.

I realized I'd been holding my breath for the past minute. I blew it out, then inhaled quietly, unable to believe my luck.

"That wasn't luck," Erica said, reading my thoughts. "That was Granddad. He brought the cat in case of trouble. He got it at the pound today. Though I'm the one who threw it over the wall."

There was no way to chirp "thank you." I had to hope silence would suffice.

"And don't get too upset about the cat," Erica added. "We're not abandoning it. It has a microchip ID tag so we can get it back."

Joshua and the mystery man were now a good distance away from me. I could barely hear their voices once they began to speak again.

"How's everything looking for tomorrow?" the mystery man asked.

"Perfect," Joshua replied. If he added anything else, I didn't hear it. They were out of range.

I chanced a look out of the pit.

They had turned off their flashlights, but I could make out their silhouettes against the lights of the rec center. They were heading directly toward it, probably going to the very same subterranean secret room I was supposed to break into. Which meant I couldn't do the break-in that night.

"We've just changed the plans, given your new information," Erica told me. "You're still to proceed according to the instructions in your package and infiltrate the subterranean room at your first opportunity, but check in immediately afterward. It'll be risky, but given SPYDER's timeline, we don't see that there's any other choice. If anything goes wrong before then, one of us will always be on the radio, ready to respond—though I hope, for your sake, that isn't necessary."

I hoped so too. My heart was still pounding from the fright Joshua had given me.

"Understand your orders?" Erica asked.

I chirped. Although my mouth was so dry, it sounded like a cricket on its deathbed.

"Okay," Erica said. "Good luck tomorrow. We're all counting on you."

And then she was gone.

INFILTRATION

SPYDER Agent Training Facility
Student Housing
September 17
0330 hours

It took me nearly an hour to work my way back to my room from the septic tank. I wasn't sure if Joshua and the mystery man had actually gone into the recreation center or if they were still outside, on the alert. Maybe they'd notified security as well. So I moved as slowly and carefully as possible. At one point, a beetle passed me.

My caution paid off, though. I didn't have another close call the whole way back.

By the time I returned, Nefarious wasn't on the couch

anymore. He'd apparently woken and realized he ought to be in bed. As proof, the door to his room was closed, as were Ashley's and Murray's.

I slipped inside my room, then went into the bathroom and locked the door.

For the first time since receiving it, I finally had a good look at the package Erica had delivered.

The ball was made of some kind of foam, painted black. Like Styrofoam, but lighter. And it smelled slightly like breakfast cereal.

A thin line ran around the circumference. I grabbed both halves of the ball and twisted them in opposite directions.

The package popped open. The inside was mostly more foam. There was a single, small rectangular gap carved in it with an electronic device nestled there.

The device was only four inches long, two inches wide, and a half inch thick. It had a screen like a smartphone and an on/off switch. Although I'd never seen a device like this in real life before, I knew from school that it was designed to break codes. Officially, the CIA referred to it as a Complex Algorithm Decryption Apparatus, but everyone just called it a "safecracker."

Tucked beneath the safecracker was a creased piece of paper. I unfolded it to find my orders, printed in an extremely small font so that all of them would fit on the page.

Step one was: "The foam ball is biodegradable. Put it in the toilet and flush it."

I did as ordered. The ball turned out to be made of some sort of wheat or corn foam. It quickly dissolved in the toilet bowl and easily flushed away.

The rest of the instructions were a bit more complicated.

The first part involved waiting until ten in the morning. No explanation was given for why this time was chosen, but I figured it had to do with when the secret underground room was easiest to infiltrate. As I'd already discovered, Joshua Hallal tended to haunt the place at night. Plus, my wandering into the recreation center in the wee hours would be suspicious, while showing up midmorning wouldn't be unusual at all.

This time, however, I couldn't get back to sleep. I was too nervous. I'd never infiltrated anyplace alone before. Not in the real world, at least. I'd done simulations in Infiltration and Escape 101, but that had never been my strongest class. (I'd received a C in it.) Whenever I'd done any real-world infiltration, Erica had been with me. Or, more to the point, I'd been with *her*. She had done all the work while I'd tailed along.

I spent the early morning reading and rereading my instructions, committing them to memory so I could shred the paper and flush the evidence. I imagined every possible scenario where things could go wrong. How would I behave if I was caught in the act? What would I say if anyone asked me what I was doing there? And if things went really, *really* wrong, how would I escape?

By seven a.m., I couldn't take it anymore. I got dressed and went downstairs.

To my surprise, both Ashley and Nefarious were awake. Nefarious was in his usual spot on the couch, already flying pretend fighter jets. Ashley was dressed for a workout in a purple leotard, blending a shake.

"Good morning!" she called cheerfully. "Want some?"

I didn't want any, but I also didn't want to get on Ashley's bad side, so instead, I said, "Sure," and grabbed a glass from the cabinet. "Why's everyone up so early today?"

"Couldn't sleep! Too excited." Ashley poured some shake for me. She'd put a lot of kale in it, so it was an unsettling vomit green. "I can't believe the big day is really here!"

"Me neither," I said, trying to sound just as upbeat. "Is Murray up?"

Ashley snorted with disdain. "Are you kidding? That kid makes sloths look hyperactive. He'll probably be in bed till noon."

I took a sip of my shake and almost gagged on it. Not only did it taste and smell terrible, it also had the texture of phlegm. It took a massive effort for me to force it down.

"Do you like it?" Ashley asked eagerly.

"It's great," I lied. "What's in it?"

"Since we need to be extra amped today, I made my special mega-protein booster: kale, acai berries, almond milk, flaxseed, ginseng, spinach, fish oil, chia seeds, chicory, maqui, goji, mangosteen, pantethine, elasmodium, and amino blasters."

"Are all those real things?" I asked. "Because a lot of them sound like Dr. Seuss characters."

Ashley giggled. "They're all real. My old coach designed it especially for me to focus my chi energy and provide extra vibrancy to my muscles. Can you feel the power churning through you?"

The only thing I could feel churning was my stomach. "I sure can."

"Good. 'Cause we're gonna need that energy today!" Ashley looked toward Nefarious to make sure he was immersed in his video game, then lowered her voice to a whisper. "If everything goes right tonight, you and I will be at Disney World soon!"

I forced a smile. "Can't wait."

"Me neither! I'm so happy I turned to crime. This is way better than gymnastics." Ashley took another gulp of shake, humming "It's a Small World" while she downed it.

I didn't think I could stomach another sip of my shake,

let alone drink the whole glass. And I was itching to get out of the house anyhow. "Mind if I take this to go?" I asked. "I was hoping to get a workout at the Rec this morning."

"Not at all. I'm gonna work out myself," Ashley said, then added confidentially, "I might as well use all this equipment while I've still got it. 'Cause after tonight, we're out of here." She flashed me a smile, unaware her teeth were filled with chia seeds, then trotted off to her private gym.

Nefarious appeared to have forgotten I was even in the room. He was in the zone, piloting his two virtual jet fighters at once on their run.

Once Ashley was out of sight, I dumped the shake down the sink and grabbed a package of Pop-Tarts instead. Then I ducked out the door.

I really did head to the Rec to work out. I hadn't been lying about that. The way I figured, it would be easier to find an opportune time to infiltrate the underground lair if I was already hanging out close by. And besides, exercising beat twiddling my thumbs and watching the clock. So I swam laps, rode the Exercycle, shot baskets. I even did a little target shooting on the firing range. I didn't manage many kill shots, but I at least winged the silhouette most times, which was enough to avoid the wrath of Mr. Seabrook. Then, at nine thirty, I shifted to the rock wall.

I tucked the safecracker in my pocket, strapped on a

safety harness, and clipped into the automatic belay device.
I opted not to use any of the loaner rock-climbing shoes
available to us, because it was almost impossible to run in
rock-climbing shoes, should that become necessary—and
besides, they all were uncomfortably tight and smelled like
foot fungus. Instead, I used my sneakers. I climbed for fifteen
minutes, during which no one else even entered the recreation center. I scaled the fake pinnacle and scanned Hidden
Forest from the top. Through the windows, I could see the
entire community laid out below me. The construction zone
was alive with activity: bulldozers shoving earth around,
cement trucks pouring foundations, carpenters putting up
frames with pneumatic hammers. However, the residential
side was eerily quiet. Not a soul moved on the streets. There
was no sign of Joshua or any of my instructors. I wondered
if they were all sleeping in like Murray, resting up for the big
day ahead.

Or they might have all been holed up in the underground lair. Unfortunately, I had only one way to find out.

I decided not to wait until ten. It was close enough, and
I wasn't going to get a better time to break in. I rappelled
down, unclipped from the rope, and checked my surroundings one last time. Then I grabbed the secret handhold and
twisted it.

The hidden door popped open.

The lights weren't on inside, which seemed to be a good indication that no one was in there. I also couldn't hear any voices from below. The place was quiet as a tomb.

I slipped inside, shut the door behind me, and fumbled around on the walls until I found a switch. The lights popped on, illuminating the staircase.

I descended quickly, wanting to get in and out as fast as possible. The less time in the lair, the less chance I had of being caught. I hurried past the conference room and the frozen yogurt machine into the main control room.

The four large monitors were off. Without them, the room was dimly lit. I could barely make out the safe on the wall, even though no attempt had been made to conceal it. There was no picture hanging in front of it. It was very obviously a safe door, a square foot of thick steel with an electronic combination lock.

I took the safecracker from my pocket. On the back, a thin strip of plastic covered an adhesive backing, like on the flap of an envelope. I peeled the plastic off and stuck the safecracker just beneath the combination lock. Then I turned it on.

The screen took a few seconds to light up. When it did, it displayed three application icons: rotary combination decryptor, electronic combination decryptor—and MP3 player. Apparently, some agents like to listen to music when safecracking. I opted to stay silent and pressed the icon for the electronic combination decryptor.

The safecracker whirred into action. Fifteen separate images appeared in a row on the screen, one for each piece of the combination. Then the safecracker began to spin through all the possibilities for each of them: not just numbers, but also punctuation marks, symbols, and letters from a variety of alphabets.

Every now and then, one of the fifteen images would freeze, indicating that the safecracker had locked in on the correct symbol: a nine, an ampersand, one of those weird *O*'s with a line through it that the Swedish like so much. But mostly, the images kept spinning. It took a nerve-rackingly long time.

I decided to check out the rest of the room. It beat sitting there, watching the safecracker work. And, should anyone from SPYDER enter, I'd probably look less suspicious wandering about than I would standing in front of the safe, staring at a decoding device.

When I'd been there before, I'd been so focused on Joshua I hadn't paid much attention to the rest of the room. It turned out, there wasn't much to it. Short of the monitors and the couch in front of them, there were only some workspaces around the walls. These all had desks, ergonomic chairs, and jacks for portable computers, but the computers weren't there; being portable, they were probably with the people who needed them.

The only other item of interest was a large joystick that sat on the coffee table in front of the couch. At least, it *looked* like a joystick. I'd never seen one like this before. It appeared to be custom-made, with more than a dozen buttons in the base.

I glanced back at the safecracker. Thirteen of the icons had been selected. Only two were still spinning.

And then the fourteenth locked into place.

It was a *U*. With an umlaut.

I hurried back over to the safe, watching the fifteenth icon spin. And spin. And spin. Whatever icon this was, the safecracker was having a nasty time figuring it out.

But then it began to slow down, sifting through fewer and fewer possibilities, as though narrowing in on the final icon. After thirty seconds, it was down to ten, then nine, then eight . . .

And then all the icons vanished.

I was expecting a nice, resounding click from the safe as the bolt slid open.

Instead, a message appeared on the safecracker's display: SYSTEM ERROR.

I groaned. However, this wasn't entirely unexpected. The instructions Erica had given me indicated as much: "There's a twenty percent chance the thing won't work. After all, it was built by a government contractor. In this case, rather than rebooting (which probably won't work either), go with Plan B."

Plan B was a bit simpler than Plan A. The safecracker wasn't merely a piece of technology.

It was also an explosive.

However, blowing the door of the safe off was much riskier than cracking the code. It was loud, disruptive, and made a lot of smoke, which meant there was a good chance it would set off either the security or fire alarm. However, my instructions mandated that I proceed with it and hope for the best. I'd already squandered too much precious time.

There was a small red switch on the edge of the safe-cracker, with a red pin lodged in it to ensure that I didn't flip the switch by accident when it was in my pocket and blow my legs off. I pulled the pin, then flipped the switch.

The SYSTEM ERROR message disappeared and was now replaced by a timer showing fifteen seconds.

I ran, dove over the couch, then curled into a ball and jammed my fingers in my ears.

The safecracker exploded with a loud bang that echoed throughout the underground lair. But thankfully, no alarms went off.

I peeked over the top of the couch.

The safe door now hung slightly ajar, charred black with wisps of smoke curling up from it.

I raced back over and swung it open.

The safe was empty.

Almost. The external drive I'd seen Joshua place inside it wasn't there. Nor was anything else, save for a single piece of stationery.

There was a message on it:

> Ben—
> I guess we can't trust you after all.
> —Joshua

And then the alarms started ringing.

DEMOLITION

SPYDER Agent Training Facility

Secret Underground Lair

September 17

1015 hours

Erica had given me one final instruction:

"If anything goes wrong, get the heck out of there."

As if I was maybe going to hang out and fix myself a frozen yogurt.

I grabbed the note from Joshua—after all, it was evidence, and I'd gone through a heck of a lot of trouble to get it—and bolted from the room.

It wasn't only the security alarm that had gone off. The fire alarm had triggered as well. Klaxons were sounding, red lights were flashing, *and* the sprinklers were spraying, dousing me with water.

I scurried up the spiral staircase, my shoes skidding on the wet steps, and burst through the secret door into the rec center.

Out the windows, I could see down into the residential area. Klaxons were ringing out there as well, and every streetlamp was now flashing red. A pleasant voice kept announcing "Security breach in central control. Security breach in central control." SPYDER agents were emerging from their tract homes and racing my way up the path through the tennis courts. Some really had been sleeping in; two were in pajamas, while one wore a robe and bunny slippers. I spotted most of my instructors. Mrs. Henderson and Coach G were leading the pack. Neither appeared nearly as kind or friendly as they had during class. Instead, they looked like they'd be happy to do some harm to me.

I couldn't see Joshua Hallal or Murray Hill among them, but then, I didn't have the time to take a very close look.

Mr. Seabrook was already inside the rec center. He raced into the room with the rock wall right after I did. Since he'd come directly from the artillery range, he was heavily armed with a semiautomatic, a bandolier of ammo clips, and an assortment of other knives and guns.

All I had to protect myself with was a piece of stationery.

I ducked into the workout room, then dodged through the exercise equipment. I reached the far side just as Mr. Seabrook entered and opened fire. Bullets pinged off the treadmills and StairMasters behind me.

I veered through the yoga studio and into the bowling alley. This had only two lanes with a small rack of balls to choose from. I grabbed two, assessed Mr. Seabrook's probable speed and the rate the balls would roll, given their size and my strength, waited two seconds, and then bowled both of them back toward the door, one after the other.

Then I ran again.

From behind me, I heard the sound of Mr. Seabrook barely avoiding the first ball as it came through the doorway, but then yelping as the second one caught him in the shin by surprise. This was followed by the thwack of him landing face-first on the floor, the swoosh of his semiautomatic skittering down the well-waxed bowling alley, and the clatter as it knocked over all the pins.

I'd bought myself a few seconds.

Beyond the bowling alley was the spa. I ducked past the steam room and the sauna to a door marked: EMERGENCY EXIT. USE ONLY IN CASE OF EMERGENCY.

This seemed to qualify.

I pushed through it and found myself back in the sunshine. The main residential area—and thus all the SPYDER agents—were now on the far side of the recreation center. However, so was the only exit from Hidden Forest. The entire area I faced was surrounded by the wall, and there was no way I was getting over that.

But I'd come up with a backup plan.

I ran toward the construction zone, hoping I had time to make it across the open ground before all the SPYDER agents showed up.

Erica's voice spoke in my ear, sounding concerned. Apparently, she'd heard the Klaxons. "Uh, Ben? Has something gone wrong?"

"Yes."

"On a scale of one to ten . . . ?"

"Twenty-three. My cover's blown. I'm heading for the eastern wall of the compound with the enemy in pursuit. Can you be there to get me?"

"How soon?"

"Right now would be good." I was almost to the construction zone.

"We're on our way," Erica said. "Er . . . How are you getting over the wall?"

Behind me, Mr. Seabrook staggered out of the rec center. He was armed with one of his emergency backup guns.

"Can't talk now!" I yelped, ducking behind a newly walled home.

Bullets plugged the stucco behind me.

The construction workers immediately stopped constructing and fled for cover. As Murray had explained, they weren't evil carpenters. They were merely independent contractors who had no idea they were working for an evil organization. They dropped their tools and scattered. Every one of them steered clear of me, as I was obviously the target Mr. Seabrook was shooting at.

I fled down the dirt path between two unfinished houses, then cut back behind one of them. Through the gaps in the wood frame, I could see several SPYDER agents coming around the side of the rec center, heading my way.

However, directly ahead of me was a bulldozer.

I clambered up the tread and scrambled into the cab. I'd never driven a bulldozer before—or even a normal car, for that matter—but I'd driven some go-karts and at least had a rudimentary idea of how the thing probably worked. Sure enough, there were a gas pedal and a brake along with a trio of joysticks to control it. Most important, the keys were still dangling in the ignition switch. I twisted them, and the engine roared to life.

Through the windshield I saw Mr. Seabrook taking aim.

I dropped to the floor. Bullets shattered the glass above my head and pinged off the metal frame of the cab.

The driver had left his hard hat in the cab. I strapped it on for good measure.

Then I shoved one of the joysticks forward.

The bulldozer didn't move. Instead, the wide metal blade on the front lifted off the ground.

I hadn't meant to do this, but it turned out to be a pretty good move anyhow. The blade rose in front of the cab window, deflecting Mr. Seabrook's shots.

I shoved the other joystick.

Now the bulldozer lurched forward. It didn't move too quickly at first, only about the speed of my grandmother with her walker. I was momentarily worried—at this rate, the SPYDER agents could catch up to me if they merely sauntered—but then I noticed a switch on the console that had two positions: rabbit and turtle. I flicked it to rabbit.

The bulldozer's engine revved and the huge machine picked up speed. Not a *lot* of speed, but at least closer to a run than a crawl.

I twisted the steering joystick toward the wall. The bulldozer pivoted that way.

My intentions suddenly became clear to the pursuing SPYDER agents. They picked up the pace, charging after me.

There was a big, clawlike device on the back of the dozer. I quickly deduced that the third joystick controlled this and raised it to block the back window of the cab. Now, with the blade in front and the claw in back, I was well-protected from gunfire. However, I was also blocking my line of sight.

Driving a bulldozer wasn't easy to begin with. Doing it blind was nearly impossible. Luckily, when you're driving a bulldozer, it doesn't really matter if you bang into things, because you can pretty much knock anything out of your way. En route to the wall, I accidentally crushed a wheelbarrow, mulched a pile of lumber, and reduced a portable generator to scrap metal.

Mr. Seabrook was still in pursuit of me, well ahead of the other agents, closing in quickly. Within another fifteen seconds, he'd be even with the bulldozer and have a clear shot into the cab. So I veered into a row of Porta-Potties and flattened them. They popped like water balloons beneath my treads, spewing sewage. Mr. Seabrook was doused by a wave of excrement. He instantly forgot all about hunting me down and ran screaming back toward the rec center, desperate to shower off.

Now all that stood between me and the wall were two newly framed homes. I steered for the gap in between them, which looked wide enough for a bulldozer.

It turned out, the gap was *almost* wide enough for a bulldozer. But not quite. The blade caught the wooden frames on both sides—then tore right through them. One wooden strut after another splintered, and without their support, the houses quickly began to buckle. The second floors tilted, sending anything that had been stored upstairs tumbling my way: boxes of nails, toolboxes, toilets that hadn't been installed yet. Some clanged off the metal roof of the dozer, while others fell into its path and were quickly pulverized beneath the treads.

Most of the SPYDER agents who had been racing after me now stopped, fearing that pursuing me through the gap between the tilting homes had become a very bad career move. Only Coach G kept coming. "Move it, you cowards!" he bellowed at the others. "He's getting away!"

The wall was getting closer, but I still had a few more yards to go, and on both sides of me, the houses were on the verge of collapse. The remaining struts were warping and twisting as they struggled to support the second floors. The wood screeched as it torqued. Some struts ripped free of the foundation while others exploded into toothpicks. Electrical wires snapped. A staircase tore apart. An opossum who'd been living in the rafters of one home tumbled onto the dozer roof and screeched at me angrily.

"Ben! What's happening over there?" Erica shouted.

"I'm almost to the wall," I reported. "Just a few more seconds."

Coach G raced into the gap between the homes behind me. He was taking careful aim with his semiautomatic when a bathtub tumbled out of a second floor and landed on him. Luckily for Coach, the tub landed upside down, so instead of getting crushed, he merely ended up entombed beneath it in the muddy ground.

The bulldozer tore through the last of the struts lining the gap. The moment they went, the houses seemed to give up any hope of remaining upright. Dozens of other struts immediately blew, and the structures came crashing down. They collapsed into the gap with a cacophony of shrieking wood and rending metal. A huge cloud of dust billowed out, enveloping me like a sandstorm. The wall vanished from sight, so I didn't even see it until the bulldozer slammed into it.

The impact was so hard, I was thrown forward. My hard hat clanged off the steering wheel. Thankfully, the bulldozer was merely slowed, not defeated. A web of cracks quickly spread through the wall where the blade had hit it. I pressed forward on the joystick, giving the engine all the power it had left.

The wall trembled, then collapsed. The entire section in front of me crumbled like a saltine. On either side, the severed electric wires writhed and sparked like flaming snakes. I was safe inside the bulldozer, though. It rumbled through the hole, and just like that, I was outside the compound.

I'd emerged onto the farm. A field spread before me, rows and rows of lettuce, which the dozer quickly began churning into coleslaw.

Behind me, the SPYDER agents were obscured by the collapsed homes and dust cloud, though I was sure they'd be coming for me soon.

To my left, on the shoulder of the closest road, a recreational vehicle was parked with the engine running. From it, Erica and Alexander Hale were racing toward me. Alexander looked completely stunned by how I'd come through the wall. Erica looked as though she were trying her best *not* to look stunned.

"Jump!" Erica yelled. "But leave the dozer going!"

I did exactly as ordered, leaping from the moving bulldozer. I tumbled through the lettuce, rolled to my feet, and ran toward the Hales. They grabbed me by the arms and hustled me toward the RV. Behind us, the dozer kept on churning slowly across the field.

Alexander looked very different than he had when I'd last seen him. He'd ditched his usual three-piece suit to go for a tourist vibe, wearing cargo shorts, a baseball cap, and a Hawaiian shirt—even though he was in New Jersey. However, the biggest change was how happy he looked. He seemed invigorated by being on a mission once again, now clean-shaven and grinning from ear to ear. "Well done, Benjamin!" he cried. "Very original! Even *I* never used a bulldozer to escape an enemy compound! Wasn't that clever, Erica?"

"It was a bit flashy," Erica replied. She was wearing her

standard outfit, all black and ready for action. Her clothes were skintight, save for her utility belt. As we ran, she kept an eye on the hole I'd made in the wall, waiting for SPYDER agents to emerge through it.

The bulldozer plowed onward, heading in a different direction from us, trailing strings of barbed wire and other detritus. A toilet was perched atop the cab like a little porcelain hat. The opossum was seated on it, seeming to enjoy the ride.

We reached the roadside and scrambled into the RV. Cyrus Hale was at the wheel. Cyrus was in his seventies but could have passed for twenty years younger, if not more. He was dressed more like Erica than Alexander, wearing clothes designed for action rather than any pretense of being a tourist. His reaction to seeing me was closer to Erica's too: cool and unemotional. He didn't so much as nod hello. "Buckle up, everyone," he said. "This could get hairy."

"I call shotgun!" Alexander cried. In the Hale family, this didn't merely mean you got the seat next to the driver. You also had to use an actual shotgun.

Erica and I grabbed the rear seats as Cyrus hit the gas.

The RV swerved onto the road—and rolled along at exactly the speed limit.

"Uh, Dad?" Alexander asked. "Shouldn't we be going . . . er, faster?"

Cyrus shot his son a disdainful look, which happened quite a lot. "An RV tearing along the road here at ninety miles an hour will look suspicious. We don't want to draw any attention right now. There's still a chance we can decoy our way out of this without resorting to gunplay."

I scoped out the interior of the RV, hoping that, perhaps, it was some sort of high-tech surveillance vehicle designed to merely *look* like an RV. Instead, it was just an RV—and an old one at that. The Naugahyde seats were stained, the linoleum floor was peeling, and the whole thing smelled like a boys' locker room. A lot of surveillance equipment had been installed inside, but not in a way that made it look sleek or cool. Instead, it was jury-rigged and haphazard. A great deal of duct tape had been used. Which meant Cyrus had probably done it; he was a big fan of duct tape.

To my surprise, there was also a cat in the RV. A scraggly calico with mismatched eyes bounded into Alexander's lap.

"What's that?" I asked.

"Mr. Wigglebottom!" Alexander exclaimed.

"It's the cat I threw over the wall to distract Joshua from you the other night," Erica explained. "Daddy wouldn't let us take him back to the pound."

"Because he loves me." Alexander gave the cat a scratch behind the ears. "Don't you, Mr. Wigglebottom? Yes, you do! Yes, you do!"

Cyrus rolled his eyes and muttered something under his breath.

Behind us, SPYDER agents began to pour through the hole in the wall around Hidden Forest. Now that Mr. Seabrook and Coach G were out of commission, Mrs. Henderson was leading the charge. Thankfully, no one took any notice of our rickety old RV. Instead, they all ran after the bulldozer, which was still chugging across the lettuce patch. A few SPYDER SUVs raced out of the front gates of the community, but they all went after the bulldozer too, quickly veering off the road and driving through the dirt.

Cyrus watched them all in the rearview mirror, then shifted his gaze to Alexander. "See what I mean? Those dinks didn't know Ben had backup close by. They still think he's on his own . . . for now."

I watched as all the SPYDER agents closed in on the bulldozer, ignoring us completely. Just as they were about to catch up to it, we rounded a bend in the road and they disappeared behind a stand of trees. Now that we were out of their sight, Cyrus hit the gas.

It turned out, the RV *had* been slightly modified. The engine had been souped up, and the RV shot down the road with surprising speed. Given that it was an RV, however, it still wasn't going to outrun an SUV—and it wouldn't be long before SPYDER realized there was only an opossum driving the bulldozer and figure out I'd hitched a ride.

"How long do you think the decoy bought us?" I asked.

"A minute, if we're lucky," Cyrus replied, then glanced back at me. "So what'd you find in the safe?"

"It was a trap." I pulled out the note Joshua had left for me and handed it to Erica.

Erica read it: "'Ben, I guess we can't trust you after all. Joshua.'" She frowned, looking as defeated as I'd ever seen her.

Alexander took the note from her and sagged as well. "They were onto us the whole time."

"Well, they were suspicious, at least." Cyrus pounded the steering wheel angrily. "Dang it! We tanked an inside man for *this*?"

He suddenly veered off the road. The RV lurched into the parking lot of a diner. Mr. Wigglebottom pitched out of Alexander's lap and landed on the floor with a yowl. Cyrus swerved around to the back of the restaurant and skidded to a stop by the trash bins. The Hale family unbuckled themselves and leapt from their seats.

"Whoa," I said. "We're eating? Now?!"

"We're ditching the RV," Cyrus grumbled. "SPYDER's agents must've seen it just now—and they've certainly realized you're not in that bulldozer anymore—so they're gonna be looking for it." He grabbed a steel case off the floor and shoved it into my hands. "Take this—and skedaddle. We don't have much time."

Erica and Alexander were already slipping out the door with similar steel cases, heading for a nondescript sedan parked by the trash bins. Mr. Wigglebottom scampered after them. Alexander opened the passenger door and shouted, "Shotgun!" again.

I followed them, piling into the backseat with Erica. Cyrus slid into the driver's seat and told Alexander, "Leave the cat."

"He can't come?" Alexander asked, upset.

"No pets on missions," Cyrus stated flatly. "You can come back for him if we survive."

Alexander sadly set the cat on the ground. "Don't worry, Mr. Wigglebottom," he said. "I'll come back for you. I promise."

Mr. Wigglebottom strolled away unconcerned, like he had already forgotten about us.

Alexander sniffled and wiped away a tear.

Cyrus muttered under his breath again and motored slowly around to the front of the restaurant.

Sure enough, two SPYDER SUVs came flying down the road, going double the speed limit. The RV was hidden well enough behind the diner that they didn't notice it and shot right past us.

Cyrus gave them a thirty-second head start, making sure they hadn't spotted us, then pulled out of the parking lot and started down the road behind them. "Ben, during your period undercover in SPYDER's compound, did you learn *anything* about this plot of theirs, other than when it's happening?"

I met his gaze in the rearview mirror. "No," I admitted.

Cyrus's gaze hardened. "Well, that's just great," he grumbled. "We all took a big risk on you, kid. Bigger than you can imagine. And for what? Nothing."

"Sorry," I mumbled, feeling completely useless.

Cyrus floored the gas angrily. We shot past two gated communities that, save for their names, looked exactly like Hidden Forest.

"Where are we going?" I asked meekly. "Back to the CIA?"

Cyrus gave a derisive snort in response.

"We've gone rogue from the CIA on this mission," Erica told me. "The Agency doesn't like rogues. If we go back there with no intel, they'll have our heads."

"Then where . . . ?" I began.

"To our only lead so far," Erica said. "Sandy Hook."

NAUTICAL EXERCISES

Lower New York Harbor
September 17
1700 hours

It took us most of the day to get back to Sandy Hook. Since there was only one road leading there, Cyrus didn't want to use it. "Too dangerous," he explained. "Know why they call them dead-end roads? 'Cause you end up dead on them. It'd be way too easy for SPYDER to cut off our escape route. If they're waiting for us there, we might as well kiss our keisters good-bye."

However, since Sandy Hook was a peninsula, there were plenty of ways in and out across the water. That was the much safer option, as far as Cyrus was concerned. The problem was, coming in by water required a boat—and we didn't have one.

Cyrus had some ideas how to get one, though. So we worked our way through the suburbs of New Jersey to the waterfront in Jersey City. This took several hours, because even though we appeared to have shaken the SPYDER agents, Cyrus was certain they were still hunting for us. He stuck to back roads, made huge detours to avoid potential ambush sites, and every time he heard a helicopter, he'd pull over under the cover of trees and wait for it to pass.

"C'mon, Dad," Alexander chided the fifth time this happened. "You really think SPYDER has choppers in the air, looking for us?"

"I didn't get to be this old by letting my guard down," Cyrus snapped. "As far as I'm concerned, there's nothing I'd put past SPYDER."

Once we finally arrived in Jersey City, Cyrus ordered us to drop him off near a high-end marina. It was located in front of some shiny new condos on the waterfront, and the slips were full of expensive watercraft: fancy wooden sailboats, gleaming motorboats, and a few yachts that were bigger than my house.

The rest of us headed south to the docks where the container ships unloaded. Cyrus had pinpointed one that was under repair, so we parked there, hiding the car in a maze of rusted old shipping containers, then went to the water's edge to wait. It was possibly the least beautiful place I'd ever been. The water's surface was slick with oil and choked with garbage, while the abandoned ship cranes loomed over us like the skeletons of dinosaurs.

A half hour later, Cyrus arrived, driving a cigarette boat. It was built for speed: thin and aerodynamic, with a pair of six-hundred-horsepower engines in the back. The cockpit was small and uncovered. There were only four seats. The boat was painted neon blue with flames on the sides.

The rest of us quickly climbed into the cockpit. There was barely enough room for us and our four steel cases.

"Where'd you get this?" Erica asked.

Cyrus chuckled. "I liberated it."

"You mean it's stolen?" Alexander demanded.

"The owner doesn't deserve it." Cyrus motored away from the dock into the Hudson River. "He's a criminal."

"What'd he do?" I asked.

"It'd be faster to list what he *hasn't* done," Cyrus replied. "The guy's dirty as they come, though the government's never been able to nail him on anything. I figure, at the very least, the guy can let us borrow his boat for a few hours. For all we know, the jerk's off on the French Riviera anyhow."

Erica looked over the paint job. "It's a little garish, don't you think?"

Cyrus shrugged. "Yeah, it's tacky. But since we're heading for the Jersey Shore, we ought to fit right in."

He took us through the channel between the mainland and Staten Island, then hugged the shoreline. He did his best not to draw attention, driving at moderate speed and falling in with other recreational boaters. The warm weather had kept up, and lots of people were out on the water, many in boats just as ostentatious as ours.

We arced along the Jersey coast, then approached Sandy Hook from the west, keeping the setting sun at our backs.

"Is anyone going to explain to me what's going on?" I asked. I'd posed the question in varying ways at several other times that day, only to be rebuffed.

Erica and Alexander both looked to Cyrus, who nodded imperceptibly that it was finally all right to fill me in on what was going on.

"Sandy Hook isn't just a beach," Erica explained. "It's also an extremely important military site."

"Since when?" I asked.

"Since 1812," Erica replied. "It's perfectly situated for defending New York City because it overlooks the main route there from the Atlantic. The United States first built a fort at Sandy Hook during the War of 1812 to protect New York from the British Navy, and it's been used for defense ever since. In the 1950s, they installed Project Nike missile silos there to fend off Soviet nuclear strikes."

"Is that what those buildings were that Murray was taking pictures of?" I asked. "Old missile silos?"

"Yes. Sandy Hook was Nike site fifty-six." Erica handed me a pair of binoculars.

I zoomed in on the peninsula ahead. Before, I had only been on the eastern side of it, my view of the west blocked by the dunes. Now I could see there were quite a few buildings on the western side: squat cement bunkers and rusted metal silos.

"I thought all the Nike missile sites were shut down after the Cold War," I said.

"Not true," Erica replied. "The military just told the public that to throw off our enemies. They even let the silos look like they're going to seed. But they're still completely functional—and there are still missiles stored inside to protect the city."

"And SPYDER's trying to steal them?" I concluded.

"That's our best guess," Cyrus said. "It's all we've got, seeing as you didn't learn any other information for us."

I sighed. Cyrus Hale might have been one of the finest spies our country had ever produced, but he could also be a real jerk. I was feeling ineffectual enough without him reminding me how ineffectual I was every few minutes.

"So . . . you suspected SPYDER was after the missiles when Murray first brought me here?" I asked.

"Of course," Cyrus said. "Why else would they be sniffing around Sandy Hook?"

"What do you think SPYDER intends to do with them?"

"I have no idea," Cyrus replied curtly. "That was what you were supposed to find out."

In the shotgun seat, Alexander glanced back at me, looking a bit embarrassed about his father. "You know, Ben actually did quite a good job, under the circumstances," he said. "This was only his first undercover mission, and it wasn't an easy one. . . ."

"What would *you* know about doing a good job?" Cyrus snapped.

Alexander recoiled, looking wounded. "I *did* save your life once."

Instead of acknowledging this, Cyrus said, "We're almost there. Time for you to get out of those ridiculous clothes."

Alexander nodded sadly, then opened the steel case he'd been carrying. Erica opened hers as well. I figured this meant I ought to open mine, too.

Inside it was everything I'd need for my mission: a black outfit that matched the ones Cyrus and Erica were wearing, night-vision goggles, and a small grappling hook. But while Erica had a gun in her case, I'd been given only a bottle of chloroform and a handkerchief.

There wasn't any place in the boat's small cockpit for

Alexander or me to change clothes in private, so Erica turned away while the two of us stripped down to our underwear and pulled on our new black outfits. The clothes were sleek and practical, though they weren't as suave and cool as the suits Alexander usually wore. Instead, the four of us looked more like a renegade circus troupe. Instead of pockets, we each had a utility belt. There were also bulletproof Kevlar vests for protection, which was nice, though I would have liked Kevlar pants and a Kevlar helmet as well.

I doused my handkerchief with chloroform, then tucked the bottle into one pocket of my utility belt and left the hankie sticking out of another, where I'd have easy access to it. Figuring out where to put the grappling hook was a little more difficult. I still hadn't had any formal training with grappling hooks—you didn't cover them until your second year at spy school (Intro to Grapples, Rappels, and other Vertical Access Methods)—and they weren't the type of thing you encountered in normal life. I'd never had much use for grappling until being recruited to the CIA. There was a revolver-size air gun that fired the hook, which had a coil of thin steel cable attached to it. I fitted the hook into the gun, then struggled to figure out how to clip it onto the utility belt.

"Here," Erica said. "Let me help you with that."

I pulled away from her. "Oh, *now* you want to help me?"

My own words caught me by surprise. I hadn't realized how angry I was at Erica until then.

Erica seemed surprised as well. She looked at me curiously. "What's that supposed to mean? I've been plenty of help to you on this mission."

"A mission you put me on without even asking if I wanted to do it," I said bitterly. I knew I probably should have been keeping my thoughts to myself, bottling them up the way Erica did, but I couldn't help it. "Instead, you just manipulated me into it. You got me booted from spy school. . . ."

"You'll be reinstated if all this works out."

"And I could get killed if it doesn't! You put me in serious danger here!"

"Danger is part of life at the CIA. I thought you wanted to be an agent."

"And I thought you were my friend."

Erica pursed her lips. For a moment, I thought I saw the slightest hint of emotion in her eyes. But then it was gone. "You can't afford to have friends in this business," she said coldly. "Personal connections compromise your ability to perform."

"Personal connections?" I repeated. "You're on this mission with your whole family! This is like a road trip for you!"

"That's not by choice," Erica said. "The unauthorized nature of this mission required using this particular team."

"So, that's all I am to you?" I asked. "Someone who you work with when you have to?"

Erica fixed me with a blank stare. "Emotions can severely complicate a mission. It's best not to form attachments. Suppose SPYDER is plotting to kill millions of people and you have the chance to destroy their operation—but Joshua Hallal takes me hostage? Now, you have a choice: Save me—or complete the mission. Which would you choose?"

I frowned, knowing what the right answer was, but not wanting to say it. "That won't happen."

"It *could*," Erica warned. "And if it does, you have to sacrifice me for the mission, not the other way around. I'd do the same thing. And so would Granddad and my father. You can't have millions of people die to save one person."

I sighed. Erica's argument made sense—and yet it seemed so *wrong*. "So, the solution is to go through life without friends?"

"Yes," Erica said.

"You're not saying that just because Joshua broke your heart?"

Erica turned on me. The temperature on the boat seemed to suddenly drop ten degrees, though I wasn't sure if it was because of Erica's cold gaze or the fact that the sun was setting. Finally, Erica said, "I don't know what you're talking about."

"Yes, you do," I said. "You liked him. Just because he turned out to be the biggest jerk of all time doesn't mean everyone else will. Friends aren't always a liability. Sometimes they're the best asset we have."

Before Erica could respond, Cyrus announced, "Can the chitchat, you two. Time for stealth mode. No talking unless absolutely necessary." He shut off the engines and handed a paddle to each of us.

Without the roar of the big motors, it was startlingly quiet. Even though New York sat only a few miles to the north of us, the wide expanse of water swallowed up the sounds of the city. When I looked south toward the modest homes on the Jersey Shore, it was easy to imagine that I was off the coast of some rural fishing village. To the east, Sandy Hook appeared completely uninhabited.

We paddled toward it. It was hard work, and we had a mile to cover. As we went, the night grew darker, covering our approach. We strapped on our night-vision goggles and scanned the shore. No one was moving. The Nike site looked like a Cold War–era ghost town.

When we were a hundred yards from shore, Cyrus signaled us to stop rowing. The current caught us, carrying us the rest of the way.

There wasn't a single light on at Sandy Hook. The peninsula was merely a silhouette that grew as we came closer to it until finally the waves slid the cigarette boat gently onto the sand.

We beached a bit north of the main building complex, where some scrub grew close to the water. We dragged some of it down to the water's edge to hide the boat, sending up clouds of pollen. Alexander wrinkled his nose at the smell and then his eyes opened wide in alarm. He began huffing in air, building up to what looked to be an enormous sneeze.

Cyrus wheeled on him with a don't-you-dare-make-a-noise expression.

Alexander looked around desperately, spotted the handkerchief poking out of my utility belt, snatched it away, and placed it to his nose, stifling the sneeze at the last second. He sighed with relief—and then realized, a bit too late, that the rag was soaked in chloroform. "Oh shoot," he said, and then collapsed face-first onto the sand.

Cyrus and Erica rolled their eyes, then headed toward the silo complex, leaving Alexander snoring softly on the beach. I felt a little bad about leaving him behind, but he wasn't going to wake anytime soon, and I knew we couldn't delay our mission a moment longer. It was coming up on eight o'clock.

Even with the night-vision goggles, Cyrus and Erica were almost impossible to see as they slunk along. They melted into the shadows, becoming a part of them. I did my best to mimic their movements, praying that I wouldn't screw up like Alexander had.

There were three missile silos on the property, sunk deep in the ground, covered by large round metal lids that would slide open when the time came to fire. The access was through three cement bunkers, which were the low, squat buildings I had seen at the beach.

We were almost to the first bunker when we finally encountered some guards. Unfortunately, just like Alexander, they were sprawled on the ground. They were unconscious, rather than dead, though this did little to relieve my fear. SPYDER had obviously beaten us there.

Cyrus pressed a finger to the neck of one of the guards, taking his pulse.

"How long has he been out?" Erica whispered.

"At least half an hour," Cyrus replied, his voice laced with concern.

I shifted my gaze to the nearby bunker. There were no windows and only one door, five feet tall and made of rusted steel.

It hung open. Cyrus led us through it.

A metal staircase plunged downward, almost exactly like the secret one at Hidden Forest. It was as though any organization that needed a covert underground lair used the same architect. We crept down it, spiraling several stories into the earth, until we arrived in a large room.

While SPYDER's underground lair had been tastefully decorated and homey, this room was cold and industrial. The walls, floor, and ceiling were all concrete. It was lit by bare bulbs dangling from electrical wires, and the furniture all appeared to be relics from the Cold War: metal desks, folding chairs, a water cooler. However, the missile systems had been upgraded relatively recently. The computers on the desks were only a few years out-of-date, which qualified as modern for the government, and the large screens that would be used to track incoming missiles were of decent quality.

Except for us, the room was empty, which was unsettling in a command center that was supposed to be staffed twenty-four hours a day, weekends and holidays included.

Cyrus and Erica seemed worried by this as well.

There was only one other door besides the one we had come through. It was a thick steel affair, like you'd expect to find on a bank vault, rigged with all sorts of alarms and marked by dozens of signs saying that it shouldn't be opened for any reason.

It was open.

Since the alarms weren't ringing, I assumed they'd been dismantled.

Cyrus headed for the door. Erica and I followed.

We passed through a cement wall several feet thick and

found ourselves at the base of the missile silo. The missile was still there, towering above us. I didn't get a very good look at it, though.

I was too distracted by the explosives.

A ring of dynamite was strapped around the base of the missile with duct tape. I'd never seen dynamite outside of a Bugs Bunny cartoon, but it looked exactly as I expected: foot-long red tubes with wires sticking out of them. All the wires snaked to a small electronic device that was also duct taped to the missile. There was a timer on the device. It showed there were four minutes and thirteen seconds left until everything exploded.

SPYDER wasn't planning on stealing the missiles after all. They were destroying them instead.

Cyrus Hale considered all the dynamite—and then ran. "C'mon!" he yelled, bolting out of the silo. "Move your butts before they get blasted off!"

Erica and I followed right behind him.

"You're not going to defuse it?" I asked as we dashed back through the control room. Now that Cyrus had spoken, I figured I had free rein to speak as well.

"How many great CIA bomb defusers have you ever heard of?" Cyrus demanded.

"Er . . . none," I answered.

"Exactly! There aren't any! Because people who try to

defuse bombs get killed." Cyrus pounded up the staircase ahead of us.

"But if SPYDER's trying to destroy the missiles," Erica protested, "shouldn't we be trying to thwart their plans?"

"Defusing that bomb would take way more than four minutes," Cyrus explained. "I'll bet you SPYDER's up to more than just blowing up those missiles. And we're not gonna be able to thwart them if we've been reduced to smithereens. Standard operating procedure in this case isn't to risk our lives with the bomb. It's to get the holy heck away from it." He burst through the door at the top of the stairs, then stopped so suddenly that Erica and I slammed into him from behind.

I started to ask Cyrus what the problem was, but then noticed he had his hands in the air.

And after that, I noticed the twenty men aiming guns at us. They were arrayed in a semicircle around the door of the bunker, cutting off any route of escape.

"Cyrus Hale," a voice announced from the darkness. "This is the CIA. You and your associates are under arrest."

"Nuts," Cyrus said.

EVACUATION

Site 56

September 17

2000 hours

I raised my hands the same way Cyrus had, hop-ing he knew how to get us out of this mess—and do it quickly. Due to my innate sense of time, I was well aware there were only two minutes and thirty seconds left until the dynamite blew.

If Cyrus was worried, though, he didn't show it. He simply squinted into the darkness at the CIA agent who had spoken and asked, "Rafferty, is that you?"

"That's affirmative," Agent Rafferty replied. He was middle-aged and pear-shaped, standing behind his men in the center of the line.

Cyrus said, "Think we could lower the guns and continue this discussion a few hundred yards from here? This silo's rigged to blow in a couple minutes."

"Yeah, right," Rafferty said. "I'm not falling for that old routine. You think I'm an idiot?"

"I don't think that at all," Cyrus said. "I *know* you're an idiot."

Rafferty sputtered angrily, then exclaimed, "I'm not the one who defected from the CIA and then illegally infiltrated a top-secret military base!"

"I did no such thing," Cyrus shot back. "Don't you think it's suspicious that you showed up here exactly when I did? Let me guess what happened. About fifteen minutes ago, you received a classified Double-A red alert from Internal Affairs detailing my arrival here along with a warning that I'd left the Agency to pursue some evil scheme or another. Furthermore, this alert told you exactly where and when to find me."

"Er . . . yes," Rafferty admitted.

"Does that sound like something that I'd do?" Cyrus demanded. "After everything I've done for this country? I would never betray the Agency! I'm on a classified mission, hunting down the subversive organization that has rigged this silo to blow. That same organization sent you the red alert, not the CIA! And by keeping your guns on us right now, you're playing into their hands. They've set us all up."

For a moment, Rafferty almost looked convinced. But then he shook his head. "The alert I got couldn't possibly have been a fake. It had an official code that checked out."

"These guys have infiltrated the CIA!" Cyrus exclaimed. "One of their moles sent that to you!"

Rafferty shook his head and clucked his tongue. "Listen to yourself, Cyrus. You're saying I'm a fool to think you'd go join the enemy—but instead, I should believe some top-secret evil organization has infiltrated the entire CIA?"

Cyrus sighed, then muttered to us under his breath, "Like I said, he's an idiot. How much time till detonation, Ben?"

"Fifteen seconds."

"Get ready to run for the boat." Cyrus returned his attention to Rafferty and the CIA. "Agents, all of you know who I am and what I stand for. I swear, I'm telling you the truth. So before you back Rafferty over me, there's one thing you ought to know. . . ."

At which point, the silo exploded.

Cyrus, Erica, and I were prepared for it. Or at least, we were as prepared as you can possibly be for an entire missile complex to detonate beneath your feet.

The other CIA agents were completely caught by surprise. Apparently, none of them had believed Cyrus's warning.

A column of flame erupted behind us, shredding the silo and sending huge sheets of rusted metal cartwheeling through the air. The ground trembled as though an earth-quake had hit. Cracks spread through the earth at our feet and fractured the cement bunker into pieces.

And then the other two missile silos at Sandy Hook blew as well. The explosions were farther away, but just as big, turning night into day and spewing dirt and metal.

Many of the CIA agents were thrown to the ground by the blasts. Others were temporarily blinded by them. Most of the rest scattered, gibbering in fear.

I ran for the boat as I'd been ordered. Erica and Cyrus were right there with me. We barreled past the startled agents blocking our way. Two regained their wits long enough to try to stop us, but Cyrus and Erica made quick work of them. There was a sudden flurry of arms and legs, and the next thing either agent knew, they were on the ground, wheezing in pain.

A little farther away, a third agent was wheeling toward us with his gun.

I defended myself with the only weapon I had: my grappling hook. I fired the air gun, launching the metal grapple at the enemy. I'd been aiming for his head, hoping to knock him unconscious, but as usual, my aim was off and I nailed him in the groin instead. It worked, though. The agent dropped his gun and doubled over, whimpering.

"That's not exactly the recommended way to use this," Erica chided, snatching the grapple off the ground as we ran past.

"You know a better way to take out the enemy with a grappling hook?"

"Watch and learn."

The ground was collapsing behind us, forming a crater where the missile had once been. A huge chunk of the bunker sheared off and tumbled inside. We sprinted as fast as we could, trying to stay ahead of the expanding hole. Craters were also growing where the other explosions had occurred. Lit by fire and flame from within, they looked like volcanos sprouting on the beach.

By now Rafferty and a few of the other agents had realized we were on the run. They came after us, steering clear of the craters as well. Rafferty shouted something that might have been "Curse you, Cyrus!" though I couldn't hear it clearly over all the noise.

Erica reloaded my grappling hook into the air gun, then fired it at a tree a few feet away. The grapple whipped around a low branch and held tight. Erica then jammed the gun into the crook of another tree, yanking the wire tight across the path five feet above the ground. She did this so fluidly, she didn't miss a step. Even with all the explosions and fires around, the thin wire was almost invisible in the night. You'd only notice it if you knew to look for it.

Rafferty and his men didn't know to look for it. They were too focused on us—or on the exploding missiles or the flaming craters or the random smoking objects that were now beginning to plummet from the sky. Behind us, I heard Rafferty yell, "If you don't stop, I will order my men to . . . Waughhhh!" There was a metallic twang as he and all his agents caught the wire in the chest simultaneously and were knocked flat on their backs.

Erica flashed me a cocky smile. "See? You only took down one person with it."

We kept on running, leaving the imploding missile base behind as quickly as possible. The cigarette boat was right where we had left it—as was Alexander, who had somehow slept through all the noise. He woke as we shoved the boat back into the water, still woozy from the chloroform, and blinked in confusion at the fire and chaos down the beach. "Ooh!" he said groggily. "Fireworks! Is it Independence Day already?"

"And he wonders why I never invited him on a mission before," Cyrus grumbled.

Erica grabbed Alexander by the arm and helped him to his feet. "C'mon, Dad. We have to go."

"On a boat ride?" Alexander asked. "Sounds delightful!"

We got the boat off the sand, then angled it toward the middle of the bay and clambered into the cockpit. Alexander tumbled in face-first, his legs sticking up in the air.

Several more explosions suddenly flared in the night. They were so far away, we didn't hear the booms until fifteen seconds later, but the blasts were bright and clear, orange mushrooms blooming on the horizon. Three were to the northeast of New York City, and three were to the northwest.

"What's that?" I asked.

"Sandy Hook wasn't the only active missile site near New York," Cyrus said, firing up the engines. "Looks like SPYDER just hit the others, too."

Rafferty and his agents had gotten back to their feet and were charging our way again. Down the beach, I saw them readying their guns. Cyrus revved the motor and we roared away, kicking up a huge rooster tail of water just as the CIA opened fire.

I breathed a huge sigh of relief and sagged into my seat.

"Stay alert!" Cyrus warned. "We're not out of this yet!" He pointed behind us.

The CIA had called for backup. Three boats were coming from the direction of the missile base. Gunfire erupted from them. Bullets stitched the surface of the water behind us.

Erica grabbed for her gun to return fire, but Cyrus shook his head. "No shooting back. They're fellow agents, not the enemy."

"*We're* agents too," Erica protested. "And they're shooting at *us*."

"They've been hoodwinked by SPYDER," Cyrus said. "And SPYDER would probably like nothing better than for us to do their dirty work for them and blow one another away. But we're not playing that game."

"What game are we playing, then?" Alexander asked. "How about Parcheesi? I *love* Parcheesi!"

"If we can't fight back, what's our plan?" I asked.

"I didn't get this boat because it looked pretty," Cyrus explained. "I got it for the speed. We ought to be able to outrun them."

"And them, too?" Erica asked, pointing to our port side.

More boats were coming. It was hard to tell in the dark, but it looked like the New Jersey police had mobilized their marine division as well.

"Dang it!" Cyrus growled. "SPYDER wasn't taking any chances with this. We played right into their devious little hands." He yanked hard on the wheel, veering away from the Jersey police boats as well.

"How's that?" I asked.

The motors were roaring so loud, Cyrus had to shout his response. "There's no way the NJPD would have boats out this fast if the CIA had just called them. Those silos went up only a few minutes ago. That means SPYDER probably tipped them off well ahead of time too, the same as they did with the CIA."

"You think they have moles inside the Jersey police too?" Erica asked.

"No," Cyrus replied. "I don't think they're *that* big. They probably just phoned in a tip and got the police on their toes, so when the missiles went off, they were ready to roll."

"But with the CIA, they definitely used an inside man?" I asked.

"Rafferty wouldn't have been able to mobilize an Agency team that big unless he thought word was really coming from on high." Cyrus shook his head, looking annoyed at himself. "SPYDER played us just like they played you. They fed us a single crumb—Sandy Hook—knowing that we'd bite. Then they rigged the missiles and set us up so that *we'd* take the fall for it. They probably hoped we'd all get killed in the blast, but this still works out for them just fine. We're the only ones who know SPYDER's plotting something—and now they've got the CIA chasing *us*, freeing them to pursue their evil plans. It's deviously brilliant, really."

Thankfully, the CIA and the Jersey police weren't gaining on us. Our boat was going so fast, it seemed to be skipping across the water. It wasn't very comfortable, though. We kept slamming up and down on the surface hard enough to rattle my teeth. Salt water pelted us as we smashed through wave after wave, leaving my eyes stinging from the brine and my body shivering from the wet.

Only Alexander seemed to be having fun, and that was because he was still zonked from the chloroform. "Whee!" he cried. "This is fun! We should go boating more often, Dad!"

"This might be naive," I said to Cyrus. "But is there any sense in letting them *catch* us? After all, you're a legend in the CIA. Wouldn't someone higher up listen to you if you explained what was going on? How could they even think that you, of all people, have joined the enemy?"

Cyrus sighed, and for a moment he looked much older. "Sadly, there's precedent. I wouldn't be the first highly regarded agent to switch sides. Especially at my age. People get packed off into retirement and have a tough time adjusting to the real world on a skimpy pension. After you've spent your whole life fighting for freedom and democracy, early-bird specials and bingo nights don't really cut it. In fact, I suspect SPYDER already has a legend or two working for them. It'd explain how they have such good intel on how the Agency works. And the top brass probably has come to the same conclusion, which means I wouldn't be above suspicion."

"We could prove we weren't behind this," Erica argued. "I'm sure there's surveillance footage showing SPYDER entering the silos long before we got there. . . ."

"It's probably been blown to bits," Cyrus said. "Along with everything else at Sandy Hook."

"Even so," I protested, "if they grill us, we all have the exact same story, which should indicate we're not lying. . . ."

"True," Cyrus agreed. "They'd figure it out eventually. But you've been grilled before, kid. You know how that goes.

By the time we finally sell them our story, SPYDER will have already launched phase two of their plan—and I can guarantee you there's a phase two. They didn't decimate Sandy Hook right now just to take us out of the game."

"What are they going to do?" Erica asked.

Cyrus shrugged. "Don't ask me. Ask Ben. He's our undercover man." Unlike before, Cyrus wasn't trying to be dismissive of me with this statement; he was too upset at himself for being manipulated by SPYDER to be upset at me as well. But I felt guilty just the same.

I glanced back toward Sandy Hook, wondering what could be going on. I was sure that I'd encountered *some* clue or another as to SPYDER's ultimate plans during my time at Hidden Forest. Unfortunately, I hadn't made sense of it yet.

Sandy Hook had dropped far in the distance. The blazing fires were now mere dots of orange on the horizon. But the CIA and the Jersey police were still keeping pace with us. Their boats were as souped up as ours was. As I watched, they unleashed another fusillade of bullets, one of which pocked the stern of our boat.

"All right," Cyrus said determinedly. "Time to shake these guys."

We had reached the narrow gap between Staten Island and Brooklyn and the going suddenly became much more treacherous. There was a lot more traffic: fleets of fishermen and pleasure boats returning home after a day out on the water, as well as massive container ships from Jersey and a cruise ship from Manhattan on their way out to sea. We were a minnow beside these whales and were probably supposed to give them right of way, but we didn't have time for that. Instead, Cyrus slalomed through them, trying to lose our pursuers, resulting in some terrifyingly close calls. We barely avoided being flattened by one outbound freighter and nearly got pureed by the rear propellers of another.

"Woo-hoo!" Alexander yelled.

Behind us, the CIA and the NJPD got lost in the shuffle. Only one boat—the lead for the CIA—managed to follow us through, only to get clipped by the cruise ship. It was as though a kid had capsized his bathtub toy. The CIA boat was flipped on its side, catapulting the agents into the harbor.

Cyrus chuckled to himself. "That ought to keep the Agency off our tail."

"But what about the New York police?" Erica asked, pointing ahead of us.

I looked in that direction and groaned. I think Cyrus might have even done the same.

Sure enough, the NYPD had been alerted about us as well, and they were coming in full force. It looked as though Homeland Security and the U.S. Coast Guard had also joined the hunt. A dozen boats were converging on us, as well as two helicopters, which shot overhead, spotlights sweeping the water.

"Hang on," Cyrus warned. "This might get dangerous."

"*Now* it's getting dangerous?" I gasped. "What was that before?"

"Mildly treacherous." Cyrus suddenly veered wildly to starboard. This kicked up a wall of water, which temporarily shielded us from view while Cyrus quickly switched direction again. We blasted through our own wave and bore down on our attackers, aiming for a narrow gap between two police boats.

The police shouted warnings at us through their bullhorns, and when we didn't stop, they opened fire.

We dropped onto the floor of the cockpit and curled up tight, pulling our Kevlar vests over our heads like safety blankets.

Bullets raked both sides of us as we zoomed between the police boats. I could hear things cracking and splintering above my head. One shot must have glanced off my Kevlar. It felt like someone had pounded it with a hammer.

And then the shooting stopped. We were through the gap and the other boats were struggling to pull U-turns and come after us. I sat up to find the neon blue paneling of our cigarette boat shredded, the windshield riddled with holes, and one engine trailing smoke.

"Hey," Alexander said, his chloroform haze finally dissipating. "Those people were trying to kill us! This isn't fun at all!"

"Nice of you to join us." Cyrus turned toward the pier in New Jersey, where we'd started out that night, but now saw there were reinforcements coming from that direction. A lot of reinforcements. Twelve boats in all.

Alexander's eyes grew as big as golf balls with fear. "They've cut off our escape route!"

"I noticed." Cyrus cursed under his breath and reoriented us toward the tip of Manhattan.

All the other boats slewed in the water a bit as they changed course behind us, then revved their engines and rejoined the chase.

"Without an escape route, we can't escape!" Alexander babbled. "What do we do now?"

"Keep your pants on. I have a plan." Cyrus kept his eyes locked on the city ahead.

"What is it?" I asked.

"Leave the getaway to me," Cyrus said. "You focus on figuring out what SPYDER's up to. Without that, everything we're doing here is for naught."

I racked my brain, struggling to make sense of everything I'd seen and heard over the past few weeks. It would have been difficult under normal circumstances, but I found it almost impossible to concentrate with the bullets flying and the boat jouncing over the water and Alexander whimpering and the constant threat of death everywhere around us. The fact that Erica was staring at me expectantly also didn't help.

After a mere fifteen seconds had gone by, she asked, "Well? Any ideas?"

"No," I admitted. "None."

"Then think harder."

"What is that even supposed to mean?" I snapped. "How could I possibly think harder? That's like telling someone to see harder or taste harder. The problem isn't that I'm not thinking hard enough! It's that your stupid plan to send me undercover wasn't any good!"

Erica's cold stare grew even colder. "Our plan was perfectly fine."

Cyrus sliced directly behind another container ship, which had left a cavernous wake in its path. We launched into the air, sailed across it, and came down hard on the far side. One of the boats pursuing us wasn't as lucky. It plunged into the trough and flipped stern-over-bow, landing upside down in the harbor.

"SPYDER never believed I was really working with them!" I argued. "They knew I was a mole the whole time. Any information they fed me was false!"

Erica shook her head. "They might have *suspected* you

were a mole, but they weren't sure. They wouldn't have brought you in merely to set us up. That'd be far too risky. They *wanted* you for something."

"No, they didn't. I was just a patsy."

One of our motors coughed and died, cutting our power in half. The pursuing boats quickly started gaining on us.

"You weren't a patsy!" Erica told me. "SPYDER has always wanted you on their side. Because you're not as incompetent as you believe you are! So *think*! What did they want you for?"

"I don't know!"

"Did they train you for anything special?"

"No!"

"Did they ask you to do anything unusual?"

"No! I haven't done anything for the past few weeks except workouts and math problems!"

The moment the words were out of my mouth, I had a sudden flash of understanding. Everything that had happened at Hidden Forest fell into place. Everything I hadn't grasped instantly came into focus.

Erica seemed to sense this. In the sweep of the helicopter searchlights, I saw her cold stare fade. "What is it?"

"I know what SPYDER's up to . . . ," I said.

But that was as far as I got. As we passed Liberty Island, another police boat ambushed us. This one was built like ours, and it came up fast, looking to broadside us. Cyrus wrenched us to the right to avoid it, but with the other boats closing the gap and the helicopters overhead, there was nowhere for us to go. Gunfire rang out and something sparked off our bow. Both engines went up in flames.

"Abandon ship!" Cyrus yelled.

"What?" Alexander cried.

Cyrus slammed into him a second later, lifting him up and over the side of the boat. Erica lunged for me in the same way, although I was already moving when she hit me.

The engines blew as we jumped. The shock wave sent us cartwheeling through the air. I saw the city skyline flip over twice and then the surface of the harbor smacked me in the face. It was like being punched in the head. I was dazed, only vaguely aware of the cold embrace of the water and the fact that I was sinking. I tried to swim, but something heavy snagged around my foot, dragging me down toward the bottom.

Above me, at the surface, I saw the bright flare of the explosion, the churn of the bubbles as boats raced overhead, and a vision of a woman's face . . . all fading quickly as I was pulled farther and farther away.

And then the darkness swallowed me.

SECURE LOCATION

Liberty Island
September 17
2300 hours

I was only vaguely aware of being pulled from the water, the experience a jumble of images: the sensation of being dragged back up from the darkness and emerging into the light and noise once again; the roar of helicopter blades in the distance; the feeling of being hauled, wet and cold, onto muddy ground; Erica yelling, "Fight, Ben! Fight!" and then leaning over me; a woman with a stoic gaze looming behind her; the groan of stone against stone as a passage opened in a rock; a Komodo dragon in a pink tutu, doing pirouettes atop an elephant.

It's quite possible that I dreamt the last one, as I lost consciousness more than once.

I came to lying on a cold granite floor. A voice echoed nearby while footsteps paced. Erica. She must have been on the radio with someone, because I couldn't hear their half of the conversation.

"He hasn't regained consciousness yet, but he's stable. . . . No, I'm not going to try to rouse him. He needs time to recover. . . . Yes, I understand what's at stake. What's the situation there?"

I opened my eyes and immediately wondered if I was still dreaming. Directly in front of me was a toe the size of a bathtub. It was bronze, part of an enormous bronze foot, which wore an enormous bronze sandal, draped by the fringe of an enormous bronze dress.

"Let me guess," I groaned. "We're inside the Statue of Liberty."

"He's up," Erica reported into her radio. "I'll call you back."

I sat up, confirming my suspicions. We were inside the museum in the statue's base. The giant foot I'd been staring at wasn't part of the real statue; it was a scale model.

Erica stood by a smaller model of the entire statue in the middle of the room. She had traded her wet clothes for souvenirs from the gift shop: a tacky T-shirt and a beach towel, which she'd wrapped around her waist like a skirt. Without her usual, primed-for-action outfit, she looked more like a normal teenage girl than usual.

I realized that my wet clothes had been removed as well. I was cocooned in souvenir towels, naked save for my underwear.

Erica hurried to my side, apparently relieved that I was conscious again. "How are you feeling?"

"All right, I guess." I met her eyes. "You saved me?"

She nodded. "The anchor rope snagged around your leg. By the time I got you free, you were . . . Well, it could have been bad."

"You had to resuscitate me?"

"Yes."

I felt my face grow warm as blood rushed to it.

Erica immediately understood why I was blushing. "Don't get all worked up. Yes, our lips touched. But it wasn't kissing. I was only forcing air into your lungs."

"I know," I said, wishing I could remember it better. The bizarre thought occurred to me that it was almost worth dying to have my lips touch Erica's. "How'd we get in here?"

"There's a secret entrance. Granddad knew about it."

I'd had enough experience with the Hale family to guess what this meant. "Are you telling me that the Statue of Liberty is really part of some top-secret New York City defense system?"

"Yes. Although, unlike the Washington Monument, it's

not really that big a secret. The military started using this island back in 1807. The fort's not even hidden. They put the statue right on top of it." Erica pointed to a photo mounted on the wall, a bird's-eye view of the statue.

I'd never seen the Statue of Liberty from above before. Now that I did, I was startled by how obvious the fortress was. What I'd always thought was an exceptionally large base for the statue was, in fact, a massive defensive structure shaped like an eleven-pointed star.

"There were soldiers stationed here right up through the Civil War," Erica continued. "And this wasn't the only place. There were more than a dozen forts around the city at one time or another: Governor's Island, Battery Park, Fort Washington, Fort Brooklyn. Eventually, during the late eighteen hundreds, the military decided it needed a lookout tower so it could see threats coming from out at sea."

"So they built the statue?"

"You didn't really think it was a gift?" Erica laughed. "From *France*? Why would France give us a giant statue of a woman?"

"To celebrate our nation's hundredth birthday."

"Oh, please. I can't believe you bought that story."

Now that I thought about it, the tale of how the United States had ended up with the Statue of Liberty *did* seem kind of odd. And yet I couldn't help feeling defensive. "I'm pretty sure *everyone* bought that story. Even the park service."

I pointed to a placard on the wall, which was all about how the French had donated the statue to us.

"All part of the disinformation campaign," Erica informed me. "It was actually pretty brilliant, making the tower a statue. They put an observation platform three hundred feet up around the torch, high enough to see for thirty miles in any direction—and convinced the whole world it was some crazy art project."

"Is that where Alexander and Cyrus are right now?"

"The torch is too exposed. They're in the crown, keeping an eye on our surroundings, waiting for the coast to be clear."

"Aren't they worried that someone else in the CIA knows the statue is a fortress and will come looking for us here?"

"No. Apparently, most of the history of these places has been forgotten, even by the government itself. Back when this statue was built, it was the tallest structure for miles. But once skyscrapers started going up in the city, they offered better vantage points and this place lost its purpose. The government stopped using it, and over the years, they bought their own disinformation about it. Granddad knows the truth only because *his* father told him. And Granddad hasn't told anyone about it except *us*."

I got to my feet, keeping the towels wrapped around me, taking in the entire museum. It was amazing to be inside it at night. Just as it had been amazing to be inside the Washington Monument at night with Erica. There was something almost magical about being let in on such great national secrets, to be one of only a handful of people who knew the truth.

"Is there any iconic American monument that *wasn't* secretly built for national security reasons?" I asked.

Erica pursed her lips, considering this. "I don't think the Gateway Arch in St. Louis was. It's too wobbly. And frankly, what's the point of a lookout tower in the middle of the country?"

"How about the Seattle Space Needle?"

"A big tower right near the border with Canada?" Erica asked. "C'mon. That's definitely for security."

"Really? We're worried about *Canada*?"

Erica shrugged. "You can't trust anybody. How's your strength? Do you think you can climb?"

I took a few tentative steps. To my surprise, despite everything that had happened, I felt perfectly fine. "Yes."

"Then let's go up. They're waiting for us."

I'd been to New York City once before, on a family vacation when I was eight. I'd wanted to see the Statue of Liberty then, but my parents hadn't thought to get tickets in advance and it had been sold out. I'd had to settle for taking the Staten Island Ferry past the island and jealously staring at the tourists whose families had planned ahead. Now I was getting a private tour of the statue itself. True, I'd been duped by SPYDER, pursued by the CIA, and nearly drowned in the harbor, but for a few minutes, life was pretty sweet.

After picking out a T-shirt and fashioning a beach towel skirt for myself, Erica and I took the elevator up through the statue's base, then climbed the rest of the way. The inside of Lady Liberty was a web of steel struts going in every direction with a double staircase spiraling through it all like a coil of DNA.

We arrived at the viewing platform inside the crown to find Alexander and Cyrus pressed against the glass, keeping an eye on the goings-on outside. Both wore T-shirts and beach towel skirts as well. Alexander smiled warmly upon seeing me. The effects of the chloroform appeared to have worn off. "Ah, Ben!" he exclaimed. "You're looking well, all things considered."

Cyrus, on the other hand, glowered at me. "Glad to see you've finally decided to join us."

"He wasn't slacking off, Granddad," Erica protested. "He was unconscious."

Cyrus waved this off, as though there wasn't a big difference. "You'd never catch *me* losing consciousness in the middle of a mission," he grumbled.

Erica frowned. "He almost *died* because of that stunt you pulled."

"I did what I had to do to shake our pursuers," Cyrus said. "I didn't know he was going to get tangled up in the anchor line."

"You could have at least given us some warning," Erica retorted.

"Wait," I said. "*You* blew up the boat? Not them?"

"I didn't have any other choice," Cyrus replied. "They had us surrounded. So I faked our deaths."

"Did it work?" I asked.

Cyrus shot me a nasty glance. "Do I look like an amateur to you? Of course it worked. I must've faked my own death fifty times over the years. I once convinced the entire KGB that I'd been buried in an avalanche in Kamchatka. No one can die like I can."

"The Feds are still searching the area," Alexander said. He waved us over to the windows, then pointed almost directly down, to where five boats were sweeping the water with spotlights. "But Dad chose the perfect spot to blow the boat. The water's quite deep right there. Very tough to drag for bodies."

"Looks like they're searching the island, just to make sure," Erica observed.

Sure enough, a few teams of men were moving about the perimeter of the fortress at the statue's base, scanning island with flashlights.

"Of course they are." Cyrus sniffed. "But they won't

search here. The front doors won't show any sign of a breach, because we didn't come through them, and they don't know there's any other entrance. They've been hunting for hours now and haven't found diddly-squat. Pretty soon they'll decide this is a goose chase and draw down till daylight. That's when we'll make our move."

"How?" I asked.

"That depends." Cyrus turned me away from the window to face him. "Right before the boat blew, you said you knew what SPYDER was up to. Care to finally share that with us?"

With all the excitement, I'd forgotten all about my revelation. Almost dying can have that effect.

"Oh, right," I said. "SPYDER's going to launch missiles at targets in New York City."

The Hales looked from one to another, then back to me.

"You're sure?" Erica asked.

"Ninety-nine percent," I told her. "You were right. SPYDER did want me for something, but they were so sneaky, I didn't even realize what I was doing for them. The whole time I've been there, they've been giving me all these math problems involving missiles. I thought they were for class, because they were tucked away with a whole bunch of other evil math problems about ballistics and projectile parabolas and stuff like that—but they weren't for class at all. They were for real missiles."

"What kind of problems were they?" Cyrus asked.

"Complex targeting issues, mostly. Like, *really* complex. I gave SPYDER everything they'd need to program their missiles to hit precise targets around here."

Cyrus scowled, not quite convinced. "And they recruited a *kid* to do that?"

"Ben isn't a normal kid," Erica told him. "When it comes to math, there's not many *adults* who can do what he can. And we practically gift wrapped him for SPYDER."

I blushed. This was the closest thing to a compliment Erica had ever given me. "Plus, I had the added bonus of secretly working for you. Not only did they use me to feed you information, but they also got me to do their dirty work for them."

Erica frowned, angry at herself. "They're always one step ahead of us. If not twenty."

I felt angry at myself too, upset at being used. But I was determined not to let SPYDER get away with it. "We know what their plan is," I said hopefully. "So that's something, right?"

"We only *think* we know what their plan is," Cyrus muttered. "I haven't heard much evidence to support this idea yet."

Erica turned to me. "What else do you have?"

"I'm pretty sure Joshua Hallal programmed the missiles himself," I said. "I think that's what he was doing in the underground lair the night I saw him there, when he was using Russian. SPYDER got Russian missiles before. They could do it again."

"But you don't speak Russian," Cyrus reminded me. "So you can't be sure."

"True." I nodded, then thought of something. "But I do remember numbers well. Two of the ones Joshua entered were 40.7057 and 73.9964. If he was really programming missiles, then those are probably coordinates."

"Let's see." Erica whipped out her phone, which was sealed in a waterproof pouch, and typed the numbers into it.

"Wait," I warned. "Can't SPYDER or the Feds find us if you go online?"

"I scrambled the GPS function," she told me. "Anyone tries to track us through this and they'll think we're in Parsippany. Okay. Got a match." Her face suddenly filled with concern. "You were right, Ben. They're coordinates, all right . . . for the Brooklyn Bridge."

We all reflexively looked out the windows and across the harbor, to where the Brooklyn Bridge was lit up in the night. Cyrus now looked far more convinced I was right—and far more worried as well.

"They had me do problems about how much explosive was needed to blow up bridges too," I said. "I worked out the payloads and the best places to strike the targets to provide maximum damage. . . ."

"Why would you give them that?" Cyrus demanded angrily.

"It was for class!" I snapped back. "I was trying to be a good student! You wanted me to fit in, so I was doing it! I didn't ask to be sent undercover to evil spy school! That was your idea!"

Cyrus recoiled angrily, unhappy with how I'd spoken to him. But before he could reply, Erica stepped between us. "Ben's right, Granddad. About everything, I think. That day at Sandy Hook, Murray wasn't only taking pictures of the missile silos. He was also photographing the bridges in Manhattan."

"Oh," I said. "I thought he was taking pictures of you and the other girls."

"So did I," Erica admitted. "But he was only pretending to do that to hide what he was *really* taking pictures of: SPYDER's targets. SPYDER just destroyed the NIKE missiles designed to protect New York City. So now there's nothing to stop them from attacking the bridges here. Except us."

"I can't believe this," Alexander said, stunned.

"It has to be what they're planning," I said. "All the evidence adds up."

"Oh, I get that," Alexander replied. "It's just that SPYDER used missiles in their last big scheme. And now they're using them again? That's not very creative."

"Maybe they got a good deal on missiles last time and had a lot left over," Erica suggested.

"This isn't about creativity!" Cyrus barked. "There's no rule that says bad guys can't use the same weapons two times in a row. This is about causing chaos and mayhem, and nothing does that better than a missile." He swung back toward me. "So please tell me you know where they are."

"Back at Hidden Forest," I said.

Cyrus narrowed his eyes. "That's not possible. We've been watching that place for weeks."

"The missiles have been there the whole time," I told him.

Alexander looked skeptical as well. "You're telling us that SPYDER hid a bunch of stolen missiles in a suburban housing development?"

"It's not a *real* housing development," I explained. "It's camouflage for the missiles. SPYDER's hiding them in plain sight."

"But there's no silos," Erica told me.

"There *are*," I countered. "They're just disguised as septic tanks."

Cyrus and Erica were taken aback for a moment, but then nodded understanding. Alexander didn't. "What are you talking about?" he asked.

"There are huge holes all over the property," I explained. "Easily big enough to hold missiles underground. They're marked as being for septic tanks—and they even look like there are septic tanks in them—but the other night, I was on top of one, and there was a big hinge on the edge of it. The only reason you'd have a hinge there is if the top was supposed to swing open, and you don't need the top to swing open on a septic tank. . . ."

"But you *do* on a missile silo," Cyrus concluded, shaking his head in amazement. "You have to hand it to SPYDER. They're clever. I looked at the satellite photos of that place a dozen times and never thought twice about the septic tanks."

I said, "I'll bet if you pulled up the sewer grid for the area, you'd find that Hidden Forest is attached to it and that they don't need a septic system at all."

"I don't think that's necessary. Your logic sounds right on this." Erica brought up an image she'd saved on her phone. "This is a satellite photo of Hidden Forest from two days ago. Looks like there are ten separate septic tank holes, meaning they've got ten missiles."

"Ten bridges down means a lot of chaos and mayhem." Cyrus stared out the windows at the city. "Far more than anything SPYDER has done before. It'll bring New York to a standstill for months." He glanced downward and checked the scene at the base of the statue. "We can't afford to waste another moment. Let's move." He headed for the stairs.

Alexander glanced out the window himself. "But there's still a search party down there."

"That's only the shadow force." Cyrus started down through Lady Liberty's head. "Looks like most everyone else has been sent home. Besides, we need at least one team here so we can get off this island."

"How so?" I asked, following him.

"Because we're gonna steal their boat," Cyrus replied.

Erica fell in behind me. "How are the four of us supposed to infiltrate Hidden Forest by ourselves? The security there was tight enough to begin with, and I can guarantee you SPYDER's going to jack it up for D-day. The control center is in the middle of the whole complex, two stories underground. It'll be impossible for us to penetrate that."

"Plus, most of our weapons are now at the bottom of the harbor," Alexander added.

"We'd need a whole platoon of agents to even make a dent in that place," Erica said morosely. "Is there *any* CIA agent we can trust? Anyone we can explain the situation to?"

"Not that I can think of," Cyrus muttered.

I stopped on the stairs halfway through the Statue of Liberty's neck, struck by a thought. "I don't think we need to explain anything," I said. "I know how to get the CIA there. We just need the right bait."

"And what would that be?" Erica asked.

"Us," I said.

BAIT

Liberty Island
September 18
0000 hours

Our clothes were all hanging in the bathrooms in the museum in the base of the statue. Cyrus had dismantled the hand driers and rejiggered them to blow hot air constantly over our things. It had been only moderately effective. The shoulders and lower legs of my outfit were still cold and damp, while the area around my crotch was so overheated, I could have baked a potato in my pants. However, there was no option but to suit up and move out. There was little chance of escaping the island and overthrowing SPYDER while wearing beach towel skirts.

The secret passage out of the statue began in a long-forgotten storage room and tunneled to a trapdoor hidden deep in the largest clump of trees on the island. We emerged and set off after the lone crew of CIA agents still hunting for us. There were six of them, but they were spread out in three groups of two, and after hours of repeatedly wandering the same fifteen acres without finding so much as a trace of us, they had decided this was a pointless assignment and dropped their guard. The island wasn't well lit and there were plenty of shadows to lurk in, so Cyrus and Erica were able to quickly reduce the number of conscious agents to four, then two, and then none.

Alexander and I tied them all up, then stripped them of their weapons, badges, and communications devices.

Their boat was moored at the ferry dock. The CIA had commandeered a Coast Guard vessel along with a Coast Guard captain, who didn't look very happy about the assignment. He was sitting in the bridge, playing a game on his phone. He didn't pay much attention when Alexander wandered onto the boat, looking like any other CIA agent, until Alexander jammed his stolen gun in the guy's ear and ordered him to take us to the mainland. The captain quickly agreed and even dismantled his radio himself so we understood he wasn't going to try anything stupid and get himself killed.

The few boats still trying to find remnants of us in the

water were on the other side of the island, so no one noticed when we pulled away from the dock.

New Jersey isn't far from Liberty Island. Parts are so close that, if the water hadn't been full of garbage and toxic waste, we could have swam it. The trip back to where we'd left our car didn't take long.

On the way, I borrowed Erica's phone and dialed Zoe Zibbell. I never forgot a phone number. Especially that of the one person in the whole world I was certain I could trust.

She answered groggily, roused from sleep. "Hello?"

"Hey," I said. "It's Ben."

"Smokescreen?!" Zoe was instantly awake. She had lowered her voice to a whisper, but I could still hear the mix of excitement and concern in it. "What's happening out there? The word is you and the Hales have joined the dark side. I don't believe it, of course, but the rest of the CIA seems to."

"Believe it," I said. "I *have* joined the dark side."

"No, you haven't. If you'd really joined the dark side, you certainly wouldn't be telling me that you had. You'd be telling me that you hadn't."

"So if I said I hadn't joined the dark side, then you'd think I had?"

"Never. I know you, Ben. Better than any of these other idiots do. No matter what you tell me, I know you're not a traitor."

"I am, Zoe. I swear. I'm a traitor to my country and very, very dangerous. So I need you to alert the school administration that you know exactly where I'm going to be two hours from now."

Confusion now edged into Zoe's voice. "I'm not going to do that. You're my friend. Why would I turn you in?"

"Because I'm working with SPYDER now, and we're about to launch missiles at New York City."

"What?!"

"Get a pen. I'm going to give you the exact coordinates."

I heard Zoe fumbling around her desk for a few moments. "Okay."

I gave her the exact latitude and longitude of Hidden Forest, which Cyrus had calculated while keeping an eye on the place. Then I had her read it back to me, just to make sure she had it right. I didn't want her to send a CIA team to attack an innocent gated community by mistake.

"I need you to report this right away," I told her. "Tell your resident adviser and have her wake the principal and every professor she can find. Don't tell them that I asked you to turn me in, though. They'll be suspicious of that. Tell them that you figured out where I've been. Tell them you always suspected I was no good, and so you put a tracer in my old phone. You've known where I've been all along, but you didn't know I'd joined the enemy until you heard the news a few hours ago. And now you're tracking me and you know I'm heading back to SPYDER's secret headquarters."

"They'll never believe that I was suspicious of you," Zoe argued. "I'm always going on about how great you are."

"Which you only did so that I'd drop my guard around you and let you get close to me. Very sneaky of you, really. Probably worth some sort of commendation when the CIA follows up on your tip and captures me. By the way, just so the CIA doesn't get confused when they get there, SPYDER's top-secret headquarters looks like a gated residential community."

"You're kidding, right?"

"Nope. You know how sneaky they are."

The boat was pulling up by the dock where we'd left the car. It was deserted.

Cyrus thwacked the captain on the back of the skull with his gun and the man collapsed in a heap. Erica trussed him like a rodeo calf.

Zoe said, "Ben, this is crazy."

"Not really." I thought back to everything that had happened since I'd had to steal a bulldozer that afternoon. "Honestly, it's not even in the top three craziest things I've done today. But I need you to do it. You have to convince everyone you know where I am and that they need to send a big force out there to stop me. Let them know the Hales and I are holed up inside the compound and that we're plotting something very big with SPYDER. Something that'll make everything else SPYDER's tried look like a Sunday school picnic."

Cyrus steered the boat up against a small pier and cut the engine. Alexander leapt ashore and tied the mooring lines. Erica signaled me to move quickly.

Zoe asked, "Can you at least explain what's going on?"

"It'd take way too long," I said, scrambling off the boat. "You'll just have to trust me. I need you to do this *right now*. Every second counts."

"All right," Zoe said. "I'll turn you in."

"Thanks. You're a good friend."

Just past our car, there was an enormous construction site where a huge section of the pier was being rebuilt. There were four cranes, mountains of steel beams, and a fleet of a dozen cement trucks.

And a large sign proclaiming: LEW BROTHERS CONSTRUC-TION.

I froze in midstride.

Until that moment, I'd assumed that Lew Brothers was a tiny company created by SPYDER solely to build Hidden Forest. But now I realized what it really was: a huge corporation that did multimillion-dollar government projects.

"I have to go," I told Zoe.

I had just figured out the rest of SPYDER's plan.

21

SIEGE

SPYDER Agent Training Facility

September 18

0200 hours

Cyrus laid out his plans for thwarting SPYDER on the drive back to Hidden Forest. I had been hoping that my assignment would be something along the lines of "Wait in a nice, safe place while the rest of us infiltrate SPYDER's compound and do all the dangerous work." Instead, I was told I'd be playing a crucial role in the attack. It was my job to lead the way into the underground control center.

"Frankly, I'd prefer a greenhorn like you stay well clear of the action," Cyrus admitted. "But you're the only one who's been inside SPYDER's lair and the only one who knows all the people on the other side. That makes you our key asset. And we can't just have you sitting on the radio, talking us through it. You need to be there in the thick of it in case things change—or we lose radio contact. Don't worry, though. We'll protect you as well as we can, seeing as you won't be much use to us if you're dead."

I didn't find that very reassuring, but I accepted my fate and girded myself for battle.

Thankfully, we now had some equipment: the weapons and walkie-talkies we'd liberated from the agents on Liberty Island. And Cyrus had left one last steel case in the car, filled with assorted other supplies he'd amassed over the past weeks: everything we'd need to infiltrate SPYDER's compound.

By the time we arrived back at Hidden Forest, the CIA was already there. They'd moved faster than I'd expected, although we'd had to make a pit stop at a White Castle in Newark. None of us had eaten since lunch, and Cyrus said it was a bad idea to fight the enemy when you were hypo-glycemic.

The CIA had shown up in full force, led by Agent Rafferty, who obviously had a chip on his shoulder as far as Cyrus Hale was concerned. There were more than sixty agents spread out around the perimeter of the gated community. We had to park well down the road and slip quietly through the fields so they wouldn't notice our approach. However, they weren't very focused on what was behind them; they were focused on Hidden Forest instead. We slipped into a clump of trees along the CIA's line, not far from where Rafferty had set up his command center.

I couldn't see any SPYDER agents on the far side of the wall, but I had no doubt they were there, watching the CIA closely. In an odd way, the whole setup reminded me of a medieval siege. SPYDER was holed up in the modern-day equivalent of a walled city, and the CIA was looking to breach it the same way an army of knights would. Beyond the wall, I could even see the rec center high in the middle of the compound like a glass-walled castle, complete with a dungeon beneath it.

The CIA was ready for battle, every agent bristling with guns and knives. Armored cars had towed in mortars as well. Once they were all in position, Rafferty got on a bullhorn and spoke to everyone at Hidden Forest: "This is Agent Harold Rafferty of the Central Intelligence Agency. We have you surrounded. Cease all hostile acts at once or we will have no choice but to take you by force!"

"Do you believe this guy?" Cyrus muttered. "Time is of the essence and he's giving warnings like a hall monitor. We need to kick this assault in gear." With that, he whipped out his gun and took a few potshots at the community wall.

SPYDER agents reflexively returned fire. The wall around

Hidden Forest turned out to be more medieval than I'd thought; there were secret holes built into it to shoot through, the same way castle walls had slits for crossbows. The CIA agents immediately shot back. Rafferty shouted at everyone to stand down, but Cyrus blasted the bullhorn out of his hands, muting him. After that the assault spiraled out of control. Most of the activity took place at the weakest points in the community's perimeter, where the CIA hoped to break through: the front gates and the spot where I'd driven the bulldozer through the wall that afternoon. SPYDER had hastily patched the hole in the wall with plywood and strung electric wire across the top, but it had been a rush job; they apparently hadn't expected the CIA to show up.

Everyone was so busy trading shots, they didn't notice us. During their days of observation, Cyrus and Erica had pinpointed the perfect place to breach the perimeter: a towering oak tree thirty feet from the wall. We scrambled up it as high as we could go, then unloaded the supplies Cyrus had amassed to create a homemade zip line. First, Erica fired a grappling hook over the wall. (It was amazing how handy those things were once you became a spy.) It caught in the upper story of an unfinished, framed house, after which we fastened our end of the wire around a tree branch, cinched it taut, then clipped onto it with carabiners and rock-climbing belts.

Cyrus and Alexander went first to make sure it was safe. No one from SPYDER or the CIA seemed to notice them as they glided silently toward the wall.

The moment they crossed *over* the wall, however, alarms went off. Sirens wailed so loudly they could even be heard over the gunfire.

"Shoot," Erica muttered. "They must have some sort of laser system to detect intruders. We better move now."

"Now?" I repeated, though in a much more frightened tone of voice. "But SPYDER knows we're coming over the wall."

"No. SPYDER knows someone just *came* over the wall. So they'll be looking for invaders inside the perimeter. Not above it."

"But won't *we* be inside the perimeter soon?"

Rather than argue the point, Erica simply launched herself down the zip line and dragged me along with her.

The ride down the wire took only a few seconds, but it felt like weeks. En route, I could see SPYDER agents racing through the darkness, converging on the frame house where Cyrus and Alexander were now holed up. I kept waiting for someone to spot us on the wire, where we were sitting ducks—or at least, gliding ducks. But Cyrus and Alexander started shooting, grabbing SPYDER's attention, and we slid to safety unnoticed.

We alighted in the upper story of the frame house. Cyrus and Alexander were on the far side from us, taking cover behind a stack of plywood. "Get going!" Cyrus ordered us. "We'll draw their fire!"

"We will?" Alexander asked nervously, but Cyrus had already started shooting again.

SPYDER's agents shot back at them, filling the stack of plywood with more holes than a loaf of Swiss cheese.

Erica and I went in the other direction, leaping out the back of the house and skulking away before anyone could see us. We then worked our way toward the rec center, moving in a wide arc around the SPYDER agents trading shots with Cyrus and Alexander.

Despite all the firefights around us, it wasn't that hard to steer clear of the enemy now that we were on the inside. All of SPYDER's men were busily fending off Cyrus, Alexander, or other CIA agents. Even so, we did our best to be stealthy.

Two helicopters raced overhead. They were unmarked, so it was impossible to tell whose side they were on.

As we crept through Hidden Forest, I managed to catch a glimpse of some of SPYDER's agents. I recognized a few of my instructors among them, like Mrs. Henderson and Mr. Seabrook. I didn't see Joshua Hallal or any of my fellow students, but then, the compound was large and there were plenty of places they could have been.

Our route took us past one of the "septic tanks." There was a loud, mechanical hum coming from inside the hole. I peered in to see that the cement lid was opening, raised by hydraulic pistons, revealing that there was, indeed, a missile silo hidden beneath it. The shaft dropped several stories down into the earth. The missile was a big, metallic Cold War relic with Soviet lettering on the sides. I'd been right; SPYDER had Russian missiles.

"C'mon!" Erica ordered. "They're preparing to fire! We don't have much time!" She dropped any attempt at stealth and bolted for the rec center.

I took off after her. We raced out of the construction zone and cut across the croquet lawn.

In the distance, some agents from SPYDER spotted us. They yelled something. We were too far away and there was too much other noise to hear it properly, but it was probably something along the lines of "Stop or we'll shoot!"

We didn't stop. So they shot.

We dove over a decorative hedge. Bullets whizzed over our heads and shattered the glass walls of the rec center, which saved us the trouble of going through the door. Erica shot back, laying down cover fire as I scrambled across the carpet of glass shards, racing for the rock wall.

It occurred to me that I wasn't panicked. I wasn't screaming, like I'd done while being chased by a horde of first-year students during the SACSA. Maybe this was because I'd matured into a better spy since then—or maybe it was because the simulations at spy school had prepared me well for a real-life action sequence—but I was impressed by how well I was handling the situation, all things considered.

I reached the rock wall and twisted the proper handhold.

The secret door hissed open. I held it that way while Erica raced for it.

In the distance, well past the croquet lawn, I could see the muzzle flares as our attackers opened fire again.

Erica slid through the doorway and spoke into her walkie-talkie. "Granddad, we've got some company en route to the rec center. Think you can hold them off?"

"Sure thing, sweetheart," Cyrus replied. "I'm on it."

Erica then led the way down the stairs. I knew it wasn't very chivalrous of me to let her do this, but then, Erica was adept in all forms of combat while I had the martial arts skills of a bowl of Jell-O. She swept the hall at the bottom, then signaled to me that it was safe to follow while she moved on to the kitchenette and the conference room. There were no enemy agents in either one.

"You can stop poking around out there!" Murray called from the control room. "The party's in here!"

Erica frowned, then led the way to the control room.

There were fewer people inside than I expected. Joshua

Hallal wasn't there—or any of the other adults. Instead, there was only Nefarious and Murray. Nefarious was seated on the main couch, staring at the TV screens, which were displaying dozens of security camera feeds from all over the property at once. Most of them were showing the battles outside, though a few were trained on the missile silos as their hatches opened—and one filmed the hall we had just come through. Nefarious was so focused on the screens, he didn't so much as glance at us. From the doorway, I could see only the back of his head. He was holding the custom-made joystick I'd seen on my previous visit to the lair.

Murray was seated in a lounge chair to the side of the couch, his feet propped up on the coffee table. He had no weapon, only a half-eaten frozen yogurt sundae. Being Murray, he had raided the toppings bar, choosing everything from crumbled Oreos to sour gummy worms. "You didn't really think you could sneak up on us in here, did you?" he chided. "We've got cameras everywhere. But then, I pretty much expected you to show up, Ben. That's your standard move, isn't it? SPYDER's about to put a plan into action; you arrive just minutes before it happens and try to thwart it. Like clockwork."

Erica aimed her gun directly at Murray's smiling face. "Oh, we're not *trying* to thwart your plans. We're thwarting them. Shut off the missiles."

Murray shrugged helplessly. "It can't be done. Everything's preprogrammed. And after that little stunt you pulled on the last mission, Ben, we've hardwired the electrical systems, so you can't just yank the plug and be done with it."

"I wasn't talking to you," Erica growled. "I know you're not smart enough to control the missiles. I was talking to your pal on the couch. Nefarious, abort the missiles or I shoot both of you."

"How about this instead?" Murray asked. "You drop your weapons, or Ashley shoots both of *you*."

There were two foreboding clicks behind us.

I spun around to find Ashley there, holding a gun in each hand, one for me and one for Erica. She looked like she felt pretty bad about this, though. "Sorry," she said. "I really don't want to shoot you, but I will."

"How did you . . . ?" I began.

"Get behind you when you'd already swept the area?" Ashley finished. "There's a secret hiding place behind the sundae bar. I guess you never got the full tour of the complex." She looked to Erica. "You're still holding your gun."

Erica released her weapon, letting it clatter to the floor.

"Much better!" Murray said, scooping more yogurt into his mouth.

"You're pathetic," Erica told him. "I can't believe you're using missiles again. Where's the creativity in that?"

"Well, we got a good deal on them," Murray admitted. "They're cheaper when you buy in bulk. And after we'd gone through all the trouble to smuggle them into the country, we figured we might as well use them. Plus, we've learned from the mistakes we made last time. Sorry, Ben, but there'll be no thwarting our plans tonight."

At that moment, the room began to shake. There was a tremendous rumble from behind the walls. On the TV screens, the ten missiles each blasted off, streaking toward New York City.

We were too late.

NEGOTIATION

SPYDER Underground Lair
September 18
0230 hours

The flares from the missiles' rockets were so bright, they bleached out the TV screens and bathed the entire control center in a pale, eerie light.

Erica looked to me. I wasn't used to seeing her worried, but she was worried now. "How long will it take those to hit their targets?"

"The first will strike in eight minutes," I said, feeling sick to my stomach. After all, the reason I knew this was because I'd done the math that had allowed Joshua to program the missiles. When they struck and did their damage, I would be partly responsible. I had naively gone undercover, hoping to defeat SPYDER, and had instead been manipulated by them into doing their dirty work.

This wasn't a very good feeling.

But then, I still had eight minutes to fix things.

On the TV screens, cameras mounted on the missiles themselves tracked their progress across New Jersey. The landscape flew past beneath them at rocket speed: farms and suburban communities and clumps of forest. It looked weirdly like the images from the video games Nefarious had spent all of his time playing: the view from a pilot as his plane hurtled into battle.

I turned my attention to Ashley, because unlike Nefarious, she was making eye contact with me. And because I suspected she wasn't really evil at heart. "Put down your guns," I said. "Please. You can still abort the missiles. If you don't, you're going to have the blood of thousands of innocent people on your hands."

Ashley shook her head. "Innocent people aren't going to die. You don't know what we're really doing here. . . ."

"I know exactly what you're doing," I replied. "You're blowing up all the major bridges around the city so that you can get paid billions to rebuild them."

Ashley's eyes widened in surprise.

"Holy cow!" Murray cried from the couch. "You figured

out our evil scheme *again*! Every time I think we've got you fooled, you still work it out. How'd you do it this time?"

"I saw a Lew Brothers construction site in New Jersey," I told him. "A big one, rebuilding an entire shipping pier. Which meant SPYDER's construction company was much bigger than I realized. So we Googled the company. With the exception of this community, Lew Brothers only does government work. Mostly large infrastructure projects. Like bridges."

"Nice work, as usual." Murray grinned, revealing several rainbow sprinkles stuck in his teeth. "To be honest, SPYDER didn't even see the potential of the construction company at first. We originally started Lew Brothers as a money-laundering scheme, but then found that being evil was standard procedure in the large-scale construction business. In fact, we were shocked by how corrupt and deceitful some of our rival companies were—and we're terrorists! To get jobs, everyone uses bribes, blackmail, kickbacks, and threats. We started to do the same thing, and we were good at it. Before you knew it, Lew Brothers was bringing in more money than our illegal schemes. So then we started thinking, why wait for the government to come to *us* with construction jobs? Why not create the jobs ourselves? I mean, if some shady international organization paid us to blow up a bridge, we'd get paid a few million, tops—while some lucky construction company would get *billions* to rebuild it. The real money isn't in knocking things down; it's in putting them back up again. So why should we let some other sleazeballs make big profits from our terrorism when *we* could be the sleazeballs making the big profits ourselves?"

"You're creating a fake terrorist attack just to cash in on the emergency rebuilding funds?" Erica asked.

"Yes!" Murray crowed. "And a real doozy of an attack, too. The ten major bridges and tunnels into Manhattan all going down at once! The way we figure it, if you only knock out one route into the city, it's a crisis, but New York can still get by. But if you take out *ten* routes at the same time, you cripple the place. Doomsday will have nothing on this. The city, the state, and the federal government will be desperate to get everything rebuilt as quickly as possible, and they'll have to pay through the nose to do it. It just so happens that Lew Brothers is perfectly prepared to handle such an cataclysmic event, with all the connections, personnel, and raw materials on hand necessary to rebuild quickly—and for maximum profit."

"So, you see," Ashley added gleefully, "what we're doing here isn't so bad, really. It's not slaughter-thousands-of-innocent-people evil. It's more like inconvenience-millions-of-people-for-a-few-months evil."

"People are still going to die," I told her. "You're

detonating ten missiles around the biggest city in America!"

"But we're doing it in the middle of the night," Ashley countered. "No one's going to be on those bridges or in those tunnels at two thirty in the morning."

"We specifically picked this time to minimize human pain and suffering," Murray added. "So there."

On the TV screens, the missiles were screaming over the outskirts of the New York metropolitan area. The farms were gone. Now there were only suburban homes, shopping malls, and supermarkets. In the distance, the skyscrapers of Manhattan were getting closer every second.

"That doesn't mean *no one* is going to be on those bridges," I said, keeping my eyes locked firmly on Ashley's. "What's going to happen to those people when they explode? What's going to happen to the people in the tunnels when they collapse and flood? And what do you think is going to happen to everyone in Manhattan after you cut them off from the rest of the country? There'll be panics. Food shortages. Power outages. What you're doing here is going to lead to death and riots and agony, just so you can make some money off their misery."

Ashley shook her head violently. "No, you've got it all wrong."

"I don't," I told her. "And deep down inside, you know that's true."

"No," she said again. "You *are* wrong. We're not going to just make *some* money off their misery. We're going to make *an incredible amount* of money off their misery."

The moment she said this, any trace of doubt or concern in her eyes faded. So did any trace of the sweet, good-hearted girl I thought she was. Instead, she showed her true self—and it was evil. As though all the death and destruction SPYDER was about to cause was thrilling to her.

"You think those people are going to suffer?" she asked. "Well, no one's suffered like me. I trained my whole life for the Olympics! I gave up my entire childhood to practice sixteen hours a day! I never had fun! I never had any friends! I never had a single piece of candy! And for what? So that some stupid judge could make a mistake on my score and keep me from my rightful place on Team USA!"

"Don't blame the rest of the world for your failure," Erica said coldly. "That judge was right."

"She was not!" Ashley roared. "She was blind!"

"I saw the Olympic trials," Erica informed her. "You blew that landing."

"I did not!" Ashley was trembling with rage now, her arms shaking, her face twitching. I half expected fire to explode from her eye sockets. "I stuck that landing! I stuck it!"

I was terrified that, in her fury, she would blow Erica and me away. And she very well might have, if Cyrus and

Alexander hadn't shut the power down at that moment.

We'd planned that part. The idea was, Erica and I would try to deal with SPYDER via negotiation while the others would try to simply stop the missiles by hitting the power supply. The entire room went dark in an instant as every light, TV screen, and piece of electrical equipment went out.

Erica and I were prepared for this, while the others were caught by surprise.

From beside me, I heard the distinct sound of Erica going on the attack, followed by the wheeze of Ashley getting punched hard somewhere painful, and then the clatter of her guns on the floor as Erica disarmed her.

Then the backup generators whirred into action. The lights and TVs and electronics came back to life and the room looked almost exactly the same, save for a few small changes.

Instead of holding us at gunpoint, Ashley was now fighting Erica. And despite having started at a severe disadvantage, she was fighting well. Normally, Erica would have knocked her opponent unconscious by this point, but Ashley had proved more formidable than expected. She was using her personal combination of gymnastics and martial arts, blocking Erica's attacks and launching her own.

Nefarious and Murray were exactly where they'd been before. Nefarious hadn't moved. Murray had spilled his sundae down the front of his sweatshirt. For the first time since our arrival, he looked peeved. "Aw, great," he muttered. "Now look what you guys made me do!"

The one other thing that had changed was that, on the TV screens, the landscape was still hurtling past, but now an emergency message was flashing in big red letters: AUTO-PILOT DISENGAGED. The missiles began to drop from the sky, moving toward homes and schools, rather than the bridges.

"The navigation systems are blown," Nefarious said, the first words he'd spoken all night.

"Guess it's up to you, then," Murray told him.

Nefarious flicked a button on the side of his customized joystick.

The emergency message disappeared, now replaced with the words MANUAL OVERRIDE ACTIVATED. The missiles straightened up and resumed their flights.

Suddenly, it was evident what Nefarious had been doing on the couch all those hours. He hadn't been playing video games. He'd been training to pilot multiple high-speed missiles to their targets at once. It couldn't have been easy, but he was doing it perfectly. As usual, he was also giving a mumbling commentary on what he was doing. "Adjustaltitudeon-missilefivereorienttrajectoryonnineincreasethrustfortwo." On the screens, the missiles moved steadily over New Jersey, closing in on Manhattan.

I lunged toward Nefarious, but Murray moved faster, producing a gun from under a throw pillow and aiming it at me. "Oh no," he taunted. "It's not gonna be that easy, Ben."

"Just shoot him!" Ashley shouted, launching another flurry of kicks at Erica. "Kill Ben before he thwarts us again!"

"He's not gonna thwart us this time," Murray said coolly. "It's out of his hands."

"So what?" Ashley screamed. "Do it anyhow! He's the enemy!"

"You actually had a crush on this girl?" Erica asked me, fending off Ashley's attacks. "She's psychotic."

"Apparently, I misjudged her," I said sheepishly.

"Gee, you think?" Erica asked.

I tried to keep calm, but my head was spinning. I was reeling from discovering Ashley's true colors and desperately trying to figure out what I could possibly do to stop the missiles.

The missiles neared the Jersey Shore. Sandy Hook was coming up fast. If there had still been Nike missiles there, they would have already been launched to take out the ones en route to the city, but of course, they couldn't be launched because SPYDER had destroyed them. Soon, there'd be nothing between SPYDER's missiles and their targets except open water.

And the kid who was still controlling them.

Now that Ashley had proven to be more evil than I'd realized, I turned my attention to the other evil spy school student, hoping he might be more reasonable. "Nefarious, think about what you're doing. This isn't a game anymore! When those missiles strike, it will happen in the real world."

"And you'll make *real* money!" Murray cried. "Tons of it!"

"No, you won't," I warned. "SPYDER only told you guys that to get you to do their dirty work for them."

For the first time, Nefarious took his eyes off the screens in front of him. It was for only a fraction of a second, a fleeting glance my way, but there was concern in it.

"Don't listen to him!" Murray warned. "No one at SPYDER conned us! They wouldn't do that to me!"

"Then where are they?" I asked. "I haven't seen them anywhere around here tonight. Joshua told us himself that SPYDER was going to get away with this because all the evidence would point to some fall guys. Well, *you're* the fall guys."

The missiles cleared Sandy Hook and barreled over the harbor toward Manhattan.

Erica and Ashley were still battling for the upper hand.

Murray shook his head, though it seemed like he was trying to convince himself I was wrong as much as he was trying to convince Nefarious. "SPYDER's blaming terrorists for this."

"No. SPYDER's framing *you*," I told him. "Joshua and

the top brass will make billions—and you'll end up in jail. Unless you abort those missiles!"

Murray suddenly didn't look so sure of himself anymore.

Instead, it was Ashley who yelled at Nefarious. "He's lying to you! Stay on course!"

The missiles were approaching the lower tip of Manhattan. The ten of them suddenly veered in different directions, each homing in on a different target.

"Nefarious," I pleaded, "I know you have trouble fitting in and that makes you angry, but this isn't the solution. The people at SPYDER aren't your friends. They're using you. If you want to make *real* friends, you don't do it by being the bad guy. You do it by being the hero. And this is your chance. You can be the hero right now. You can save the city!"

The missiles were bearing down on the southernmost bridges now, so close that we could see individual cars on each span. And then the people in the cars. And then . . .

The missiles dipped under the bridges at the last second, missing their targets.

Nefarious had barely moved. He'd made only a few subtle flicks of his wrist. But it had been enough.

For the first time since I'd met him, he was smiling.

"Noooo!" Ashley cried. "You idiot! What are you doing?! Bring them back around!"

"Ben's right," Nefarious said. "SPYDER set us up. The

CIA has us surrounded. We'll never get away. But Joshua and all the other leaders will."

The missiles—whether they had just avoided their targets or were still en route—suddenly angled sharply upward, rocketing high into the night sky, away from the city and all the people in it.

Ashley unleashed another flurry of kicks at Erica. "So we'll get caught. They'll find a way to spring us!"

"Why would they?" Nefarious asked. There was a confidence in his voice I'd never heard before. "Then they'd just have to share the money with us. And they're not going to do that. After all, they're evil."

The missiles were still climbing, rising through the atmosphere, leaving the city far behind.

Murray's eyes went from the screens to me and back again. He seemed so stunned by SPYDER's betrayal that, for the first time in his life, he was speechless.

Ashley grew even more apoplectic, however. She redoubled her attack on Erica while screaming at Nefarious the entire time. "You can still fix this! Even if you only hit a few of the targets, we'll still be rich! Don't let Ben confuse you! SPYDER isn't the enemy here! He is! He's—"

She didn't finish the rest, because Erica punched her in the stomach. Ashley gagged in pain, bending forward, and then Erica nailed her in the jaw with an uppercut, sending her flying. Ashley slammed into the wall and crumpled into a pile.

On the screens, miles above the earth, nine of the missiles exploded. There was a huge flare of fire and then their feeds disintegrated into static.

But the tenth missile didn't blow. Instead, it arced around and started hurtling back for earth.

Murray looked concerned, but he still kept his gun on me. "What's happening there?" he asked Nefarious. "What are you doing with that one?"

Nefarious jiggled his joystick, concerned. "I'm not doing anything with it. I don't have control over it anymore."

"Then where's it going?" Murray asked.

"Here," I said.

Everyone turned to me, worried.

"I did the math for this, too," I explained. "It was for extra credit. There's a fail-safe built into that rocket in case things go wrong. A homing device."

Murray's eyes went wide. "Why would they send a missile *here* if things went wrong?"

"No loose ends," I told him. "You all know too much. But the CIA can't make you talk if you're dead."

"You mean they're going to kill me?!" Murray gasped. "*Me?* That's not possible! They promised me a house! With a Jacuzzi tub!"

"They lied to you," Erica said. "They *are* the bad guys."

Murray looked as though he'd been punched in the gut himself. "How much time do we have?"

"Eight minutes," I told him.

"Then let's get out of here!" Murray dropped his gun and ran for the exit. Nefarious, Erica, and I fell in right behind him.

We made it only a few steps.

Then we noticed Ashley. She wasn't crumpled on the floor anymore. She was blocking the only exit and she'd recovered her guns, which she was now pointing at us.

"No one's going anywhere," she said.

MASS DESTRUCTION

SPYDER Underground Lair
September 18
0240 hours

"Aw, come on, Ashley!" Murray cried. "This is really uncool!"

"*I'm* being uncool?" Ashley screamed. "I'm not the one who just tanked all of our plans and triggered SPYDER's doomsday scenario! You guys are traitors—and so you're going to die here with these doosers from the CIA."

"Doosers?" Erica asked.

"Dorks plus losers," Nefarious translated.

"Ashley . . . ," I began.

"Don't you start with me!" she shouted. "You're the

biggest traitor of them all! You made me think you were my friend! You said you'd go to Disney World with me! But you were lying the whole time! You're a jerk!"

"You should talk," Erica muttered. "You're evil."

"That's not really helping," I told her.

"I'm not evil!" Ashley roared. "All I want is what's due to me! I deserve to be rich for all that I've been through. I worked my whole life only to get screwed! I deserved to make the U.S. Olympic team. I stuck that landing! I stuck that—"

She didn't finish the thought, because someone whacked her on the back of the head with a tennis racket. Ashley crumpled into a heap once again, revealing her attacker behind her.

Zoe Zibbell.

"Hey, Ben!" she said cheerfully, as though we'd just run into each other in the school cafeteria, rather than in a secret underground enemy lair that was about to blow up.

"Zoe?" I said, stunned. "What are you doing here?"

"I'm on a field trip!" she exclaimed. "The CIA let me come on the mission as a reward for turning you in! I came up here on a helicopter with some big-shot agents from Washington. It was supercool!" She glanced at Ashley, sprawled on the floor, and suddenly grew a bit self-conscious. "It's okay that I knocked her out, isn't it? I mean, it looked like she was going psycho on you guys."

Murray spoke before I could. "You did great, Zoe. Really great. Can we get out of here now?" He tried to rush past her, but Zoe cocked the tennis racket over her shoulder like a baseball bat and he stopped dead.

"One more step and I'll be more than happy to knock you out cold too," Zoe snarled.

I couldn't help but flash Erica a cocky grin. "I told you friends could be assets."

Erica rolled her eyes, then told Zoe, "We have to evacuate. A missile's en route to blow us up."

Zoe's eyes grew even wider than usual. "What?! Why?!"

"It's a long story." Erica pried the gun from Ashley's hand and trained it on Murray and Nefarious. "Let's go," she told them. "Quickly. Though if either of you tries to escape, I'll shoot you somewhere very painful, got it?"

Murray and Nefarious nodded obediently, then hurried out of the secret lair.

"Wait," Nefarious protested. "I saved New York. I thought the hero was supposed to make friends, not get arrested."

"You saved New York?" Zoe asked him. "That's amazing!"

Nefarious now broke into a huge smile. Even though he was about to go to jail and was fleeing for his life, after getting a compliment from Zoe, he looked like the happiest person on earth.

I stopped on the way out of the lair and hoisted Ashley onto my shoulder.

"You're rescuing her?" Erica asked. "She's the bad guy!"

"I'm not leaving her to die," I said.

"She just tried to leave *you*," Erica pointed out. "Carrying her is going to slow you down."

"I'll be all right," I said, hoping it was true.

Erica looked concerned, then hustled after Murray and Nefarious. I followed as quickly as I could. Since Ashley was small, she wasn't very heavy, but carrying her still wasn't easy.

I took a final glance at the TV screens in the control room. The remaining missile was still racing our way.

Zoe stayed back to help me with Ashley, though she looked nervous about it. As we passed the kitchenette, she gasped with surprise. "Whoa. They have a sundae bar in their secret lair?"

"With toppings," I said.

"We don't even have a sundae bar in our mess hall," Zoe groused. "And this rec center is way nicer than ours."

"I know," I admitted. "But on the other hand, they're evil and we're not. How'd you find me down here?"

"Oh, it was Jawa's idea to search this building."

"Jawa's here too?" I stumbled on my way up the stairs. Not out of surprise, really. It's very hard to carry an unconscious human up a spiral staircase.

"Yeah. Spy school let me pick three friends to come along. So I brought Jawa, 'cause he's almost as smart as you; Chip, 'cause he's tough; and Warren, because he'd have thrown a fit if I didn't pick him. Technically, we were only supposed to observe the mission, but Chip said it would be lame if we came all this way and just sat by the helicopter. So he ran off and we came after him, and then Jawa noticed the rec center and said we ought to check it out. We split up to cover more ground. The secret door to the underground lair was open and I heard you and Murray and then spandex girl here going crazy, so I grabbed this tennis racket from the equipment room and came down to see what was going on."

"Thank goodness you did," I said. "You saved us."

Zoe's face lit up with pride. "Yeah. I guess I did."

We emerged from the lair and raced out of the rec center. Erica, Murray, and Nefarious were a good distance ahead of us, although I could still hear Murray. "How could they even think of me as a loose end? I'm not a loose end! I'm a core part of the team!"

"Maybe they got tired of hearing you whine all the time," Erica told him. "I've only been with you a few minutes and *I'm* ready to blow you up."

High up in the sky overhead, I could see the missile. It looked somewhat like a comet, a red streak of fire and smoke bearing down on us.

Hidden Forest was eerily quiet. The battle wasn't raging anymore.

"Did the CIA win?" I asked.

"Big-time," Zoe told me. "It was pretty much over by the time we got here. All SPYDER's guys were surrendering. Although most of them claimed they didn't even know what SPYDER was. They said they were all independent contractors."

"Most of them were. Where's everyone now?"

"They evacuated," Jawa said, running up from the basketball courts. Chip and Warren were with him. Chip had a large duffel bag slung over his shoulder that appeared to be crammed full of equipment.

Despite the urgency of the situation, I couldn't help but smile upon seeing my friends.

"We should evacuate too!" Warren informed us. "It seems like something bad is about to happen to this place."

"Then why are you still here?" Zoe asked.

"We were looking for *you*," Chip told her.

"Aw," Zoe gushed. "You guys are so sweet!"

"It was my idea," Warren said.

"We have to move fast," I told them. "There's less than four minutes left till detonation."

We all fell in together and ran for the closest exit, a hole the CIA had blasted in the wall in the construction zone.

"Who's the dead chick?" Chip asked, pointing to Ashley.

"She's not dead," I told him. "She's unconscious. And she's a junior SPYDER agent."

"She's cute," Chip said.

"Ugh!" Zoe cried. "Chip, she's evil!"

"Maybe on the inside," Chip told her. "But she's cute on the outside."

"Is that Ashley Sparks, the gymnast?" Warren asked.

"Yes," I replied. "Though now she's an evil gymnast."

"She was my favorite!" Warren exclaimed. "She really should have been on the U.S. Olympic team. The judge was blind. She stuck that landing."

"So I've heard," I said.

We raced through the sports courts into the construction zone. Now, in addition to the usual construction detritus of bent nails and wood shavings, there was also a great deal of spent bullet casings.

Jawa glanced at the duffel bag Chip was carrying. "What's in there?"

"Sporting goods," Chip replied. "I got some primo rock-climbing gear, a couple of footballs, some bowling shoes. . . ."

"Hold on," Warren said. "While we were busy looking for Ben and Zoe, you were stealing stuff?"

"If you take stuff from the bad guys, it doesn't count as stealing," Chip said proudly. "It's payback."

Warren started to argue this point, but he was interrupted by a sudden yelp of surprise from ahead.

"That sounded like Erica!" Jawa exclaimed.

I glanced across the construction zone and caught a glimpse of Nefarious and Murray sprinting for the hole in the wall. Murray was always easy to pick out because he had a very distinctive gait. He ran like he had a permanent stomach cramp.

However, Erica was nowhere to be seen.

I heaved Ashley off my shoulder and shoved her into Chip's arms. "Take her to the authorities," I ordered him, then told Jawa and Zoe, "Catch Murray and the other guy. I'll find Erica." I ran off before anyone could protest.

Jawa and Zoe took off after Murray and Nefarious. Both of them were good sprinters and they moved quickly. Chip wasn't far behind them, even while holding Ashley. He was so strong, carrying the gymnast was like carrying a bag of potato chips. Since I hadn't asked Warren to do anything, he simply ran for safety as fast as he could.

Above me, the fireball in the sky was growing quickly as the missile came closer.

I ran across the construction zone, trying to approximate what Erica's route had been. "Erica!" I yelled into my walkie-talkie. "Where are you?"

Instead of using her own walkie-talkie to respond, Erica

simply shouted through the construction site. "Never mind me! There's no time! Save yourself!"

I scanned the dark landscape around me but couldn't find any sign of her. "Darn it, Erica. Just tell me where you are!"

"No!"

I pinpointed the sound. It was coming from my right. I ran in that direction—and almost pitched into one of the missile silos. The hole was just darkness in the other shadows, perfectly concealed.

Erica was four feet down, clinging to the cement rim of the silo. There was nothing but a three-story drop below her.

I'd expected that she would have been thrilled to see me. Instead, she frowned. "Go away!" she yelled. "If you try to help me, we'll both die!"

"I'm not leaving you!" I yelled back, searching the area for anything of use. "You're my friend."

"I told you, having friends in this business only causes trouble."

I ignored her. There was a generator nearby. It had been shot to pieces in the battle, but the electrical cord was still attached. I tore the cord loose, wrapped one end around my waist, and tossed the other end into the hole. "Grab this!"

"No. I'll pull you in."

"Just grab it! Or we'll die!"

The missile was now close enough to see, silhouetted against its own flame.

I sat on the ground. There was nothing to hold on to nearby except grass. I grabbed on tight and hoped for the best.

It didn't work. The moment Erica put her weight on the cord, the grass tore free. I slid quickly toward the hole, desperately digging my heels into the dirt, and barely managed to stop myself mere inches from the edge. The cord tightened around my waist, squeezing my abdomen so hard I though my organs might get forced out my nose.

Thankfully, Erica was quick and agile. It took only a few seconds for her to scramble out of the hole. Instead of relief, there was embarrassment on her face. "You're an idiot," she told me.

Then she helped me to my feet and we ran.

"What happened back there?" I asked.

"Murray got the jump on me."

I started to ask how, but she told me, "Save your breath. We'll talk later."

It was good advice. Since I'd arrived at spy school, there had been several times when I'd had to run for my life—but this time, I had to run even faster. My legs pumped harder than ever before, fueled by fear and adrenaline. Construction sites and earth-moving machines flew past us. Then we were out the gap in the wall I'd made with the bulldozer and into the field beyond. But as fast as we were going, it still wasn't enough to outrun the missile.

It was coming in with astonishing speed, growing exponentially in size as it hurtled down out of the sky.

Erica's hand was suddenly holding mine, clutching it tight. "Take cover!" she yelled, then yanked me into an irrigation ditch.

I curled into a ball and, before I could stop her, Erica curled around me protectively.

The missile came down right on the rec center.

I had my eyes shut tight, but I still felt almost blinded by the flash of white light that surrounded us. The noise was so loud, my whole body vibrated, and then the shock wave from the explosion pummeled me as well. The ground shook. A wave of heat rolled over us. I could sense things tearing apart and flying past.

And then, maybe because of the explosion, or maybe because I'd already almost drowned once that night and was in a delicate state, or maybe because I was just completely and totally exhausted . . .

I passed out.

I regained consciousness sometime later, but I was still disoriented and groggy. There was an incredible amount of activity going on at once, and I was able to process only snatches of it all. My ears were still ringing from the blast, so I couldn't really hear anything anyone was saying.

I was in the diner down the road from Hidden Forest, lying on top of a table.

CIA agents were everywhere. Apparently, they had commandeered the place.

I had an IV stuck in my arm and a few bandages, but otherwise, my body seemed fine. All my arms and legs were accounted for.

Erica was lying next to me. She appeared to be in similar condition, although she was still unconscious.

Our hands were still clasped together tightly. I thought about pulling mine from hers, then decided against it.

A bank of TV monitors had been erected near the soda fountain. They were showing the local news. On every station, there were helicopter shots of the gaping hole the missile had left in the ground. Bits of Hidden Forest were still there: collapsed homes, burning lawns, a few stretches of wall. The gatehouse had somehow managed to escape unscathed. The rec center and all the missile silos were gone, though. The missile had vaporized them all, wiping any trace of SPYDER off the earth.

The news crawl at the bottom of one screen said GAS LEAK DESTROYS GATED COMMUNITY. CIA disinformation at work.

Nearby, Cyrus and Alexander were seated in a booth with several CIA agents around them. It didn't look like they were in trouble. In fact, the agents were shaking their hands and slapping them on their backs. One man, who looked a little older than Cyrus and somewhat important, was laughing and shaking his head, as though he was amused by everything that had happened.

Mr. Wigglebottom sat in Alexander's lap. Evidently, the cat had stuck around the diner after we'd left it there yesterday. Alexander wasn't paying much attention to anyone else. He was too focused on the cat, lovingly stroking its fur and making kissy faces at it.

Agent Rafferty stood nearby, scowling at Cyrus.

The principal was with him, looking confused. He'd gotten himself a new toupee to replace the one that had been burned when his office blew up. Amazingly, this one was actually worse. It looked as though a hamster had died on his head.

Out the window, a CIA paddy wagon was parked in front of the diner. Ashley Sparks was being loaded inside, her hands cuffed behind her back. She had regained consciousness and was screaming at everyone. I thought I could make out the words "I stuck the landing."

Zoe, Chip, Jawa, and Warren sat in a corner booth, away from the action. To my surprise, Nefarious was with them.

He was cuffed as well, but he looked far happier than Ashley. He wasn't an outcast anymore; he was the center of attention. He was talking animatedly—spilling his guts about SPYDER, perhaps—and my friends were hanging on his every word, fascinated.

There was no sign of Murray Hill. He had apparently escaped. And Joshua Hallal certainly wasn't there. He'd probably been in another country when the missiles fired. Along with the rest of the higher-ups at SPYDER.

I was too tired to feel frustrated about this. Instead, I felt proud of myself. Maybe the bad guys had escaped to fight another day, but for the time being, I'd helped thwart their plans once again. My first undercover mission had been a success.

Suddenly, Erica's hand tensed in mine. I looked over at her.

She was awake now. Or at least, kind of awake. Her eyelids still drooped and she seemed a bit zoned out.

"Hey," she said. She sounded oddly far away, even though she was only a few inches from me. It was probably due to my ears still recovering from the blast.

"Hey," I replied. "How are you feeling?"

"Excellent. But that's probably because they've given us painkillers."

It occurred to me that this was probably why I felt so calm myself.

"Thanks for saving me," Erica said. It was the type of comment she never would have made unless she was doped up on medication. "I owe you one."

"How about this," I suggested. "Next time you decide to bring me on a mission, you tell me about it first?"

"It's a deal." Erica's eyes began to slide shut again. "In fact, next mission, I'll ask them to make us equal partners."

"Really?" I asked. "You'd do that for me?"

"Of course. That's what friends are for." Erica gave me a dreamy smile, then dozed off again.

I wondered if she'd ever remember saying that. But for the time being, I was too tired to care. Even with all the chaos around me, I closed my eyes and drifted back to sleep as well, Erica's hand still firmly clenched in mine.

September 20

To: CIA Director █████████████

Re: Operation Bedbug Mission Recap

While Operation Bedbug achieved its main objective—the discovery and subsequent thwarting of SPYDER's plans—I hesitate to call it a success.

The identities of the top members of said organization remain a mystery, while ████████ and ██████████ managed to escape. The people we did capture were mere pawns of the organization, though Nefarious Jones has been eager to share what he knows. Given his aid in deflecting the missiles, he might have some value as █████████████████.

Sadly, Mr. Jones is unaware of what SPYDER's future plans might be and any further evidence concerning those was destroyed in ████████████ ██████████████████. Thus, it will require ███████████████████ to determine what they are plotting next, although we can assume the organization suffered a severe financial loss from the failure of this endeavor.

Although Agent-to-be Ripley ████████████████████████████████ ██████████, he certainly proved his mettle on this mission—and I'm not saying that simply because he saved my granddaughter's life. Given their key contributions to Operation Bedbug and ██████████████████ ██████████████████████, I suggest that both Erica and Benjamin should be reinstated as students at the Academy of Espionage—and be given top grades in Undercover Work as well.

In addition, I would highly recommend the services of Ben Ripley for future missions and suspect he would be a very good selection for Operation ██████████.

One last item: I am somewhat concerned about this Mike Brezinski character. How much does he know? Let's discuss options.

Sincerely,

██████████

Turn the page for a sneak peek at
Ben Ripley's next adventure.

Activation

Bushnell Hall

CIA Academy of Espionage

Washington, DC

December 6

1130 hours

The summons to the principal's office arrived in the middle of my Advanced Self-Preservation class.

Normally, I would have been pleased for an excuse to get out of ASP, as it was my worst subject. I was only getting a C in it, even though, in real life, I had been quite good at self-preservation. Over the past eleven months, my enemies had kidnapped me, shot at me, locked me in a room with a ticking bomb, and even tried to blow me up with missiles—and yet I'd survived each time. However, my instructors at the CIA's Academy of Espionage never seemed very impressed by the fact that I was still alive. They just kept giving me bad grades.

"There's a big difference between running away and being able to defend yourself," Professor Simon, my ASP instructor had explained, shortly before the call from the principal came. Georgia Simon was in her fifties and looked like someone my mother would have played canasta with, but she was an incredible warrior, capable of beating three karate masters in a fight at once. "So far, all you have done in the field is run."

"It's worked pretty well for me so far," I countered.

"You've been lucky," Professor Simon said. And then she attacked me with a samurai sword.

It was only a fake sword, but it was still daunting. (The academy had stopped using real swords a few years earlier, after a student had been disarmed in class—by actually losing one of his arms.) I did my best to defend myself, but lasted only twenty seconds before I was sprawled on the floor with Professor Simon standing over me, sword raised, ready to shish kabob my spleen.

Which was all the more embarrassing, as it happened in front of the entire class. ASP took place in a large lecture hall.

My fellow classmates were seated in tiers around me, watching me get my butt kicked by a woman four times my age.

"Pathetic," Professor Simon declared. "That's D-grade work at best. Would anyone here like to show Mr. Ripley how a *real* agent defends himself?"

No one volunteered. My fellow second-year students weren't idiots; none of them wanted to be embarrassed like I had. Or hurt. Luckily for them, at that moment, the announcement from the principal came over the school's public address system, distracting Professor Simon.

There were plenty of other, far less outdated ways to deliver urgent messages to the classrooms at spy school, but the principal didn't know how to use any of them. In fact, he wasn't very good at using the PA system, either. There were a few seconds of fumbling noises, followed by the principal muttering, "I can never remember which switch works this stupid thing. This darn system's a bigger pain in my rear than my hemorrhoids." Then he asked, "Hello? Hello? Is this thing on? Can you hear me?"

Professor Simon sighed in a way that suggested she had even less respect for the principal than she had for me. "Yes. We can hear you."

"Very good," the principal replied. "Is Benjamin Ripley in your class right now? I need to see him in my office right away."

A chorus of "ooohs" rippled through the room: the universal middle-school response to realizing that someone else has just gotten in trouble.

Professor Simon gave the class a warning glare and the "ooohs" stopped immediately. "I'll send him right now," she replied. Then she looked down at me and said, "Go."

I leapt to my feet and hurried for the door, pausing only to snatch my backpack from my seat. Zoe Zibbell, my best friend at spy school, was in the next seat over. She looked at me inquisitively with her big green eyes, wanting to know if I knew why I'd been summoned. I shrugged in return.

Next to Zoe, Warren Reeves snickered at my misfortune. Warren didn't like me much; he had a crush on Zoe and saw me as competition, so he was always rooting for my downfall.

I made a show of hustling out the door for Professor Simon—and promptly slowed down the moment I was out of her sight. I was in no hurry to get to the principal's office.

I had been summoned to the principal four other times, and it had always been bad news: Previously, the principal had sent me to solitary confinement, placed me on probation, informed me that my summer vacation plans were cancelled in favor of mandatory wilderness training—and expelled me from school. (I'd been reinstated, however.) So I dawdled, wondering what trouble lay in store for me this time.

I exited Bushnell Hall and entered Hammond Quadrangle on my way to the Nathan Hale Administration Building. It was the week after Thanksgiving. Fall had been mild and beautiful in Washington, DC, but now winter had arrived with a vengeance. Frigid winds were stripping the trees bare of leaves, and a crust of icy snow carpeted the ground.

As I slowly made my way across the quad, my phone buzzed with a text. It was from Erica Hale:

STOP DAWDLING AND GET YOUR BUTT UP HERE. WE'RE WAITING.

I stared up at the gothic Hale Building, wondering if Erica was watching me—or if she simply knew me well enough to presume I was dawdling. Either was a likely possibility.

Erica was only a fourth-year student, but she was easily the best spy-in-training at school. However, she'd had a head start on the rest of us: She was a legacy. The very building I was heading toward was named after her family. Her ancestors had all been spies for the United States, going back to Nathan Hale himself, and her grandfather, Cyrus, had been teaching her the family business since she was born. When I'd been learning how to assemble Legos, she'd been learning how to assemble semiautomatic machine guns. Blindfolded.

I picked up my pace, hurrying toward the Hale Building. If Erica was waiting for me with the principal, that probably meant I wasn't in trouble. Plus, I was excited to see her.

I had a massive crush on Erica Hale. She was the most beautiful, intelligent, and dangerous girl I'd ever met in my life. I knew Erica didn't like me nearly as much as I liked her, but the fact that she liked me even a *little* was a big deal. Erica regarded most of her fellow students—and professors—with complete disinterest. As though they were rocks. And not even pretty rocks. Boring, gray rocks. Gravel. Even though her text to me had been curt and cold, it was still a text from her, which was practically as much human contact as Erica ever parceled out. There were plenty of guys at school who would have killed to get a text from Erica Hale. Literally.

I burst into the Hale Building and took the stairs up to the fifth floor two at a time. The security agents stationed there quickly waved me through to the restricted area. "Come right on in, Mr. Ripley," one said. "We've been expecting you."

I stopped and spread my arms and legs for the standard frisking, but the second guard shook her head. "No need for that. They want to see you ASAP." She pointed me toward a door.

This was a different door than the usual one for the principal's office. A piece of paper was taped to it. It said PIRNCIPAL. Given the misspelling, I figured the principal had written it himself.

The principal was very likely the least intelligent person in the entire intelligence community. We had a lot of decent teachers at school, most of whom had been decent spies earlier in their careers. Meanwhile, the principal had been a horrible spy. He had failed on every single mission. No one wanted him teaching anyone anything, so he was made an administrator instead. He mostly handled paperwork that no one else wanted to deal with.

The principal wasn't using his normal office because I'd blown it up by firing a mortar round into it. (It was an accident.) The damage had been extensive, and since the government was in charge of the repairs, they were taking a very long time. The official completion date was set for three years in the future, but even that was probably optimistic; my dormitory had been waiting to have its septic system replaced since before the Berlin Wall fell. In the meantime, the principal had been moved down the hall.

Into a closet.

It was a rather large closet, but it was still a closet. Given the pungent smell of ammonia, I presumed that, until recently, cleaning supplies had been stored there. Instead of a nice, big imposing desk, the principal now had a card table. He sat behind it in a creaky folding chair, glowering at me from beneath the world's most horrendous hairpiece. It looked like a raccoon had died on his head. And then been run over by a truck. The closet would have been crowded enough with only the principal and me, but three other people were crammed in there as well, waiting for me. All of them were Hales.

Erica stood beside her father, Alexander, and her grandfather, Cyrus.

Alexander Hale had been an extremely respected spy for years, despite the fact that he was a complete fraud. The Agency had finally caught on and kicked him out, but he had subsequently proved himself on an unsanctioned mission and been reinstated. Now he was back to his usual debonair self, wearing a tailored three-piece suit with a perfectly folded handkerchief and a crisply knotted tie.

Meanwhile, Cyrus Hale was the real deal, as good a spy as there was in the CIA, even though he was in his seventies. He'd been retired but had recently reactivated himself. Cyrus didn't bother with fancy suits, which he considered impractical. Instead, he wore warm-ups, sneakers, and a fanny pack; he looked like he was about to go walk around the mall for exercise.

Erica wore her standard black outfit, her standard utility belt, and her standard bored expression. She barely glanced at me as I came in. "Nice of you to finally join us."

"Sorry I kept you waiting." I realized the closet didn't have a window. Which meant Erica *hadn't* seen me dawdling. She'd simply known I was doing it.

"No worries, Benjamin," Alexander said cheerfully. "I just got here myself."

"That's not exactly something to be proud of," Cyrus told him disapprovingly. "Seeing as you were supposed to be here half an hour ago."

Alexander winced, the way he usually did when his father dressed him down, then tried to save face. "I was doing some important prep work for this mission."

"What mission?" I asked. In the cramped closet, there was barely room to move. "What's going on?"

"You're being activated!" Alexander announced excitedly.

Cyrus grimaced, as though Alexander had said something he wasn't supposed to.

"What?" The principal snapped to his feet, flabbergasted, obviously unaware of this news. "You're activating this little twerp? For a *real* mission?"

"It wouldn't make much sense for us to activate him for a fake mission, now, would it?" Cyrus asked.

"Well, he can't go!" the principal declared childishly. "He blew up my office!"

Cyrus exhaled slowly, trying to be patient. "As I have explained to you multiple times, that was not entirely Ripley's doing. It was a setup to make our enemies at SPYDER believe that he had actually been expelled so that they'd recruit him. . . ."

"He nearly killed me!" the principal protested, immune to Cyrus's logic. "It's bad enough that I had to take him back here as a student . . ."

"He *was* instrumental in thwarting SPYDER's plans," Alexander pointed out.

". . . but now you're going to send him out into the field again?" the principal railed on. "He hasn't even been at this academy a year yet! He's not qualified for the field!"

"He is," said Cyrus. "He's proved it."

"But—" the principal began.

"It doesn't really matter if *you* agree with me on this," Cyrus interrupted. "Because the chief of the CIA agrees with me. And he's the one who authorizes the missions, not you. The only reason we're even having this meeting here is that, as the principal of this institution, you officially have to be informed when students are being sent into the field."

If there had been anyplace to sit down in the office, I would have sat down. It was surprising enough to hear that I was being activated by the CIA. But I was completely floored to hear Cyrus defend me. Cyrus didn't give out praise easily. In fact, it was a good bet that he'd never given any to Alexander at all.

The principal sank back into his folding chair, glowering even harder at me.

I tried to avoid his gaze, shifting my attention to Erica instead. "You're being activated too?"

Erica arched an eyebrow at me but didn't say anything.

"I mean, you're *here*," I explained. "And your grandfather just said '*students*' were being activated. So it's not only me. . . ."

"Excellent deductive work, as usual!" Alexander pronounced, patting me on the back. "You're right. Erica will also be with you on assignment, as will my father and I!"

Erica's expression didn't change. I had no idea if she was pleased with any of this or not. She might as well have just been told she needed a root canal.

I was pleased, though. Even more than pleased; the idea of being on assignment with Erica was thrilling. In the first place, there was no one I trusted more. Second, it meant I now had an excuse to spend a lot of time with her.

In theory, I should have had plenty of other excuses to spend time with Erica, seeing as we both went to the same top-secret boarding school. But Erica could be as cold and distant as Antarctica. While the other kids at school bonded over pickup games of capture the flag or James Bond movie marathons, Erica kept to herself. Even though I was considered her closest friend on campus, that didn't mean much. A few months before, at the end of our last mission, when we were both doped up on painkillers after nearly being vaporized by a missile, Erica had said a few nice things to me and held my hand. But since then she had behaved as though that had never even happened. There had been weeks when she hadn't so much as glanced at me.

So I was excited for an excuse to hang out with her. Even one where my life might be in danger. As far as I was concerned, it was worth the risk.

"What's the mission?" I asked.